P9-DWF-201

The Exhibitionist

ALSO BY CHARLOTTE MENDELSON

Love in Idleness

Daughters of Jerusalem

When We Were Bad

Almost English

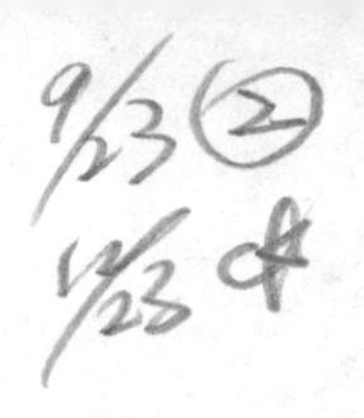

The Exhibitionist

Charlotte Mendelson

ST. MARTIN'S PRESS
NEW YORK

This is a work of fiction. All of the characters, organizations, and events portrayed in this novel are either products of the author's imagination or are used fictitiously.

First published in the United States by St. Martin's Press, an imprint of St. Martin's Publishing Group

www.stmartins.com

Designed by Jen Edwards

Library of Congress Cataloging-in-Publication Data

Names: Mendelson, Charlotte, 1972– author.
Title: The exhibitionist / Charlotte Mendelson.
Description: First U.S. Edition. | New York : St. Martin's Press, 2023.
Identifiers: LCCN 2022056760 | ISBN 9781250286932 (hardcover) | ISBN 9781250286949 (ebook)
Classification: LCC PR6113.E53 E94 2023 | DDC 823/.92—dc23
LC record available at https://lccn.loc.gov/2022056760

Originally published in 2022 by Mantle, a division of Pan Macmillan, UK

First U.S. Edition: 2023

10 9 8 7 6 5 4 3 2 1

For Elaine, Jane, Jean and Martha, who know.

I am glad it cannot happen twice, the fever of first love.

Daphne du Maurier, *Rebecca*

He looked into the hole, and like any hole it said, Jump.

Susan Sontag, *The Volcano Lover*

PART ONE

FRIDAY, 9 FEBRUARY 2010, AFTER LUNCH

1

"Tolstoy was an idiot."

This is how he always begins. Then, when somebody responds, laughing or demurring, Ray will say: "All that crap about happy families. It's the unhappy families who're alike. Uptight, cold . . . ugh." He'll gesture merrily at the havoc: books everywhere, wizened tangerines and cold coffee, heating on full. "Poor bloke had never met us lot. We're famously happy, aren't we. Aren't we? And totally unique."

"I'm not actually sure he m—"

"And no, before you ask, I haven't read whatever the book is, *Crime and* Bloody *Punishment.*"

This weekend is his chance to prove that, despite recent troubles, the Hanrahans are still enviable; with Ray Hanrahan, like a fiery prophet, above them all. Tomorrow will be the private view for Ray's first solo show since the mid-nineties; a miracle, given his pain and suffering, the medication-induced fog, and, whisper it, the recent critical attention for Lucia, his wife. They're having a celebratory dinner tonight; the usual relaxed surfeit but even his brothers, even his tricky younger daughter Jess, who abandoned him, will be there. On Saturday morning, Ray and his other, devotedly loyal daughter, Leah, will finish the preparations and then, in the evening, the show will finally open. If his guests have any sense, paintings will be bought, Ray's unfairly occluded career will resume, and the Hanrahans' glory days will begin.

Please, she is thinking. Let it be bad news.

Lucia Hanrahan, the artist's wife, is lying on the concrete floor of her own studio, listening to the telephone ring. Her strong forearms are terracotta-red; stone-chips and clay-clots press into her back. She is trying to be calm, to ready herself for an entire weekend of alert self-containment, of giving nothing away: two nights, almost two full days, of solid dishonesty. But faking it, she has recently discovered, is easier than one might think. She's a much better liar than anybody guesses; she's been doing it for decades.

With appalling timing, Lucia has come back to life. The thought of why makes her throat swell, her knuckles ache. Heartache is coming, it is already here. She is beside herself, whatever that means.

She needs to focus on keeping tonight's plans straight, not obsess about whether a tiny meeting, even ten minutes, could be crowbarred in.

When will the ringing stop? It's the landline, which can only mean Marie-Claude at the gallery. No one else uses it. It should be exciting.

Lucia is not without ambition; this used to be her only secret. Protecting Ray from this, keeping him confident, unfurious, has been her life's work; he's not above estimating how successful her day has been from the plaster-dust under her nails. A phone call from the gallery will only bring upset, because she'll have to tell him all about it. He too was represented by a gallery, once.

He tends his grudge like a sacred lamp. He'd been spotted

by Dolly Chastin at art school; was, for a time, one of Chastin's stars. He claims that the postcard sales from his big success at the RA Summer Show, *Screw* (1971), funded their St. John's Wood renovations.

Ray thinks he introduced Lucia to Dolly Chastin. In fact, Dolly's wooing of Lucia herself began earlier than he knows, in 1977 after she'd won the Hooper Prize. Dolly took her to a bar. Lucia was living largely on dry cereal and Dolly didn't buy her dinner; Lucia got drunk quickly, kept slipping off her stool. She explained about her name, that her mother, Carmel Brophy, three years married, deliverer already of over a hundred other women's babies, had gone to the Vatican to pray for fertility and a lovely nun called Lucia, "but with a 'ch,'" had shared a bag of apricots on the steps. Soon, lo! Carmel was with child.

"She called me *Lu*-seea, though. Never explained why." Dolly didn't praise her work, not once, but she pronounced her name correctly. Then she sent a note: *I'm fucked if I'm going to let anyone else take you on.*

Lucia did not respond. How could she have? She had already found her calling: Ray, her teacher and Dolly's client, needed her. She was devotedly dealing with all his letters, cleaning his brushes and mixing his colors, filling his sparky brain with ideas, reassuring and encouraging: the perfect assistant, honored to be elected to serve the genius. He was, amazingly, torn with self-doubt and suffering, needing constantly to be buoyed up. He hated dealing with collectors, so she wooed them for him; making him great was their joint project. Whenever the reverberation of a new idea, the tuning-fork thrill, began in her chest, she'd squash it, loyally. His career came first. Everyone fancied him, and he had his pick; he was posher, cleverer, better, and he allowed her, Lucia Brophy, to choose his blues and browns. Of course she was wildly in love. And she had Patrick already, pee-soaked, delicious, fatherless;

soon her other two babies. Somebody had to take care of them, and she wanted to, sort of, and every moment she could snatch when they weren't staggering into washing-up tubs of acrylic, or wailing about biscuits, was required by Ray.

And he did encourage her enormously; she must not forget that, she thinks now, tense for the phone to ring again. It's getting dark; he'll be upset that she isn't home, all systems go for the dinner. But she doesn't move homeward.

"But why don't you paint a bit when you can?" he'd say. "My golden girl, you should." In the long years before all three children were reliably in school, Leah already Ray's little twin, Jess a roaring toddler, Patrick still holding her knees, it was beyond her. The work, in her head, was much too big to squeeze between forgotten chapter books, opticians, chicken pox, three meals for five people, scrubbing the bath; not a little scribble at the kitchen table but huge creaking joists and tautness and howling space. She'd feast on the smooth curves of her children's cheeks and temples, the minuscule quivering of a lower lip, wondering: am I awake but unconscious, or conscious but not awake? Like a good mother, she'd stroke and inhale them, whispering: "You are entirely beautiful. I love you so much. I will stare at you all night."

But her thoughts would drift: to art, to her dream studio, a big plywood mess far from anywhere, to child problems and the current Ray crisis. He hadn't yet decided he wanted yet another baby; once that happened, there was upset every time a buggy passed.

So she gave up completely, not even a sketch for months. Then Ray made an announcement: when the storeroom beside his studio at the Angharad Bevin Community Center became free, he'd persuaded the landlord to let it to Lucia, to store her stuff.

She'd press against the cold whitewashed wall between them, breathing cottage-pie steam from the Pensioners' Club, the dampness from the cemetery trees close by, in, out, and try to sense how his own painting was going. She'd think: I'm so lucky. Now I have a room, I could work in here forever.

No one could say that Ray didn't help her, wasn't loving and supportive at the start. He'd explain, kindly, that she had much to learn about the World of Art. It was just that by the time he began to regret it, it was too late.

His conviction grew that no couple can succeed in the same world; one—Lucia, obviously—must step back. He insists that, had she been more grateful, more respectful of his seniority, they could both have stayed at Chastin's. The truth is that Dolly tolerated his delays, the increasing opacity and repetitiveness of his work ("why should I have to explain it?"), stood by him. Then, at the private viewing for the Hayward's Unbound, Ray was so pissed, ranting about sidelining and neophilia that, despite Lucia's increasingly desperate explanations of the power of his vision, Chastin's quietly dropped him.

Lucia had a small piece in that show: *Bloody Perseus*. "I had to tell her who Perseus was!" he says. "Didn't have a clue!" She can't think of it without sweating; his shouting, her pride derailed.

Then Dolly died, launching both Lucia and Ray into the backwaters. Eighteen years later, the unheard-of Marie-Claude rocked up. Obviously, Lucia has tried to persuade her to take Ray on too.

Lucia used to visualize a future point when everything would be easy. Ray says she's a shark, a ligger, a user, yet she loves him, has loved him so entirely. She always expects him to say he's met someone else.

If Marie-Claude did take on Ray, Lucia would surrender, if necessary. Oh, even that word: surrender.

Is this what it's like to be a man?

2

The phone has stopped. Lucia, still on her back, breathes through her nostrils: linseed, cold clay, solder. She keeps her head still, moves only her eyes in the frame of her skull to see the mess that used to excite her: wire everywhere, curled on hooks, thick with beeswax. There are nails, the rustier the better, in coffee and mustard tins lined up against the narrow window, so cluttered with cannibalized maquettes that it barely sheds light, when daylight—where it strikes, what it changes—is the point. Balsa and hazel poking out of a pub fire-bucket; bamboos in a Laphroaig canister; deconstructed beach mats and Venetian blinds continually crashing to the ground; matchboxes by the score. Lined pebbles and sea urchin fossils, for holding up to see their angles in sunlight; knuckly plane-tree twigs, bones and cones. Cheap teabags, caustic soda, pans full of solidified wax, crunchy lung-destroying nubs of florists' foam, as much plywood as she can fit in; the single hotplate, stolen in 1974 when she was young and ferocious and so, so hungry.

No wonder she can't start anything new. She needs to earn, not stare out of the window imagining what, if she could coax a person here, silently, breathing quickly, they could do to each other.

Rain bursts against the window. Fool. You should be working.

Usually fear is the poke she needs. She is fifty-four, almost dead, and has wasted her life faffing, fretting, obsessively wondering what, say, a huge commission could do for her. What it would do to her marriage. Her current piece, another group but more birdy, more arrowy, which she wants to call *And Then They Came* but Ray will say she's straining for profundity, remains soggy and unrecoverable. She can only think of him, her husband; how much he'll hate it, if it's good.

So instead she dreams of filthy acts against blond-oak cupboards, in an office above Westminster Tube station. She can't leave her phone alone. Her mind has gone beyond the reach of caffeine. And, like a spider, flinging silken threads over the chasm of debt, she's also trying to think of something big, buyable, but ideally mediocre, to keep them all afloat. Her kiln failed again this morning: its lying thermostat and dodgy door humiliating, at this stage in her career. Tina Erzinger keeps banging on about her magnificent new Sorensen Deluxe CZ200, but Tina can work as she wants: no children, no husband, only pure dedication to her art.

Artists need wives; everyone tells Ray this, or no ties at all. She thinks of Henri Gaudier-Brzeska, selfishly rootless, or that gorgeous bastard Modigliani, sleeping in his studio, mallet beside his humble cot so he could work upon waking. Other artist heroes—Lee, Isa—knew that women with children cannot do this. Long grainy nights of colic and nappies after the bedlam of art school, sinking stunned onto the floor bundled in blankets, sleep broken by nightmares, wet sheets or, when Patrick became free range, her own terror. It wasn't drugs; he was even scared of Calpol. He'd say he was out with his mates, her silent boy: really? And, when he would talk, or at least endure her chat, her carefully light arm, there was always Ray, furious that she was claiming him for her own.

She should stop worrying about Patrick and hurry home before the phone rings again.

But Lucia's children are in trouble. She has to bribe her adult son with all-day breakfasts to assess his mental state, as if coaxing a deer. Her elder daughter, Leah, who hates her, barely leaves the house; the younger, Jess, barely comes home. The fluffy heads she used to press her mouth to on the bus, who'd trot around galleries while they played "Art or Fart?," are lost. Yet she still can't leave them for long, or whatever careful tranquility has built up will start to crack. And the worry, the ache, follows her here.

She thinks of peers, competitors, their children launched, leaving them to months of solitude and focus. She's twenty years behind, has wasted so much time, lost so many ideas.

The phone has fallen quiet. She watches her chest rise, and her mind drifts away from perpetual worry to other skin, other breath. Instant, raging desire: her hands burn with it, her heart stings. She'd never before realized that lust makes one's body hurt.

Stop it, she thinks. Not that.

But by now she is lost in the second night they kissed, absurdly recent, when they'd been saying goodbye by the Tube and she'd whispered: "What happens if we fall in love?"

"Then we fall in love."

And so she'd walked into disaster.

3

Jess is cutting it fine.

She's told her family again and again she'll be on the first possible train south after Friday lessons, yet everyone's still outraged. Her elder sister, Leah, refuses to believe she can't leave earlier; her father takes it personally, particularly because Martyn, her boyfriend, asked the Head for the afternoon off, so he could be on the twelve o'clock sharp.

Martyn's been pressing her to take the same train: five and a half solid hours of chat about their shared colleagues, their life.

"You know it's History Club," she said. "I can't let them down."

"What about Ray, though? He'll be so delighted, why not spend more time with him?"

She stared at Martyn: his amazing unawareness. "I'll be on the four o'clock, I'll race there from the station. It's fine."

"You don't even seem excited."

"I . . . I'm just nervous," she said. "It's complicated. Don't forget Dad hasn't done this, shown his work, for most of my life."

"So?"

"So it might be a disaster. No, it really might. They have completely overhyped it, he and Leah. All those guests, I don't know.

It's a bit hostage-to-fortune, how much they're counting on it to turn things round for him."

"Rubbish," said Martyn. "It's going to be fantastic."

Men always fall in love with Ray Hanrahan; he makes them laugh at his daring, his rudeness, and they swoon into his arms. When she and Leah are being united and brave, they carefully tease him about the devotion of the postman, their old headmaster's postcards, heterosexual middle-aged men who pay what Ray calls homo-age. Adoring fans are always with him; "like," Ray says, "herpes." Sometimes he's amazingly generous, even as he mocks them. In return they praise his cooking and Paisley, his cat; denigrate his rivals; attribute every success of younger artists to his influence. Tonight there'll be several, criticizing the Auerbach show (Auerbach has never been friendly enough to Ray), agreeing that the latest batch of art-school graduates is talentless. Plus, for extra stress, months ago Ray bonded with some curator from Texas over bratwurst, and invited him to stay, in the house, for the exhibition. Eric Nakamura has artists in LA, Nice, Shanghai; now his sights are set on Ray, allegedly.

Leah is convinced this will be Ray's rebirth.

"But what if he doesn't take him on?" Jess said to Martyn. "If this man's any good, it's not . . . likely. Dad's not even represented at the moment. God, wait until he sees the house. And the work might not sell, or . . . It's going to be grim. You haven't seen Dad at h—"

"This guy would be lucky to have him. It's Ray Hanrahan! You wait," he told her, with the confidence of the wrong. "You moan about going to London, seeing the family. But the minute you arrive, you'll relax. How could you not? And the exhibition will be a sellout. It's bad we can't travel together, though. What will you do? Won't you be sad?"

"I'll be fine," Jess said. "Don't worry." Often she pretends not to understand him, unfocuses her eyes. Mental Teflon: it buys her a few moments of peace.

If he's missed his train, she's sunk. But it's safe; he's already texted excitedly from past Peterborough. Martyn loves her. He wants her with him, all the time. She catches sight of her reflection and sees a sad, withered girl; the more she frets, the worse she looks, which will put him off. This should be helpful, but the more she withdraws, the tighter his grip.

She's torn at a new cuticle; blood is welling around the nail. She sucks it clean, presses it against the skirt she spent nearly an hour choosing this morning. Ray will hate it; he'll guess she wears it for teaching. What adult woman worries about what her father will think?

"So what's this weekend going to be like?" asked her friend Astrid Pringle at lunch. They were buying biscuits for yet another engagement party; Dalziel's teachers are very marital, often with each other. "Give me detail."

"Martyn is jazzed."

"I bet."

"But, for me, it'll be more: 'Hello, are you all still mad? OK, bye.'"

"Could it be fine?"

"No. Also, I was thinking of telling my mum about me and Martyn. Our . . . well, my . . . worries."

"As in your obsessive ruminating about how to chuck him?"

"No! Shhh. Come on, it's not straightf—"

"Yes it is. And you must."

"But I've told no one else. And I'll cry."

"You know my views," replied Astrid.

But she doesn't truly understand. Astrid is desirable; she teaches Spanish. Whereas Jess can't leave Martyn because no one else will want her ever again. It's simply a fact.

She's already been in almost every shop on the station forecourt, but there are always reasons to visit a chemist. The London train makes her nervous; Pepto-Bismol. Can you drink on top of that? Or some sedative to take the edge off: cough medicine, antihistamines?

Maybe it's just a shopping urge, the quick fix she yields to more and more often. She wants something all the time: a fillip, a tonic, a way to break up lunch in a pub with Martyn, or before a long evening at home, even though Martyn says there's nothing wrong with their relationship.

"It's as good as anyone gets. Why don't you say you love me as often as you used to? Want to know the problem with you?" he'd asked Jess this morning.

"Not rea—"

"The problem with you is that you're an Angry Young Woman. Which isn't actually a thing."

He says that the wear on their love is normal, easily removed, like panel-beating. He claims she's always the one who starts their rows. "You can't resist lighting the fuse. Actually, these days it's always lit."

He's got this from Jess's father. Ray has nicknames for her: Bolsh, for bolshy. Moo, for cow. Piece, for nasty piece of work. He claims they're affectionate but forgets that she asks him to stop. He used to say she'd inherited his fire.

So she tried to stay small and quiet with boyfriends, to avoid becoming him. When she first brought Martyn back to London, and Leah asked: "Is he strong enough to take care of you when Dad dies?" and her mother said, "Do you not want to be single for a bit?", her father called him Martina or "that short-arse," then asked loudly: "Who'd have her? Must be a glutton for punishment. Fiver says she'll scare him off by the end of the month."

But Martyn persisted. She knew she was lucky, even if thirty felt young to feel old; or was that stupid? When she was growing up, they were forbidden sleepovers "in case you're needed." She never brought friends home after school. So Martyn is right. She is fortunate that he wants to stick around.

They've announced the platform, the luggage racks will be filling up but now, when it's almost too late, she steps through the door of the big Boots at the back of the station. She's simply browsing, roaming aimlessly up Vitamins and down through Bath and Body. The station smells fumy, as if the train is idling close by. Through Face, past Cold and Cough, and she's barely set foot in Women and Family Planning when a voice behind her says, "Oh, Jessica," and she turns to look into the beady face of Sally Ornand, Chemistry: the Head's Cardinal Richelieu; Martyn's chief fan.

Steadily, as if caught stealing honey by a bear, Jess withdraws her hand. Sally Ornand has definitely seen where she was reaching; her little mouth is pursed, thoughtfully.

"I . . ." Jess begins.

"Am I interrupting?"

"'Course not. I'm late, in fact; going to London to see my—"

"Ah yes." Sally Ornand smiles. "Martyn told me. I've heard so much about your wonderful father. Hush now," she says, gesturing at the shelf. "Your secret is one hundred percent safe with me."

4

If Lucia had gone when she'd promised, Marie-Claude might have given up, left her alone. But selfish Lucia is still here. Her hand rests on her breastbone; her breathing slows, but she wants more.

Please, she thinks: it's you I want.

And then, inconveniently, she has her vision.

It is fully formed; brief, sufficient. It seems to be made of what looks like quartz, the texture of a red ice lolly with the flavor sucked out; inherently red but somehow frosted, glaucous, although not wetly glistening, nor, she thinks, eyes open now, steaming with dry ice. No. It is huge, monumental, its shape essentially a beveled block, like her beloved vertebrae (Ray says she's repetitive, that everyone does bones) heavily grooved, like old-fashioned radiators, a sperm whale's plankton-filtering grille. It has a hint of life, like a giant brain or liver and its rounded upper edge resembles the lip of the terracotta-tiled step of the mansion block where, four months ago, her world atomized.

She should sketch it, but Ray—

And the phone begins to ring again: three times, four. Then the answerphone clicks on.

She waits, throat dry, fingers damp. The machine was Ray's present when she moved into the studio: a shocker now, a tombstone encrusted with dust and paint, yellow fingerprints on the 7 and 2. The red light is flashing; he's upset if you ignore it.

What if it's doom, with a French accent? Marie-Claude is inexorable. She knows that Lucia avoids the telephone, and does not care. She never says hello or goodbye, wears loads of eyeliner and always Converse high-tops and, when Lucia says she's her gallerist, people have started to look impressed. Lucia adores her, as an erring priest adores God the Father. They have never discussed certain issues but Lucia knows that Marie-Claude knows everything, including why she usually dodges her calls.

A long whirr; a click. Then she hears Marie-Claude, sounding odd: "Call me immediately. And sit down. I have news, very urgent. We must talk."

Lucia sits, but only to quell the fizzing in her chest. She tells herself it'll be a Customs problem with the piece heading to Cologne, or the mystery buyer for *Rabbits* has decided casting is too expensive.

Or what if Marie-Claude wants to discuss the idea Lucia recklessly mentioned last year: a series of strangeness. She'd envisaged a fast-moving sliding slice of Perspex and was ruminating about ways to install it. Marie-Claude may be old-school but it's such a young gallery, fixated on provenance; of course they'd want something fresh but cheap to make and store. Could Lucia deal with Ray's derision; his misery, if the idea proved to be good? Or, worse, the risk that she's overlapped with one of the subjects he has annexed: mothers, sons, sex, nature, time?

It's like playing Jenga: any threat to his self-esteem, a tiny wobble and the whole thing comes crashing onto your knuckles. Sometimes he cries, and what woman can resist a crying man? They're so bad at it; it takes so much.

What if Marie-Claude is the bearer of good news?

There have been some difficult moments: the fallout from the

Hooper Prize, when Ray was officially still only her teacher; the talk in Düsseldorf and then the Nova Scotia lectures; the awkwardness with Basel, where he still swears she was only offered the Statements show because she flirted. The group show at the Whitechapel, one of her proudest moments, was followed by a fortnight of recriminations. The trips she's sabotaged, the collectors, friends she has dodged, for the sake of peace. At the Roche Court private view, all she could see was his distraught face; he wouldn't even come to Münster, and so her hotel phone bill was over three hundred pounds.

Münster: the year after the most horrible year of her life. Ray still insists that he did what he did because she wouldn't turn it down.

Their rows do not vary in temperature; all that differs is the spark. His gloves are never on. He says whatever he likes: that her protectiveness of Patrick is basically grooming; that Leah agrees she's a career vampire; that she's ruined Jess's life by turning her against her loving father. Lucia's always sucked in to defending herself, trying to reason, apologizing, vowing to change, but it's always weak and unsuccessful, like a worm holding up a little sign.

He's very hot on keeping things private, which is why Lucia's told no one about Sukie Blackstock, or their other troubles. Also, she didn't want her friends to think less of him. He still wrote her love notes, bought presents, made her laugh into the night.

Rushing now to pack her bag, she allows herself to notice, fleetingly, the excitement in Marie-Claude's voice. If only she could press a button and pause Marie-Claude for the weekend: not a work drama, not now.

———

What if it is the thing she has dreaded, success, come at last?

Say that Marie-Claude has good news, who would understand why that was bad? Gillian? Dr. Gillian Fine, married to Ray's younger brother, is an elegant researcher into the digestive enzymes of giant tortoises, and notices everything. She runs a lab, applies for enormous grants. She once said, "Ray, you really need to be nicer to Lucia," and everyone went quiet. She says Ray's reactions are "extreme" and that's without knowing some of the worst; that he lay in bed for days, grinding man-sobs, after Goldsmiths finally made Lucia a professor, although he insists that degree-teaching bonsais and stifles. Or that Lucia spends hours, weeks, after every small bit of professional success, trying to explain that it doesn't reflect badly on him, that no one will consider him diminished; not critics, collectors, galleries. Ray is intransigent. "I'm sorry. I'm sorry," she always ends up saying, her chest aching as if he has pushed his fingers in under her ribs and pulled.

Oh God: could Marie-Claude have been talking to Bobbie? Ray would think it treachery.

Bobbie von Usher is currently number two on the *Telegraph*'s list of Philanthropists in Art. Whenever her name comes up, Ray claims that she's bankrupt, has dementia, that everyone knows "her taste has gone." But it's possible. Bobbie, after overlooking Lucia all last century, out of the blue offered to help with the production costs of *Old Mother* for Roche Court.

Lucia said no.

Please, she thinks, locking the studio door, the damp hallway air like a little punishment, let it not be something that hurts him.

If not a collector, could she be ringing about a journalist? That might be worse. Has Marie-Claude heard that, when Norman

Bank approached Lucia last Frieze, she panicked and cut him dead? People do want to know how it works: two artists, together. They ask loudly, "Isn't there ever competition?" They refer to his ego, his pride, in front of him. "How do you two manage it? Isn't there tension?"

"Not at all," she'd say. How could there be competitiveness between them when he was so clearly on top? Ray had drawn his extremely famous *Screw*—a naked leaping woman, an orange and blue and apple-green squiggle of life—when he was her tutor. The model was rumored to be Lucia; merely another pupil scrabbling in an established artist's wake. It made his name. Pray no one mentions *Screw* tonight; it always sets him off.

Possibly people don't mean to pour petrol on her marriage by mentioning having seen something of hers.

"I can't understand," Ray always says afterward, "why you keep pretending. Everyone knows you're the megastar now. People fighting to shake your hand—no, don't shrug, I saw—when we went to the Dulwich Picture Gallery. Although maybe if you hadn't elbowed me aside, if you'd bothered to introduce me . . . Have you any idea how painful it is? And my God, there's so much I haven't told them; I'm just protecting you, but they'd be shocked. Remember our wedding photo, me a god in my velvet suit and you a terrified pregnant child-bride. The other day someone asked how it feels for me to be married to you," and there they are again, on their hamster-wheel, puffs of blond curly shavings stirred endlessly, without purpose.

Am I lonely, she asks herself, pushing open the fire door and out into the night, if I have no one to talk to?

Of course not; I'm married.

If only he would tell her what he's planning to show. She's been trying to spur him on for weeks; usually he wants to discuss every detail, summons her for a chat under his Duchamp poster (living artists destroy his resolve), all his necessities to hand: Scotch; the kids' white Nintendo; fig rolls; scummy tea; ashtrays, most of their missing cutlery. He has an enormous collection of paints and pastels, brushes, sponges, resins, but the right palette knife is always in Lucia's studio. Yet he hasn't rapped on the wall for days. Oh Ray, Ray, what are you doing? Or not doing? How will you be ready for the exhibition, if you carry on farting around?

His happiness, theirs, rests on guest numbers, sales, reviews, if any. Please let there be sales. He'll be so wound up already. Better to ring Marie-Claude back tomorrow, hope she can stall until Monday. Although what if it is an interview on this, his weekend?

Lucia is weak, and full of wanting. That little flare of vanity, the chip of ice, has never entirely thawed, despite the blazing sun. She's wicked to want it, when whatever it is that's happened might push him into despair: to leave her, or worse. With Ray, there is always the dread of worse.

Now she wants a cig, which is ridiculous. Until a couple of months ago, she lived in fear of the carcinogens in every breath of exhaust, each unwashed lettuce. Now she wants toxins: brandy, steak, the minor high of a Marlboro Light. Ray, who smokes mainly to irritate people, would be furious if he smelt it. And it would make her even later home. Welcome to wifehood.

But Lucia's world has become richer: the sound of rain easing, a bus driver's tight glove. Everything has a wash of sex. London unfolds, its quiet corners shimmering with potential. She's been learning which cafés have a decent phone signal and she's never the only one; there'll be somebody else murmuring into their phone, eyes darting, distracted, then transfixed by a single word.

And shops are full of promise. Like a fool, she's bought knickers, shyly lacy; she tells herself it's about self-respect. Never a reader, she now aches in bookshops: seventeen again, soulmates with Emily Dickinson. The heart wants what it wants. She read some of Louis MacNeice's *Autumn Journal* one lunchtime, hungry for another's pain; when she reached "All of London littered with remembered kisses," she moaned aloud.

As if he senses something, Ray says she's overspending. Their income grows ever tighter, like tugging a belt-strap into the next hole. There's a startling gas bill, possibly because Ray leaves all the windows wide open. Every lunchtime there's tension, at best; he insists that going to Clive's, the local café, is his basic human right. She wants to save money; to work; to eat healthy food from home; to be alone, all of which offend him.

"You're my tiny wife," he will say, "why don't you want a romantic greasy date?"

He'll knock on the wall after eleven; by twelve-ten he's in the corridor and she'll have to go out and explain herself, or there'll be a row in the café, on the street; he is not shy about public shouting. All of London littered with unforgettable arguments. A couple of months ago, going round the RA, he saw a "Courtesy of the Hertz-Chamaut Gallery" cartel beside a Manuel Greeson, and he started ranting there and then; at the slightest reminder of her two solo shows, he's off. There have been so many days, at least hours, when, children safe, boiler functioning, she could have worked but, instead, needed to placate him, explain why whatever-it-was did not matter, why praise was meaningless, commissions merely the consequence of selling out.

Also, his work is timeless, when hers does nothing but . . . sit. Hers is made of rubbish; it frightens people. At least, she hopes it does.

"Think of all you've sold," she'll say, and he'll grouch that it's only friends, out of kindness, well, and investment, but he does smile. She's talked him up to Marie-Claude and everyone else she can think of, coaxes him to the studio, strenuously praises every passing idea. Sometimes, in extremis, she suggests doing prints of *Screw*, another run of lithographs but, last time, this led to terrible accusations in a car park, Ray screaming at her by the ticket machine that he might as well be dead, so she's keeping quiet.

And he's given up the evening classes at Archway Technological College, where he was casting his pearls, as he puts it, on the primeval swamp of the old and weird. He's suggested that she go back to teaching full-time.

People assume that her art makes money; as if production costs are funded by magic, or collectors turn up at the studio with bags of cash. But a quarter of, say, £15,000 doesn't go very far; publicity doesn't help with the cost of smelting, gold leaf, vans, cherry-pickers. It doesn't stop Goldsmiths suggesting cutting her salary for next term.

But he still knows how to entertain her; it kept them alive for so long. When he's happy he's more fun than anyone she's ever known; much more fun than she is. Tonight they're having people over like any other couple. Maybe they'll be like a normal family, getting on, proud of each other.

Please, she thinks, possibly to her mother's God, let this weekend be a success, so he's cheerful. So I can be free. Please, let me be free.

In the soft hours of the night, when they were first together, they promised to tell each other everything. It was impossible; she sees that now. Marriage is about the stronger protecting the weaker, cushioning their secret vulnerability. How her heart aches for him, his brutal fragility, his frail boyish ego; has ached.

Her mother devoted herself to guarding and soothing her undeserving father.

Lucia tries to keep her father out of the studio. If she spots a Ford of his era, a Cortina, even a Zodiac, any of Dagenham's finest, she still winces.

"He wasn't so bad," says Ray, who never met him. "Whereas Carmel Brophy is a saint." But she's old and tottery, back in Limerick, and unmentionable, because Ray cries instantly at the thought of his own mother, "Mother," whom Lucia took care of because Ray found it too upsetting.

"Haven't you got anything better to wear," Ray had asked this morning as she left, prodding her collar. "Remember who's arriving tonight."

"I'll change later," she said.

"But not too . . ."

"Not too flash. I know."

"The Nakamura bloke isn't here for you, although he'll probably chance it. We just have to accept," said Ray, "that, when we met, I was the star, gave you endless leg-ups and now, thanks to me, your time has come."

"But yours has! It hasn't gone! And it will again. This is the start."

"Yeah, yeah," said Ray.

It's a lot of space to fill: the brand-new gallery in the Guildworkers' Hall. Larry Nathaniel, who claims to own it, says there's room for "fifty small or thirty medium, if you hang them right."

Last year, when Ray decided her tiredness was getting ridiculous, she went on a conservators' *kintsugi* course in Oxford; the lizard-colored canal, horse chestnuts and church bells, lacquer ground with gold dust to fill in the cracks in broken porcelain. She wanted to stay but he said he needed her in London, so she took the train there and back all week.

Is she dawdling, or thinking of art? Here are those horrible mottled hydrangeas; she touches a petal, considers all the Snow Whites poisoned by sugared almonds, apples, rings and combs and grapes, wipes her finger on her trousers. Not every sculptor dies young. Moore: eighty-eight. Hepworth: seventy-two and perhaps she was careless; Rodin: seventy-seven; Caro: eighty-nine. But Lucia will. Given her predisposition, the nasty little insight she has already had into her genes ("Think of them as a book," murmured the too-intimate doctor, his knees almost touching hers as he zipped round her in his office chair, "whose language we are only beginning to interpret"), she won't live long enough to be what she used to want to be.

The same looping thoughts; here's the lovely moss-wall, here is the certainty that she brought it on herself. Her family history, for which a weary nurse-practitioner printed out a key (⊕ for certain cancers; ⊗ for accident; ⊙ for suicide) showed nothing, as she put it, of interest.

The whole experience was very upsetting, Leah had pointed out, for Ray.

"Why for Dad," Lucia asked her daughter, "particularly?"

"Think about it," said Leah. "Intimations of mortality, yeah?"

"But it's my dead relatives."

"I know," said Leah. "But he feels it so much. He cried, Mum. You know family is everything to him."

None of the hospital leaflets mentioned this constant scratching-away at sanity, the omnipresent fear. Death hums everywhere, planting its seeds. Was her own doom sealed by the industrial washing powder Ray insists they buy at Costco? Or the economy matches she uses for her endless pointless maquettes? Sometimes she can feel malicious fibers multiplying, accreting calcium cases. Could the blackness have begun in her own childhood: pounds of penny sweeties, no sun cream ever, leaded petrol, everything fried and crispy-crumbed and sugar-dredged?

And the anxiety; isn't that fuel for those bastard cells? What about right now: WiFi and diesel; progesterone in the tap water; toxic deodorant; urban blackberries; the hormonal disaster of milk, yogurt, all her favorites; the impossibility of affording organic food, of eating food at all?

No one warned her about sex, either. If they had, she might have been prepared.

Early on the morning of Lucia's operation, she went to be injected with radioactive dye. Ray came too, with Leah; "Dad'll need support."

He charmed the nurses, explaining how he had tried to come to all of his wife's appointments; it was just that work, or his legs, or long-booked tickets to see Bob Dylan in Manchester, conspired to keep him away.

Then the handkerchief came out. "To think that I could lose her, when I—"

"Dad," said Leah, "I know. Poor man, it's so horrible for you. But she's not actually dead. Why don't I get you a lovely Coke?"

They had arrived as Imaging opened; an elderly cleaner pushed a mop carefully around every chair leg while Ray dozed. When at ten the scanner was free, Leah, who had been a first-aider at school so is, in Ray's eyes, virtually a doctor, confidently reassured her mother, then hurried back to Ray behind a rubbery curtain, designed to protect family members from gamma rays while they waited.

Lucia, on her back in the machine, was in a desperate trance, like a rabbit hearing the hawk. The actual surgery was scheduled for one. The male technician, wearing stained blue scrubs, approached her to insert something into her breast, possibly the sentinel-node tracing wire—it felt like a nail—then inject the dye and she realized nobody had mentioned whether or not it would hurt.

It did.

Three years later her mind still winces at that searing pain, like a burn around which the skin whiskers and puckers. Other men in blue were holding her down, forcing the needle in, but, to their collective surprise, it was unable to penetrate her areola. They pushed again. That was only the first time. They had to do it twice more.

Lucia screamed. She knows this because afterward, gown removed, dressing taped on, back in the clothes she had decided were appropriate for this, her last day of womanliness, and will never wear again, as she weakly followed her husband and daughter back down the passages toward the mini-cab (Ray had insisted they all rushed home before the surgery "for a good lunch"), Ray and Leah discussed what they had heard from the waiting area. Ray was sweet. He took Lucia's arm. Then, as he arranged himself in the passenger seat, Leah expressed concern about the trauma he'd just endured.

"They didn't even shut the door," she said. "Just that carwash flappy thing. We could hear everything. Jesus. My poor Daddy. How's he supposed to cope with that?"

5

Jess is on the wrong side of the carriage, of course, gazing at the East Coast over a pitiful Year Nine Anne Boleyn essay. Everything looks better from the other direction. The idea of London makes her skin feel sticky, as if lunacy is catching. Is she sweating more than usual?

Definitely not. Stop looking for signs.

A pit is opening in her chest. Boots, Waverley Station, is far behind her: a lost paradise. She hadn't let herself think it through, but now . . .

It all started because she and Martyn still hadn't had sex for her birthday, weeks and weeks before, and she has always feared a sexual wasteland. In truth, they, together, are not all she had hoped. Martyn's approach is cheerfully straightforward. Sometimes she'll lose track in the middle, her mind brimming with self-consciousness, comparisons, doubt. But, despite everything, she wants action; at least, she used to. She wanted the theory. She missed getting up to pee, feeling that stirring soreness that said: he still wants me. I have been found.

Waiting for him to show interest was humiliating; trying to interest him was worse. Without sex, she'd say, we might as well be flatmates; the whispering and giggling was always their best point, discussing their friends' kitchens, their colleagues' pasts, her father's hilarious rudeness. Ray is endlessly interesting, at a distance, but, on London visits, she'd lie in bed for hours, listening to them laughing downstairs: furious as a forgotten bride.

So, Saturday night, November closing in, and she'd thought: enough missed fucks. Let's bundle them all together and have them now. I'm not ready for passionlessness. To make our love better, I have to be brave.

At bedtime, she made an overture.

Trousers off; stripey top off. Come on: knickers definitely off. Like a sacrifice, she approached the bed, pale in her black bra. Her every hair stood on end, announcing itself in the chill, as she waited for him to sense her powerful almost-naked presence.

Martyn was curled on his side, breathing deeply as if unconscious; then, with a huge sigh, he turned. Dear God, he's an awful actor.

"Is that," he muttered unnecessarily, "you?"

"No. I mean, yes." She plopped down on his costly mattress: he calls it his dowry. It doesn't shift. Jess is not, as her father says, a wisp of a girl but it is so solid, so packed with lambswool and swans' down, that it makes her back ache. "Um, hi."

"Mm. What . . . is late."

"Yes," she said. "We, I mean, I could, if you like—"

"Wha'?" But he moved his knee a little nearer. She heard him swallow, moistly.

Stupid girl. Stupid baby. "Come here," she said, dry mouthed.

He didn't respond. They looked blindly into each other's eyes. He scratched his calf with a grating sound; she held her breath. The room was thickly dark. The night was stillish. Surging out from beneath the quilt like a god, or a nightmare, he moved closer. She could hardly see him; when he touched her knee she gasped. Her epidermis, each juicy follicle, awaited the next step, but the darkness, which she had thought would help, magnified. Then he moved his hand.

"This is good," he said. "Your inner thigh."

It was like a biology lesson. Her hands moved up his narrow flank toward his hip, his waist; she stroked his chest. She expected him to say, "Why are you doing this?" but he seemed to accept that she wanted him, or something. Then she lay back. Hurry, she thought. It was too dark to see his face but she felt the presence of parts: his buttery blue stomach, the furry blackness. He kissed her neck.

"Mmm," she said. She should be excited too. She put her hand a little lower. He shifted above her; off with his pajamas. For a moment he seemed to be supporting his entire weight on one arm; he could let go and crush her. He was right there, between her thighs, doing the thing she is never quite able to believe they're allowed to do.

And afterward, in the warm almost-silence, she said: "Hey. You did use one?"

"Mmm?"

"Didn't you? You know. Love? The doctor said, because of Mum, I shouldn't be on the . . . we talked about it. We were definitely doing condoms."

"Oh . . . yes, yes. Don't worry."

She grasped his wrist with both hands. "Hang on. You did tonight. Didn't you?"

"It's OK," he said. "It's fine," and he put his arm around her shoulders, like a brother.

Nineteen past four. She keeps missing the highlights: where the sea before Alnmouth beats below a sheer rocky drop; the crime-scene farmhouse with a car-skeleton in the hedge, patio furniture facing the tracks. Her thoughts spiral around a single point: Martyn, with whom she should be happy.

She finds herself assessing little houses, the smaller the better, imagining herself alone in a signalman's cottage, an allotment shed. Quiet breakfasts; wind; solitude; she'd be the witchy-haired woman of her father's deepest scorn.

When her sister rang about this stupid exhibition, Martyn was out, running Film Club. Jess, back from work, was thinking of writing him a letter. Leah's always indignant that she can't talk during school hours; they kept missing each other, growing more irritated.

"Do I really need to be there?" she asked her sister, once she had understood that there was no crisis. "It's term time."

Normal adult children don't rush back for every family event. She needed something to break, slammed open the fridge for wine. "I can't . . . why don't I just come down for the opening? I don't mind doing it all on the Saturday."

"Don't be stupid, you need to stay at least the weekend. Dad'll feel that y—"

"It'd be a rush," said Jess, "but I absolutely don't mind." She thought of them all on top of each other, piglets fighting for the teat; took a swig from an open bottle. Cold red flooded her tongue; she licked her teeth. Careful with the sloshing noises; Leah and their father already insist she's living a life of tsarist luxury: pipers piping, oysters, velvet. Everything is a problem, because she is officially the lucky one. Leah is thirty-two, still lives at home, has never had a boyfriend, and she's extremely pretty, says their father. "I'm sorry, it's just a fact."

"You know how much Dad lives for family festivities," Leah reminded her. "The Friday will just be us lot, but celebratory. And then on the Saturday the cousins will arrive, you know he loves a house-full, and then it's the PV and a proper catered . . . Mum was angling for, you know, crap, assorted nuts, but Dad deserves a feast. Doesn't he."

"But that would cost a fortune."

When their father's at his finest, he'll insist on giving you his own scarf, or turn up with armfuls of flowers. He'll hug you in public, cry with pride. Wary daughters can be lulled into trust; this time, you think, it'll be different. Then he'll promise you a camera and buy it for your sister.

There was a pause. She could almost hear Leah choosing which card to play. "It's *family*. You have to come."

Jess thought of wives of the chieftain in his compound; brood mares. "I don't think he'd mind if I stayed away."

"He'd be gutted. Honestly," Leah insisted, "he's mellowed. His bark isn't nearly as bad as his—"

"OK, fine," Jess said, taking a gulp of wine so big she could feel its pressure against her ears. "Let's not start. But catering, seriously?"

And there was an odd warmth in Leah's voice when she said: "You know Larry's son, um, Pablo, he owns—runs—that amazing pop-up place by the Camden Overground—" but, by that time, Jess had started worrying about what to wear.

The thought of being judged by her father still makes her catch her breath; everything she does comes with his silent commentary, a one-man chorus of contempt. He's saying "fancy" when she orders coffee, or reads in the bath, or turns on a sidelight; he's there to remind her she dresses like a grandma and talks like Jean Brodie. She tries to prise his vision from hers. But now Martyn's at it too, editing their lives on Ray's behalf.

"Mm," he'll say approvingly. "Orange: Ray's favorite," or reminds her to knock when she sees a magpie.

Maybe her father would be sweet, this time. He might have changed.

"Why can't you think about his feelings?" Leah was saying tearily. "Don't make that face; I can hear it. Come on, you've done your bit. Teaching. 'Scotland.' You really need to come home."

The walls were closing in. Jess swiped wine from her chin. "I have," she began, unconvincingly, "my own life."

"*We* are your life," said Leah. "Martyn gets that; why don't you?"

Martyn denies, fiercely, passionately, that he and Leah have private conversations. He thinks Leah is angelic, just as their father does. Only Jess sees that Leah is a politician, a dark horse, a perfect courtier. She knows how to play people and Martyn, who used to support Jess in everything and now takes Leah's side, is fooled.

He's seen only the surface. He's missed the blighted Christmases, the stilted angry birthdays. As the son of a loving mother, he can't comprehend how bad it can be. When his monthly letter from Marion Clough, his mother, arrives, via the letterbox bang outside Marion's Pets on Kil-winning Road, he reads it quickly, goes quiet for about two seconds and then is his usual unrufflable self, as if a pebble has dropped into a pond. He has cleaved unto the Hanrahans and, up to a point, they have to him. Leah often wonders, aloud, how they ever did without him; they agree Jess did well. Last year, on the train back, Jess and Martyn had their worst ever row, when he quoted Leah saying: "She's much nicer since she met you."

Her chest tightened with a forgotten feeling, like a mussel closing its shell.

"I don't understand," he said, "why you just can't love them."

"I do!"

"Not enough," said Martyn.

He called her Cordelia, although he meant Regan. It stained

this journey, the castles and foam-splashed rocks, diagonal hawthorns, all the views she used to love. He says she's oversensitive; that she ought to recover as quickly as he does. "Couples fight," he says. "Look at your parents. You need to learn to bounce back, or you'll never really mature." Afterward, her diaphragm felt hollowed out, like a rotting tree doggedly continuing, in the absence of anyone wanting it to. Even when they're getting on, he asks non-questions like: "Isn't it great that your family loves me?" and "I really hardly mind your flaws. We're lucky that we never annoy each other."

The nose-ringed man opposite, on the right, i.e., left, side of the train, is reading a business book about overcoming the devil, not even glancing out of the window, let alone at Jess. Briefly, as the fiery waters of home closed over her, she forgot she's on her way there. The thin thread of self-disgust doubles back on itself, crosses, loops: another knot. He's on miniature Prosecco number three. Soon it would be reasonable to go to the toilet again. She's on high gusset-alert. Martyn's obsessed; he says he's keeping track. After sex he looks triumphant, as if he expects her to be instantly great with child. Which is stupid. She's not pregnant. She shifts in her seat, hoping for the stomach-ache that doesn't come.

Despite his lack of height and hair, his bachelor intransigence, Martyn has an attractiveness; he knows it. Other women think he's their discovery. He says he's still courted by eager school mothers, his ex-girlfriend Sam the professional viola-player and triathlete. "But we're the love of each other's lives, aren't we."

He'd been so stressed at his last school, had been sure that Dalziel's, where Jess taught, was a paradise. Then there was the incident at the York Viking Experience and bingo, Dalziel's needed a new Geography teacher. It was often difficult at lunchtime: Martyn expecting them to eat together in the corner seats, picking bits out of her lunchbox, hyper-alert to every perceived compliment and then, at home, going through it all again. Jess can't always generate the depth of interest he requires.

"You're with Astrid Pringle all the time," he says. "Why don't you spend lunches with me?"

So she and Astrid would sneak out, make excuses. On an emergency tampon-buying excursion, searching for Ultras ("I'm having a gigantic period," Astrid had explained, which had taken things up a level), they laughed at the man-vitamins, chose sandwiches, and then Astrid turned to Jess in Wellness and asked: "So what's going on?"

"What do you mean?"

"You look," said Astrid, "like a desperate woman," and Jess started crying.

"I . . . He says I'm not trying hard enough to be happy together. I'm lucky. And I know he loves me, and . . . when we met, after all that awful stuff with my mum . . . God, I was so relieved not to be out there, you know. Swirling about alone."

"Just because he wants you doesn't mean you have—"

"I can't break his heart," Jess explained. She's never admitted that, at first, she had believed she was falling in love. She and Martyn had held hands in bed, talking about their ideal tenement building, being one of those teacher couples who aged wirily well together. How can she retract it? How could she start again? "It's my fault, I'm ungrateful."

"I see," said Astrid Pringle. "OK."

"And there are no straight good free men."

"You don't know that until you've looked."

"They wouldn't want me."

And Astrid Pringle smiled. "They will."

As they pushed back through the school entrance, Astrid said: "Unless you're careful, you'll marry him simply to avoid telling him that it's over." The door whacked Jess on the elbow so hard that she gasped. "Or you'd let yourself get eaten by a lion on your honeymoon, on purpose. Admit it, this is hurting him more."

"Yes," said Jess, "I know."

Martyn says she's drinking too much, but it's the thought of what awaits her that is making her feel ill. She'd downed a supermarket vodka-tonic before they left Waverley, with a cold falafel wrap for stomach-lining but, if anything, she feels worse. When the trolley passes she copies the man opposite and buys a small warm white, a packet of salt and vinegar.

She needs another drink.

She walks the train's enormous length, swaying against laps and socked feet and puzzle magazines; somewhere between carriages C and F she realizes that not-knowing is worse. She staggers like a sailor back to her carriage and straight through it, toward the front. On a plane, the flight attendants would be murmuring in their private staffroom world; she'd ask for water, just to chat. Her aloneness hurts. She's gazing into nowhere; black wet countryside flies by.

She opens the window, to breathe certainty in. Then she makes her decision.

6

If compelled to spend long hours in bed, a woman's thoughts will turn to sex.

Mental pain; physical pain; a slow stupid convalescence. Dr. Shah and Specialist Nurse Maura at the Whittington mentioned low mood, fatigue, not months of shattering exhaustion and searing fear and no work. Only her appetite remained, with a compulsive edge: standing at the fridge eating bolognese with her fingers; crags of Edam like ancient marble; even, once, raw bacon.

Then, unfortunately, the first twitchings of desire.

People might think that the urge for textures, temperatures, pleasure barely a membrane away from pain, would disappear after maiming. But Lucia is only fifty-four, for God's sake, fifty-one when it happened, in the tiny interval between youthful self-loathing and the sorrow of age. She could have enjoyed her body for longer, if she'd known. Also, to feel lust, the mind must empty, and hers will always contain other elements: the pop a needle can make as it pierces the skin; the grubby secret folds of scanning devices. There's also the nudity problem; if she can't be naked, certain options are compromised.

But she wanted to be touched.

At first, after What Happened Happened, she'd obsess about whether Ray would want her. They used to have chemistry, didn't they? He'd say she was being ridiculous but does nothing to rectify this marital ice age. Yes, he would kiss her, briefly, he said he still—still!—desired her, although that has long been in doubt. But it always ended there: the nights unsullied, the mornings quiet. Why didn't he want to take his wife upstairs and ravish her, multiply? She would, if she were him.

He'd say: "We're not all insatiable."

She wasn't insatiable; she just wanted to be sated. She has always wanted it, if truth be told, a little more than Ray. It's often where a row began: Ray insisting that his unlibidinous calm was a more adult state, that by making him feel bad about not being in the mood, she was causing his interest to fade. Maybe he was right; if he were in her position, as it were, he'd hate him, her, for assuming she, he, oh, you know what I mean. She was too needy, too much. He'd say he couldn't be raring to go the moment she ran up the flag; that he couldn't sense exactly when she'd be receptive to him, as if she were a baboon. But she tried, didn't she, to tamp down her fears? She still wanted to be touched in general, only not, yet, there.

So she learned not to touch, or expect to be reached for. Gradually, she caught his lack of interest. It was humiliating to be so unwanted, a woman in her prime without a sex life. But who could want this strange randy creature, with her unreasonable lusts? Even in bed, in the act, he shamed her desires. The lust faded. Hope faded. And then came November.

Which is why Lucia really shouldn't care who Ray has invited to his show. She has no right. Yet, late last night, she'd blurted out: "Have you? Invited her?"

"Who?" said Ray.

"You know. Don't—"

"No. Who?"

"S-Sukie Blackstock. To your show. To see your work. Please, tell me."

"You're being silly. Sukie," said her traitor husband, as if Sukie Blackstock wasn't the ruiner of everything, a destroyer in ankle-boots, "is just a friend."

Lucia used to be ready for combat, afraid of losing Ray to a tender student, a stylish younger colleague. Yet her foe turned out to be in plain sight: an older, tighter, better version of Lucia. Sukie Blackstock had been a parent at Parliament Hill: too attentive to the husbands, showing off about hangovers, animated laughter. But divorce, and her inevitable retraining as an osteopath, her new My Partner Gareth and, perhaps, the affair with Ray, made her a different woman.

There she was, at the Euston pain clinic where Lucia had begged Ray for so long to go. He came back from his first appointment, fascinated.

"It's so sad," Ray told her, "she's had a terrible time. Hemorrhages, cancer, that horrific accident and the husband, remember him, smooth type, was a bastard." Now, reincarnated, Sukie Blackstock's smile, her picky eating and those cantilevered tits in little black jackets were all unbearable to look upon. She probably does yoga, the hot type; that waist must have taken work.

But Lucia was ten years younger; Sukie Blackstock, the Jezebel, the temptress, the vagina dentata, is definitely almost Ray's age. Shouldn't that have counted for something?

She did wonders for Ray. He was evangelical, urged everyone they knew to see her ("mention me"). He was always bumping into her outside Charing Cross Tube. Somehow, Lucia's unreasonable taking-against Sukie became the reason his phone calls were whispered, why they started going out for lunch. Still he insisted Lucia was being paranoid. To prove that they were merely friends, close friends, he invited Sukie Blackstock to summer drinks, a couple of dinners, in Lucia's own house. Every time it was horrible, like going undercover in an armed cult. Ray's enraptured gaze, his sympathy for her frequent near-death incidents, told Lucia everything.

But he said Lucia was being narrow-minded, controlling, jealous, so she endured.

She tried to be warm and welcoming, even though she wanted to raise the drawbridge, put the oil on to boil. Sukie Blackstock was like dye, blotting out everything. Lucia would think: I wish her dead. Ray's always said she has a killer's soul. She'd test herself: would I press a button? Yes. Would I do it another way? Say she was drunk near a stone staircase, would I give her a shove? Would I steady her if, thanks to her stupid high heels and man-pleasing whiskey shots, she started to topple? Where is the line?

He invited her round yet again; he wanted to make his famous chicken korma. She turned up with her nose-job, wearing one of her stretchy flimsy party-tops displaying acres of bony chest, tanned tits below. Although Lucia had promised herself not to kiss her hello, her veins running white with hatred, Sukie Blackstock managed to be the one who gracefully stepped back.

Despite Ray's insistence on her modesty, she clearly wanted to be famous. Thanks to the contacts of another ex-parent "now a friend," she appeared occasionally on Capital FM talking about Bodywork; she claimed to have celebrity private clients, which Ray believed. He'd already tried to persuade the osteopaths on Laurier Road to hire her.

Ray was, as everyone pointed out, on top form, increasing Lucia's love, and her fear. Lucia was proud of him, despite the spear sticking out of her chest, the glistening entrails. Sukie Blackstock and Gareth—who had a close-shaved hungry head and a caring smile, claimed to be a financial adviser—had brought supermarket

House Red and some clearly regifted chocolates, the eat-by date only a fortnight away.

Her laugh was a trill. She was wearing, naturally, a leather skirt. She wanted a lot of chilled white, she announced, smiling spectacularly, and Ray leaped up. They all watched her caramel haunch as she unnecessarily bent right over to straighten a rug-corner. Lucia wrenched open a packet of crisps; she could hear Ray being relaxed and cheery. Murderousness flashed in her blood, like juicy pips of lemon-flesh shot between finger and thumb. Sukie Blackstock was overpraising him, like a schoolgirl being vivacious at a disco for a boy. Was Ray, at sixty-three, the boy?

Sukie Blackstock wasn't even his first. There had been murkinesses in the past, when the children were younger; too rotten to face. But they had never been forced under her nose like this, while so hotly denied.

"She thinks you're great, you know," Ray whispered.

Even in the blurry fall of shock that followed, this dinner shines like a horrible film. My Partner Gareth was wearing a smart burgundy wool polo neck. "Bet he's a cyclist," Ray muttered. "Shaved legs; they all have that slippery look." When Sukie, plus Ray's old friend Petey, nipped into the garden for a cig, Gareth hung about near the bookshelves, skull turning at every footfall on the stairs.

How could Ray fall for someone so obvious? You are welcome to each other, thought Lucia, although she wanted to rend Sukie Blackstock's stringy flesh with her bare hands, like crispy duck.

"There's nothing, I swear," said Ray afterward. "It's unbearable that you'd think that of me. Anyway, apparently her partner Gareth is very jealous, so she says we mustn't be seeing each other for a while."

Ray was upset; he'd lost a friend. Lucia comforted him. Now

they could laugh together at Sukie Blackstock's idolatry of her only son ("Mothers and their sons!" said Ray, his mother's shining favorite); her manipulations, her manic flirting. He said he was avoiding her, by choice, and then What Happened began to happen, and Lucia receded.

Every successive hospital appointment was worse than the last; she could barely get home before the sleepiness hit. It often felt as if she were falling upward, or tottering into a pit. On the bus she'd be braced for attack; adverts made her cry. Her mind, once a tightly shuttable box, became a tree filled with stupid birds that, at the least distraction, wheeled into the sky, some in formation, others lost, taking time to settle and quiet before, at another noise, they'd be off again.

Patrick and the girls needed him; she needed him but, on the third day of hospital, when he'd queued in Marks and Spencer's for horrible wireless bras, Ray arrived so angry that a young nurse asked if she needed help. A week later, as she wept in bed, he was on the phone to her Aunt Clo, whom she has never liked, saying, "I can't deal with her emotions. And the children. Can you come up and help?"

And, afterward, long months later, when she was back supervising, lecturing, ragged with tiredness, she could not work. She'd sit in her studio and gaze at the light crossing the concrete, or nothing at all. At first it was terrifying; there is no such thing as a latent artist. Then she realized it was doing wonders for their relationship. It made work impossible: exactly what he needed in a wife.

She welcomed the anxious mornings, the unproductive afternoons, well into the next year. What a relief, to be able to report to Ray another bad day; that she had undone everything, or couldn't start. It brought him peace, while she imagined dying of paint fumes, launching herself from the stairs at the British Museum. Probably Ray was right, that she was a neglectful mother, a parasitical artist. She had been becoming a little more (within a very small world, and for several wrong reasons, and not that it matters anyway) known, and juggling all those white lies, the small omissions, was beyond her now.

Meanwhile, he betrayed her.

Even as she lay in bed, the deceits and whispered conversations seemed to be restarting, like a grassed-over burial mound being bulldozed open. How she wanted to be wrong. She was bludgeoned, half asleep; perhaps, as he suggested, she was going a little mad. So much sorrow, then finding him again; could she really have lost him once more? Now, when she could hardly stand?

The suspicion that something was up would not unstick. How likely was it that Lucia, with her sad mouth, flat bottom, lifetime of simmering worry, could be competition for the grinning untrustworthy Sukie Blackstock? Also, she was deformed. It wasn't over; there were months of procedures, drainings, dressings and, under the gauze and itchy tape, scars. She still couldn't name the part in question, look at it, bear to imagine what he would think of this grotesque lopsided horror.

He swore he was completely avoiding Sukie but took his phone into the bathroom, started going for healthy walks after dinner. Then he'd admitted they'd had a drink after "crossing each other's paths" on Gower Street. He invited her over again, once Lucia was up to smiling.

It wasn't until months later, as a lightly tapped chocolate Easter egg can fall open along the join, that he made his confession.

7

Lucia's hand clasps her phone. She mustn't ring; it's time to lock up her obsession for the weekend, not waste her energy on plans for a ten-minute assignation. A visiting relative could spot her texting; she could let down her guard. Besides, keenness is off-putting.

Unthinkingly she's taken the long way home, down Swain's Lane to see the blossom, and a fellow mother from Patrick's school is pushing a bike toward her. Lucia liked her, they were almost friends, but this woman is from the land of people whose children are Doing Well. How can Lucia face her, as an equal?

Besides, she's in another land now entirely: the kingdom of adulterers.

It's possible that Ray is simply biding his time, like a boa constrictor, lazily looped. He knows everyone; any of his huge acquaintance could have spotted a hand-touch where two Tube lines part, a glance in a bar. She constantly practices excuses, as dull as possible, about why she'd meet a politician: something involving a panel, details imprecise.

Yes, it is wrong: a crime against marriage. But she didn't want anyone else for decades: the girls' lifetimes. She gave Ray her best years. He slept with at least one of his students and she lived through it. And she was so burningly sad and small for so long. And she couldn't stop, even if she wanted to.

Maybe the fogginess of her brain has helped to disguise it. Since What Happened Happened, she isn't the woman she was. Is it something post-operative; did they leave something in, or take too much out? Was it the anesthetic, killing a small section of her mind? Logistics, multitasking, remembering directions have evaporated, although nobody believes this. She dreads the shops, coping with neighbors; the inevitable head-tilt, the sympathetic "how *are* you?," even as she yearns for kindness.

Ray will be distraught that it's raining, will worry that it'll keep people from his PV tomorrow.

If only, thinks Lucia, I could have a sighting, to keep me going.

A normal person could drive over to Chalk Farm and back. She can't even do that, would rather walk miles through seedy backstreets. Ray and Leah say she's ridiculous, that only wusses are scared of driving. She's too cowardly to mention that even the bus is almost too much, the mess of tickets and stops and strangers. Driving is far beyond her, but they refuse to listen.

"It's all about nerve," he says, about U-turns on Holloway Road, or parking wheresoe'er he sodding likes. They swap tales of convertibles stranded on speed bumps, terrified learners. He's a libertarian. Once, he decided that a neighbor had scraped the Hanrahans' scuffed car so he sat in it for an entire afternoon until the man returned, to scrape him back. And, although they've always mocked Lucia's driving, sing a special granny theme tune when she tries to park, now that Ray must be kept from the wheel he relies on her.

These days the smallest journey requires coffee, breathing exercises, dark chocolate to keep her dulled senses alert. She hides her terror for their sake but how can she possibly be safe to drive? How can she not do something lethal, reduced as she is? When she fears so much, and can't make decisions and, most of all, wants to sleep constantly, even standing; is she not unsafe?

She tips back her head for the rain on her face. Little birds are singing their heads off in the trees. No one will notice her: another solid knackered-looking woman, biting her lip. They would assume she has forgotten desire.

Yet, leaving the studio, buttoning her coat, Lucia glimpsed bra-lace under her own work shirt, and was fiercely turned on, accidentally, by herself.

Jesus, woman. Focus.

Ray was very clear about not wanting a song and dance tonight; it means he does. People, for the first time in years, are staying, witnesses to his renaissance: her brother-in-law David and his family, the Gillians; the other brother, Uncle Graeme who, according to Leah, has been banned from drinking in the Pineapple, the Cock Tavern, even the Bertram Arms, where guns are sold, which means he'll be worse than usual. There's this unknown Texan Eric Nakamura, here until Monday; God knows who else. "I adore," Ray always says, "an open house."

And, at long last, her beloved Jess, at whose shape, her fully grown survival, she longs to marvel, whose scent she wants to carry around her neck in a little bottle for free head-sniffs.

At least, she thinks, it's Friday evening. Marie-Claude won't ring home, not at the weekend. On Monday, she will deal with any minor dramas.

But, even as she tells herself this, she squirms. Her toes curl in her work boots; it isn't minor. Marie-Claude is the queen of expectation-management. Whatever she's phoning about, it's big.

She's smiled before she can stop herself.

Stop it.

Focus on steering Ray through the stomach-clenching worry of tomorrow; there's almost too much at stake to bear. What if he slumps, afterward, and it's impossible to leave the house? Anything could do it, a single tepid comment, a picture not sold; she'd buy them herself, if she had the money. She's been sounding optimistic and excited for months; it's only two more days, more bodies than there are beds, more mouths than she has organized food for and, rumbling beneath it, the gripping fear of no joy, no escape, until next week.

But later, after everyone has gone, when Ray's berated her for being too sociable or not sociable enough, and has stumped off to rest and she's emptying the bin because he hates cold cig-ash at breakfast, maybe she'll ring the studio answerphone back with her special code and listen to Marie-Claude's mysterious message again, allow herself to feel the tiny thrill. Or she might slip deep into the garden and make a phone call to someone else entirely: invulnerable to cold, looking due south to where, on unimaginable bed linen, lies the object of her every thought and breath.

Even at the thought, her skin seethes with excitement, her eyes close. She needs the owner of that voice, and no one realizes. Her mind is pornographic, her body clenched, and they think she is still merely dry-skinned Lucia Hanrahan, semi-failed artist: troubles with her children, endlessly fiddling with her amusing but disconcerting installations, her playing with time. Ray Hanrahan's wife.

If Ray does find out, it will be the end of everything. He expects her to have been faithful even before they met; to be her first, last, center. Her brief flurry with Patrick's biological father counts as the rankest infidelity, although she and Ray weren't even together. It was the grand finale to a couple of very experimental years, when she attempted to master uncomplicated sex, feed her creativity with raw edges, be alone, but fell painfully in love with several people at once.

Ray hates the idea of any of them, of Lucia feeling anything sexual other than in his arms.

And, although he considers Patrick his son, he insists that all Patrick's troubles are the legacy of his genetic father, a poor sweet rebound who helped at first, until Ray scared him off.

"Well, if you mate with a lightweight," he'd say, within Patrick's hearing. She tries to stop him but too feebly. She let Patrick down.

She cannot stand to think of it. He is her own one. She ought to have been fearless, for him.

She's almost home but can't speed up, because her footsteps will sound frightened and there are muggings around here, though Ray denies it. Whoever chose plane trees for London pavements wasn't thinking of those wide trunks. The broken streetlight makes her furious nightly, for Leah. But the world is extraordinarily beautiful and she had forgotten it: every slosh of bus-wheels through the gutter, each dripping leaf against the sky.

The corner shop: think, hurry. She has parsley, cream, more red, what else? She's not meant to carry with her right arm, still, because of the lymph nodes—she, Lucia, the packhorse—but someone has to fetch tonic water, the right vinegar, batteries, a new hammer. At least he's bought the lamb, and she's started the vegetables. Christ, has Patrick remembered the pudding? It will irritate Ray; he likes to be the cook, hates Patrick in "his" kitchen. But she wanted Patrick to feel useful. Although blueberries cost a fortune.

It's no good. On top of the usual blanketing vagueness, she's too deep in lust to think. Maybe a quick chat would help. Even now, she keeps having outbursts of smiling. Her mobile burns in her bag; she's had no texts since lunch. If only Lucia could email, but everything would be read by staff. Lucia rarely phones unscheduled, categorically never visits the office but, she thinks, I need to hear you, see you.

It makes her bones hurt. Their next meeting—she'll say she's going to a talk, maybe book-binding, Ray will never ask—isn't until Wednesday, after a dinner. She thinks of what they could do, even if they only had half an hour, and her insides lurch.

Phone back into pocket. No way, under any circumstances, will she ring.

Just before his own sixty-fifth birthday dinner, the night before Lucia was meant to go on the radio, Ray admitted that he and Sukie Blackstock had "done things."

It wasn't, he insisted, infidelity; not technically, if they didn't go to bed, which meant Lucia had visions for months of what people might do standing. Where? In doorways? She needed urgently not to know. And apparently Sukie Blackstock had entangled him, professionally, leaving him, Ray, the victim.

"It's horrible," he'd say, "for you and me both. She used us." He was so convincing: midnight discussions, backstroking, promising they'd be happy again and, inexplicably, Lucia again ended up reassuring the man who'd thrown away so many years of her love.

She takes her phone from her pocket.

8

Patrick presses his ear to the toilet door.

He's just back from the gallery, checking the pins and lights, the staging. "Not difficult stuff," Ray said. "Just basic spark and chippy. Even you can do it." But it was a huge job.

Patrick needs to hang the pictures tonight; he'd planned to fetch them on Monday. Then Leah said Ray wanted to do a tiny bit of finishing-off before he would let them leave the studio. Was three days enough? Then two? It doesn't feel right. But Ray is ignoring him; Leah's ferocious when irritated. He can't ask again.

He rolls his tender helix, then his tragus, hard against the wood. People underrate pain. Like hunger, it keeps one sharp. He's been piercing his ears himself for years, slowly puncturing up the cartilage, faithful to the fiery throb. Self-tattooing too. He's very careful; no significant infection yet, although his fossa is causing trouble. If one can strip oneself back, one realizes Me is just a layer of skin, a collection of vessels, and none of it matters much.

Ray's angry he still hasn't fixed the toilet flush, when so many people are visiting. What if someone arrives when he's in here?

Patrick has not found himself. To the disgust of his stepfather, he works as a neighborhood gardener, a handyman. Ray considers it treachery, helping other people, even though Patrick's endlessly fixing things at home. Jess says the house is still standing because of him. Patrick likes his employers, the regularity of his hours, the walks each way in different kinds of air. It's comforting to fix downpipes for their old neighbors, or to build a guinea-pig run at Bramshill Primary, where his little sisters went to school; he feels like he's stitching them all together. Simply being outside is soothing: digging up broken clay pipes and tiny fossils, seeing the echoes of lungs in leaves and trees, gives him inordinate happiness. He's in love with the perfection of beechnuts, the underside of bark, the cling of ivy, the inaudible decay of stone. He often wants to taste it. His pockets and shelves and caravan are full.

But his soul is not. He misses cooking; that's who he was meant to be. He had sincerely abandoned even the dream, but it still lives within him, makes him ache. How could he ask around, within Ray's earshot?

He had told himself it's enough. He can buy his own supplies, stay out of everyone's way. Health and self-discipline, modest eating, taking care. And at least he has ("is using," says his stepfather) the caravan. He scoured out the rust and mildew, filled it with slowly sprouting acorns, pickles firming up with oak leaves and grapes refusing to become raisins. He sleeps there now: like a spaniel, Ray says, in a nest of his own devising.

"Don't you get cold?" Ray asks.

"Yes," he says happily. "Very."

"Ugh," says Ray. "To think I'd have a . . . dependent who likes fresh air. Well, at least you're on site. In case I need you."

Jess will be here soon. She'll be happy for me, thinks Patrick. She will help me to tell Ray my amazing news.

Quickly, trying not to retch, he plunges his hand into the cistern, gropes for the washer behind the air-force valve. Infection is everywhere. When his mother was ill he kept himself ready, trying to become useful; first in the kitchen, making tempting sandwiches; then, when she edged into the garden, white-faced, he'd keep an eye on her through the back door. The readiness never wore off; being in the house has become more difficult. Something like fear is whirling him round in its icy eye: the churning awareness of loss. Even the smallest certainties are blowing away, as if he's one of those men who appear by motorways, their memories erased. Except they usually turn out to be musical geniuses, which he is not.

The idea of scrutiny, of stupid mistakes, makes him sweat, and there's more to do this weekend than he has time for. Tasks bloom like fungus. He is always in terror of Ray's footstep in the hall, of leaving some trace, like vermin. His surface is thin. There's a leaking of fear into his chest, as if a capsule has cracked. He's realized that skin is no more than a secretion, like crusty eye-sleep. Recently the outside seems to have become louder: the wind in the branches and the rain on the caravan roof. The atmosphere, which sometimes has an oddly silty smell, seems thicker, jellied, closing in.

Lately, he's wondered if he might be coming undone.

For example, he doesn't mind the dark. But on Monday evening, heading home across the Heath from fixing a gate on Tanza Road, it seemed as if nature was summoning him.

It wasn't just the knifeman in the woods, the patient strangler, but a feeling of danger crowding in. The sky was yellow-gray, murkily lit by curds of cloudy moon. He was in a gully: overhung, dead-black. The trees seemed to be edging closer; he couldn't see his hands. The sound of his boots on the frosty path was an abomination; he kept wanting to look over his shoulder, as though enemy tribesmen were waiting to leap from ditches. The path came up, a little higher than the heathland on either side, the dense but leafless hedgerows. He was in full view of the shivering trees, the open sky, as if along a spine. Such a banging in his chest; he hugged his bag to his empty stomach and stumbled onward, his footsteps like a tiny doomed army. To be fed, and warm: there was so much blackness out here. The wind was blowing harder; the trees bending as if trying to work themselves loose. It was as if a veil had blown away, revealing the true world in which trees had claws, the wind was a great breath, in, out, in, and there were pits that littered the skin of the earth, into which a man may fall. Here, close to home, was the abyss: a nest of seething menace, big enough to stop his heart.

"Hello?" he whispered.

There was a sense of swelling behind him, the woods moving nearer, the rushing air gasping, colossal and malign, as if he were straw in the wind or a blade of grass and, as he began to run, he knew that Ray would spot him bursting into the garden from the back gate, home, and the contempt poured through him like ink.

Even now he's wondering what he can do to please his stepfather. Ray is a king enthroned on a mountain, tributes being piled before him: hummingbird feathers, sacks of corn, basalt and obsidian, flayed human skin.

He needs to hide, try to recover. Ideally he'd do it forever, shore himself up in his caravan, never see anyone except his mother and Jess again. He misses Jess so much his chest hurts but she'll be on at him about moving out, getting work in a kitchen, not sticking here changing fuses for her father. She knows that's what he used to hope for, but not how scared he's become. And now it's happened.

He wasn't expecting his life to change. Then last week he'd been shifting manure, gazing forlornly at the brindled worms that squirmed in the straw, when his kindest employer, Mrs. R, called: "Your tea's on the terrace and let's have a little chat?" and, like a forest fire catching, he seemed to have been chosen for a job, doing all the things he loves, for money.

Mrs. R knows Patrick can cook; shyly he's made her lunch a few times with her beetroot or broad beans. She always praises him until he wants to hide. Mrs. R's daughter runs a vegetarian pub on Hornsey Lane: the Good Intent. And, as of Monday, she needs a chef.

The timing seems a miracle. Patrick has built Ray a gallery practically single-handed, a boxed-in sort of room on the mezzanine area. Leah says the show can't help but be a hit. Ray's fans have been waiting to buy his art for decades; he's still major. Definitely. So, full of success, aware of how hard Patrick's toiled for him, he'll be receptive. He really doesn't need Patrick on hand any longer, and he'll see what a chance this is.

9

High above Westminster Tube station, in the burrow of corridors of Portcullis House, behind the oak door with a heart-stopping name beside it, a phone begins to ring.

In this strange blazing existence, Lucia sees everything: an Italian with a big bumpy nose, which is probably the curse of her life; the pull and tuck of a stranger's bicep. Like a common-or-garden pervert, she watches the Kurdish café woman swallow, her pale throat moving, the tiny spasm, and feels a sympathetic liquidity. Yesterday on the Piccadilly Line, she was so close to the wrist of a devastating young man, deep brown skin, that she was tempted to kiss it.

Even that she could be having an affair would amaze them, let alone with whom. If th—

"Hello?"

"Oh!" says Lucia, already sounding like a fool. "Hi, hello. It's you. I mean, it's me. I just thought I'd . . . Is it OK to ring?"

"Hang on a—" There's another conversation in progress in the secretive passages, muted by carpet and those pale wood walls. Lucia strains to gather specks of information, the least sigh or breath. "Damian, hello, you arse, what the hell is going on? Hello! Hello, Vince. Yes, I'm . . . what? Oh, all right. Hello you.

God, don't ask me. Two mins." It sounds as if they're at a party. Then, closer to Lucia's ear: "I'm back."

Sex plummets through Lucia's chest, her thighs; heat and pain and the need for knowledge. Her breath is spiky, like something unwisely swallowed. "Where are you?"

"In the Palace, that corridor I showed you. The cloister one."

"Won't someone hear?"

"It's where everyone goes to whisper. There are even landlines for it, on little smart desks. With stationery."

"Wow," says Lucia.

"You see them murmuring. Resting their heads against the solemn pillars."

"I thought you'd be back home for the weekend." She has learned that, in the second half of the week, MPs are mostly in their constituencies, although those without children do occasionally stay in their London flats, alone.

"No. Keep up. I was going to but felt bad about canceling that European Humanitarian Federation thing, and some of the fun ones are still in town, so we thought we'd take them on the razzle. Maybe Golden Heaven. Imagine a Belgian eating sweet and sour ribs."

"In Pimlico?"

"That's the one."

"Oh . . . fun. Good. Excellent." The thought of friends, colleagues, makes Lucia tight with jealousy; ingrates, working within eyeshot of her lover, being able to see her smile. "With other MPs, your . . . gang?"

"Yes, that lot. Some of the Women's PLP. Or they might want Indian, which, with them, I can stand."

"What do you m—"

"They won't be all 'oh you're the expert, you'll know what to order.'"

"Christ."

"Then," says Priya, "I said I'd go to an interfaith fête thing tomorrow, meetings, blah, maybe a trip Sunday eve."

"Oh?"

"But first there's the Science Museum fundraiser. You know I'm a sucker for Deep Space."

Lucia knows. She's started researching galaxies, acquiring new interests: technology; stylish footwear; electronic music; political biographies. And every builders' radio speaks to her directly: the ache, the grinding need. No, I can't make you love me. She sits in the car to listen to Nina Simone, has twice bought lipstick but not yet worn it. Good morning, heartache.

"So, a trip?"

"Perhaps."

And it's lucky they're miles apart, so Priya can't see her face. "OK, so it isn't an issue," she says cautiously, "that you're not at home? In Coventry, I mean? Doesn't Sid mind?"

"Would Ray 'mind' if you did your own thing one weekend?"

"Who knows," she says, fun and light and relaxed. "So . . . you're out tonight?"

"Mmm. And it's just round the corner from where I rang you, when was it, last month, and we—"

"Christ," whispers Lucia at the sudden lift-drop, the thrilling devastation of her organs.

"I know. What I'd give. We could nip into that manky park again."

Lucia swallows. Since the beginning of the year, they've been writing increasingly daring messages. A torrent of filth has been unleashed; she hadn't realized what was in her mind, fermenting. "So, what do you think," she murmurs, "would happen?"

"To you? Well, I'd put my hand in your hair."

"God, don't."

"Lightly pull."

"Oh."

"Bring your mouth cl—"

"Stop." There is a deep pause. Eyes closed, she listens to their breathing. Flames are licking at her skin; her lungs are light.

"You are hot."

"God. Am I? No," says Lucia, but she could do a little jig.

"Silly, but hot."

"You are. Extremely." Then, to reduce it, Lucia says: "I've got a really stupid idea."

"Oho."

"If . . . I wanted to see you tonight, later . . ."

"I want to see you."

The mere idea is like lightning splitting her open. "Do you?" she whispers, which is the kind of risk she's always taking, not being able to stop. It's excruciating, always pushing so.

But, this time, Priya says: "Yep."

"Really?" Jesus. She swallows. "Oh. Well, we're having people over."

"You told me. If I hadn't said yes to this chaotic thing tonight, we could meet."

"We could meet," murmurs Lucia.

"Yes."

"Would . . . would you consider canceling the spare ribs?"

"It's . . . possible. I hate letting them down though."

"Of course. But . . ."

"I could. Conceivably."

The sound of her hot breath in Lucia's ear is like a fingertip. She wants to see her so badly her eyes sting. Her voice is constricted with wanting; since this began, she needs water constantly. "Christ. So, you could . . . come tonight? To mine. No one will . . . I'll think of something. God. That would be brilliant. They'll be excited, because it's you. Do you . . . say yes. Please, say yes."

10

It was the twelfth of November last year, a cold wet Wednesday. And Lucia was tired; just back from four days with the British School in Rome. Usually Ray is the one who goes on trips. It was unlike her to be invited but her usual instinct, to turn it down, was strangely quiet. He tried to make her wangle him an invitation, but she was evasive. She wanted this. Alone.

Even the journey was dazzling. From shivering in the cold dawn at Tottenham Hale station, the moon still up, to inspecting watches and caramelized nuts at Stansted, she felt in a bubble of unreachability, like a border zone. On the flight she wrote notes, as alert as a teenager; once in the city, the ancient walls reverberating with the dead, she felt peeled, absorbent, as if her brain had been unwrapped. If I lived here, she'd thought, my work could never stop.

In Rome, something happened to her. She'd expected to miss Ray; he says she gets as needy as a child. But she was skittish, light of heart. In public on a panel, then talking about her own career, like a eulogy, she did not have to make herself smaller as she does in London, where someone is bound to report on what she said. She did not wince at the applause.

On the second night, she was driven to another panel. Beside her on the back seat sat Deirdre Tomlin, who's almost won the Turner twice. Lucia had always assumed that she was fine, like everyone else. But Deirdre Tomlin told her about her own exploded lengthy marriage, the ambitious sex she was having with a student ("he's cruel, which I like"). She said "you really don't have permanent assistants?" and "I've always admired your work," as if Lucia were a serious person.

Lucia asked how it felt to be on the Turner shortlist, lightly, as if she hasn't imagined the judges phoning her and offering it, and her saying no, thank you but no, for the sake of domestic peace.

And later, over too much wine and artichokes, possibly guinea fowl, a perfect salad, Deirdre had grasped Lucia's hand and asked, "Are *you* happily married?" and, when Lucia hesitated, she said: "What are you? Fifty-two? Sixty?"

"Fifty-four, just."

"Well, I was sixty-three before I decided to be happy. Now that is scary. Don't leave it until you're as old as me."

But that was later, when Lucia may have confessed things were difficult. Before then, seven o'clock sharp, Lucia was on stage, with her own bottle of sparkling mineral water, responding to detailed questions about *Wrinkle* from master weavers and Paduan professors and a well-funded gallery in the Dolomites and she thought: this is how it could feel, being an artist, entire. Her spirit flashed into life.

She had two more whole days of remembering her old self, how it felt not being crushed into the least possible version. Then home and Ray was insisting she "showed her face" at the new neighbors' housewarming. She still avoided parties: too sad, too weary. And being near attractive women hurt her; whether young, with their plumps of perfect cleavage, or older, warm loved bodies slackening naturally with age. In any case, the sheen of her freedom had yet to wear off; he'd notice.

The rain slammed down. Patrick was assembling flat packs in Millfield Lane for a friend's mum, and Leah was at Coralie's round the corner, smoking more weed than she should; it was like standing on the peak of Darien, looking down at two hours of delicious solitude. She could have wine and tinned rice pudding in the bath, oatcakes, Stilton. Should she watch television?

Ray rang; when was she coming? It was rude. It made him look bad. One of his main issues with her is she's not friendly enough to his friends. She couldn't admit she was tired, or he'd demand information: had she done some work in Rome? If not, what had she been doing? Who had she sucked up to? Was Jocelyn Edgeworth there? Was, in fact, Eleni Stone?

"I think I've caught a cold. On the plane."

"Come on," he said, "it's only two streets away. You've got to see their chairs; they're the ones I've been wanting for years. Is it because there'll be nobody useful? I know you, you never make an effort unless it's big hitters now, do you realize that?"

So she'd caved, again, for a quiet life. She didn't even change, just rolled her sleeves to hide the plaster-smudges; her blueish shirt had bleach-spots but only around the waist, where no one would look.

The house was vast, glistening, unscuffed; there was no red wine, just cocktails served by the hostess, an events organizer from Oregon, with little turned-up trouser-cuffs. After twenty minutes, she wanted to flee. Her hips hurt, and her back, from the confused muscles; the fibers of her heart felt overstretched. Maybe Ray was right, and she's lost the trick of friendship. He's always pushing her to relax more, take time off; broaden her circle. The guests were cool: pretend work-wear or structured pleats, daunting jobs. The hostess, Muriel, needed help with a tray for the people upstairs. She looked frightened of the scale of her own house, as if there might be a floor she hadn't yet entered. So Lucia took a huge plate of cornbread and followed her toned bum, feeling sad about everything. It was quieter, in a more grown-up room; "We don't let Rudy or Ivy up here," said Muriel, and Lucia didn't at first realize these were children's names.

OK.

At least there was music. The cocktails were delicious; quickly she was on her next. "What are these?"

"Palomas. They're so easy when you have friends round."

Up here the guests wore ordinary glasses, undirectional shoes. There were apparently happy couples chatting to each other, and she felt the old sorrow again: a resigned acceptance that being not happily married was her lot.

She considered holding in her stomach, decided not to bother. Although Ray prods the lily-pad below her navel, affectionately, he says, and claims, "I like you squashy," in Rome she wondered if he was trying to keep her unwantable.

No, that's unfair. She can't look at herself in the mirror. Who would want this?

But oh, imagine it. She thought of the brutal passion of Deirdre Tomlin's student lover, the admirable orgasm-rate of her friend Angie. She pretended to look out of the floor-length sash window, barely listening to some man praising the view down to the lights of the City, the Telecom tower, uncountable red-blinking cranes all over Camden.

"That's your neighborhood, isn't it?" he said, and a woman on the sofa answered, "Probably. Could be somewhere over there; I'm not an orienteer-er."

Lucia smiled to herself. She caught the woman's eye.

Oh my God.

It was Priya Menon, MP and local celebrity. Everyone knows exactly where she lives when she's down in London, one of those mews houses off Chalk Farm Road; a sort of glamorous stable, one up, one down. They are envious of the black metal window frames, the exciting high-up hatch. They have noted fresh flowers. She has opened the annual Gilroy Street fair four years in a row; who cares about the official MP for Camden South, a drab gray beardy man? She represents somewhere in the Midlands, but she is a local; she is theirs.

The husband, Sid (Ray always says "a weak name"), was very rarely spotted, pushing his elaborate-looking bicycle, and Lucia wondered, as everyone must, what it was like for him to be married to her. Do they live together in London too? Lucia has glimpsed her in profile in a Kentish Town greengrocer's, knocking on a watermelon to test for ripeness. Once at a bookshop event she was shaking hands all around, kissing the writer on his drawn pale cheek, and her public ease, her charm was such, her lovely teeth, that everyone beamed when they saw her. Or perhaps it was fame, or the prospect of help. Like the fairy at the christening, she brought all three.

Now, in a stranger's house, face to face, Lucia saw that she was beautiful.

Cheekbones; strong jawline; firm chin: Priya Menon looked carved from warm sandstone, as if she should be holding up an Ionian column, a Modigliani caryatid, not eating chipotle corn puffs on somebody else's sofa.

"God, these cocktails."

"I know," said Lucia. "Palomas. Apparently." She took another swallow, wondered, as she does with most things, what color precisely described the skin of Priya Menon (her own is yellow and pink, like a Fruit Salad sweet): tawny? No; the inside of a toasted almond? Then she realized that Priya Menon was speaking to her.

"These sensible people are making me want a cig."

Lucia saw that she had the nose of a disappointed empress, biggish, absolutely straight from the bridge to the tip; large, very dark eyes with straight dark lashes, like a boy; a thick black-brown fringe, shiny as a horse. Then Priya smiled.

PART TWO

EARLY EVENING

11

What is Ray doing, twenty-four short hours before his exhibition opens?

He sleeps, in the house he calls "my triumph."

Once this area was all Polish piano teachers in bedsits, big houses turned into sad hotels. But the bankers are spreading through Zone Two, with fresh new second families. Sash windows are being restored, York stone laid. Ray takes such simple pleasure in London property prices, in tales of friends' children unable to afford even rent. He tells acquaintances that he paid only five grand for this "pile" of rampaging Victoriana: the end of a short terrace almost slithering off the top of Brixham Hill, facing the grassed-over old reservoir and the blur of Archway beyond. No one mentions that he grew up here; that his parents bought it in the fifties from a Maltese widow who raised rabbits, for eating, in the garden.

If Uncle David and Gillian go on about the freehold this weekend, there will be trouble. Ray insists that he bought them out fair and square, so he and Lucia, pregnant with Leah, could move in. And given that he had to organize a flat around the corner for his mother, "Mother," and help pay for his ex-wife,

Vivienne, to be set up in the corner extension, he's been very generous. Ray is a famously generous man.

The neighbors, because they have no style, despise the colossal net of Virginia creeper that darkens the front windows; it bulges over the dingy London brick, like a philosopher's beard. The hedge is a thicket of ivy, sycamore, jasmine; the red front door has faded to a liverish pink and the side gate is peeling undercoat. Jess and Leah and Patrick had to repaint it every February; Ray once made them stand out there in pajamas because they hadn't finished, until it grew dark and Patrick was crying.

Nobody dares ask Ray why, if the house is such a prize, he lets it rot. Jess says it's because of the force field around him, in which outsiders do not believe. Or they assume that they will be able to break through it, expect him to have normal standards of politeness, duty, embarrassment. But the cloud of unreason is more powerful than they can comprehend, and no one challenges Ray.

Jess says he wants the house to die with him, like a pharaoh buried with his slaves. She says the only solution is a wrecking ball.

So the house is subsiding into decay. There is a precarious crack across the cornice, daylight visible through the living-room window frame. The ceilings bulge, the radiators drip. Despite Patrick's efforts, there are grubs in the soggy window frames, moles beneath the mess of a lawn. Mold-spores multiply, obeying unfelt urges. Dynasties of silverfish live in the downstairs loo, racing around the edge of the lino; when Pat was little he thought they were eels. The house is spongy with decay. There is dramatic damp in the basement hallway, causing the jungly green paint, of which Ray is so proud, to peel in waves. Flocks of ladybirds sleep in the curtains; what Ray insists are just very big mice have tunneled into the compost bin. The washing machine needs the last few gallons of every cycle emptied by hand, like a scuttled boat. Ray keeps potatoes in the broken dishwasher; he says labor-saving devices enslave womankind, then he laughs. The garden walls and the chimney flues are hazardous. Ray's brilliant idea of varnishing behind the toilet has backfired; the mold is happily reproducing, now with an eye-catching sheen. Every time he splinters his heel on the floorboard in their bedroom, he roars at Lucia like Rumpelstiltskin. Is it woodworm, wet rot or dry?

The myth is that Ray runs the household, that he's the one with common sense. Lucia is rubbish at practicalities, as he frequently says. But Ray is exhausted. Somebody else needs to take charge.

As darkness falls on the Hanrahans' house, unwise early blossom glows palely against the ivy. You can see the concrete fort of the Royal Free Hospital from here, beyond the long lawn and tangled trees, laburnum, ash, the rotting pear. Slip your finger between the petals, blue-white under the Milky Way, and think of Patrick, how heavily his isolation weighs. Think of Leah, whose beloved is off somewhere with his girlfriend; of Lucia, already feeling like a murderer; of Aunt Gillian, bringer of sanity, of Ray. At least Jess is happy. Isn't she?

12

Leah's father needs waking in stages. Any loud noise makes his heart thump.

"The whole family, assembling in your honor," Leah tells him, balancing his fresh coffee on a Jiffy bag. "Everyone we know, all your friends. Aren't you even a little bit excited?"

Soon he'll be in the bath with his accessories: the paper and a large bacon sandwich ("Well, it doesn't affect *my* cholesterol"). Paisley will be lying pooled on the floor like a tabby carpet. The portable JVC tape-player, perilously close to his dripping back-scrubber, will be playing *Standards* by Eddie Higgins, another underrated genius. That tape is irreplaceable. She's spent weeks trying to find a back-up: no luck yet.

"*Mm-hm, mmm-hm*"; the sound of him singing along always warms her. At every crescendo his hairy abdomen will tighten, the plate tip. It will end badly. He does not care. Last night Dr. Mac gave him something extra, for the stress.

And once he's settled, muffled by the sound of pouring taps and the occasional trumpety fart, Leah will be free to ring the man she plans to marry.

There is a dry click as he opens his mouth. He sleeps so badly, barely an hour or two a night, so needs his room perfectly dark, then 100W of overhead light whenever he wakes. You'd think Leah's mother would understand, given his back and neck troubles, his poor legs, the jittering pulse and the night terrors and the new pulling sensation in his hip, but she claims the light, like his snoring, are unbearable. She says she might try sleeping in Jess's old room, except it's packed, and he was hurt.

There are smudges of light on his big nose, his brainy forehead. He's only sixty-six; that isn't old. He still has a virility, like a masterful badger: those bristly ears, the black forbidding eyebrows of a cartoon vulture, all that white hair. A handsome man, even in extremis, with none of the mistakes to which pensioners tend: the comb-over, the baggy cardigan, the tragic shuffle.

When he is dead, she will still contain his molecules. The thought makes her heart crumple like foil. No one has understood her as he does, finds her as interesting. No other man could ever compare, she'd assumed, until she met, well, saw, Pablo Nathaniel.

Ray's voice rumbles up at her, as if he can tell she's distracted: "Your mother . . . around?"

"She's—she'll definitely be back soon."

"Rubbish. She's busy, can't be bothered. So what is it?"

"What?"

"What's she working on?"

"I don't know. Is there something?"

"I bet there is."

"Really? Actually, I did notice . . ."

"Go on."

"It's probably, well, nothing. Just Coralie's boyfriend saw . . . No, you do know him, he's the one with the lisp."

"Whose brother's baby looks like a manatee? Huge child."

"Clever you, that's him. Poor Coralie. Anyway, he thought he saw Mum at Moorgate talking to som—"

"Coralie's something incredibly boring, isn't she?"

"Well, not boring. Disabled kids."

"Well, then, she wouldn't have a clue. Probably never seen a painting. I fancy something sweet. At least you haven't left me."

"Oh, Dad. Poor Dad," she says, stroking his hair. "You know I won't."

"I'm starving," he says; it's a good sign. At least when he's home she can keep track. His recklessness with his health scares her: sponge fingers in the studio, his personal toaster used to melt cheese. He's charmed the unfriendly corner shop to deliver one-liter jars of pickled chillies. Jess will be furious that her old bedroom's now a bit of a larder: two cases of Rose's Lime Cordial in the *glass* bottles, obtained at great cost, ancient jumbo packs of Californian pecans, olive oil from the dad of a man he met at the Pineapple; a pallet of his special hot chocolate.

He needs her to keep an eye on his diet, and everything else. He once called her his amanuensis. He'd write more if it wasn't for the pain. She's in charge of his archive: his scribbles on napkins, the memoir he's dictating, helping him guess how much the pictures are worth so he can stick masking tape with "Leah" or "AUCTION" on the back; sometimes he changes his mind, for fun. And, yes, tending to him, finding treats and keeping on top of his pain relief does require more care than a normal father might need.

"But who," he'd say, "wants normal?"

Jess says he's enslaved her, that Leah's a Victorian spinster-daughter. She'll arrive soon, smelling of the train, ready to judge, but she doesn't understand a thing. Besides, soon it'll be different. This weekend might be the time to tell them.

"Of course I want you to be happy," Ray often reminds her, "as long as you're still my girl."

"Always," she says. "I'll always be."

Here, in the dark beside him, she's wondering if it's a promise she can keep.

She can hear him flexing his toes. "Who else'll be here?"

"For the exhibition?"

"No, for my nude breakdancing try-out," he says, but lovingly. "Fool. I'm an excellent dancer, you know."

"I do."

"Could have done so many things. Maybe I'll make a record. Do some telly. Write a novel."

"You could. When all this is done, definitely. So . . . so who's staying? Right, so there's the Gillians. Sorry."

"'Course they are. Too tight for a hotel. Are they snuggling up with me and Mum or . . ."

"No, weirdly Vivienne's taking them."

"Oh yes? What's her game, I wonder."

"She's so uptight about her house," says Leah, "that it must be to please you. Because she's still holding a flame."

"Well, obviously," Ray says. "She is definitely coming, isn't she?"

"I told you."

"Well, she'd better not get her predatory hooves into my little brother. Or he into her, not that we'd blame him. Have you found a screen to conceal Gillian behind?"

"Dad," she says, laughing, "she's not that bad."

"Hideous."

"Shh. Sorry. Um, OK, so yes, David, Gillian and the mini Gillians; Uncle Graeme—"

"Who isn't, presumably, plus one."

"Never. And . . . Jess. Yes. She's definitely coming."

She'd better, thinks Leah, massaging his shoulders; and not upset him either. Last time she was here, Martyn let the front door slam, their father said, "It's a miracle I've kept my legendary bonhomie," and everyone, except Jess, laughed. Bitch. She plays the victim, but she hurts him; it's like she's honoring them by popping back. It can't go on. It isn't fair. This weekend, thanks to Leah's hard work, Ray will be happy, and Jess will see what she's been missing, at last.

Leah's barely sleeping. Her mind won't stop spooling. As long as nobody drags their chairs on the floor, or makes a sudden noise, or forgets one of his dislikes (cathedral towns; shrubs; supermarkets; wallpaper; exercise; English people with good French accents; umbrellas; "health food"; tomato-based pasta sauces; cut flowers; Beethoven; abstinence from anything; postwar fiction; peonies; digital clocks; thin pillows, but also overfilled pillows; all the neighbors; hoop earrings; bread-ends; pitted olives; infants being carried in slings; Italy (weak); shop-bought jam; raw vegetables; food without enough salt or butter; the council; headphones, or audible music not of his choosing; leftovers; libraries; people who do A levels; people who go to university; Wales and Scotland; loud sneezing; schoolchildren; birds "unless for eating"; teachers; the county of Essex; Germans and German art-collectors; attempts to avoid cancer; champagne; milk not in glass bottles; sorbet; illness; television newsreaders; certain women's haircuts (short/showy-off); cats other than Paisley; banks; everything pertaining to the London Irish; the dark; bad fathers; unfaithful wives), there isn't a single reason why the exhibition won't be a triumph.

Just as Leah is taking a second pill, for courage, Vivienne catches her.

Vivienne is, as Leah's father often says, a bad woman. "I'd be overjoyed," Ray says, "never to see that witch again," but she lives as close to her ex-husband as a person can. He fears her, she calls him "Poor Raymond" and exists elegantly beside them, like an unexploded bomb too unstable to move. When Lucia was pregnant with Leah, they generously converted the side section for Vivienne, with a door on the first floor between the two households, rarely used.

He says hers is England's most selfish flat because it's just three clean bare big rooms on top of each other, no storage into which his old books can creep. Leah's mother says Vivienne is cordial to her, and she's civil in return, or maybe it's the other way round. Lucia can afford to be polite; she was once a looker, has borne his children. Vivienne, however, has beauty; it's still clinging on in the deep eyes, the bony splendor of her cheekbones. And, of course, she's never got over Ray. It's hard to know who wins.

Ray kept asking if she'd RSVP'd to the exhibition, until Leah lied and said yes. And she's lending, or at least permitting, the use of her elegant home.

"I do need the airbed pump," says Vivienne. She has a large luxurious bedroom, with its television at one end, bath at the other, its questionably enormous bed.

"Sorry," Leah says. Vivienne is impossible not to suck up to. "Dad says thanks for having, putting up, the curator, gallerist, Eric thingy. And the Gillian kids."

"I never quite know how that marriage works, do you?"

"Sorry?"

"David and Gillian. They seem so . . . happy. He doesn't mind a bit that she's done so well. And *you*," Vivienne continues, "look . . . energized. Are you?"

But Leah has not come this far, to the point of true love, by giving herself away. "I'm fine," she says.

Vivienne looks a little too long, fleetingly smiles. "Oh, and my friend Lars, who's visiting, is very curious about Ray's work. So I'll be bringing him, tomorrow."

"Does Dad know?"

"Lars," says Vivienne patiently, "is on his way from Malmö. He is," she clarifies, "a very tall man. And my lover. But don't tell Ray. We'll just sneak him into the show."

"But—" says Leah.

"You do look . . . excited. I've noticed you going out more. Your mother too. Today, or tomorrow," says Vivienne, "she and I must have a talk."

Leah is a sea-captain, steering her fragile craft. When Larry Nathaniel himself suggested to Ray that his son Pablo does the catering, Leah thought she might die of hope fulfilled. The universe was aligning. Everything happens for a reason. It took so much coaxing for Ray to agree, even though he'd plainly wanted it, had been flirting with Larry Nathaniel until he agreed they could use the upstairs of the Guildworkers' Hall for free. And the Gallery, as they're calling it now, isn't much: a huge splintery platform, fiberboard walls, but it's almost as big as the main space, where they have parties and weddings and even, to her father's cheerful disgust, civil partnerships.

"As long," Ray says, "as he keeps the poofs off me."

Capacity two hundred, according to the website. Is it possible that she was too optimistic? She's lost track; if there aren't enough people, he'll be gutted. And there's no way it'll be perfect by tomorrow night. Larry Nathaniel says he's "hands off," which means he won't fix the heating, or handle any of the bits proper galleries do: taking the pieces to and from the framers, organizing price lists and biogs, hanging and lighting, consolidating the invites. Laz-Nat, as Ray calls him, is hungover most of the time, doesn't know what he's doing. It's been weeks of work, yet Leah has an uneasy feeling that she has forgotten far more than she realizes.

Because Ray mustn't be reminded that he isn't with a mainstream gallery at the moment, she keeps all this quiet.

"So this cook bloke works where?" her father had said on the way home. "Laz-Nat's son? Do we want him?"

She can't quite bring herself to say its name until he asks: "It's called . . . 'Verdisec'Oh!'"

"Jesus."

"Don't blame him, his mate christened it. I think. You know, that tiny little restaurant near the railway bridge by Camden Overground, everyone goes there, it's had amazing reviews."

"Oh," said Ray, sounding put out. "I thought it had closed down."

"Nearly. But they're hanging on, just Pablo and a couple of mates, making amazing organic—"

"Hmm. I think I've seen a review of his popper-upper in the *Camden New Journal*. By that madwoman, who asked me out, remember? Anyway. OK, if he's cheap and good. And no organic rubbish. Bet he fancies you."

Leah was unable to speak. Please, she begged her personal guardian angel, let him not guess, not see my hope, until there is something to show.

And no one is helping, not really. Her mother should have taken the day off but she puts her work first, always has: bundling them to school early, first in the playground, so she could get started; barely remembering how much they rely on her. Leah and her dad are still trying to persuade her to give up her old studio and be at home more. He needs her. It isn't fair, isn't wifely, of her to resist.

Despite his bravery, he is much more easily hurt than anyone realizes.

And what if the space doesn't do his work justice? His favorite builder, Clive Boleyn, has been jailed for smuggling cigarettes, so they're using the brother of the vet Ray is trying to befriend so Paisley can have free ear-detanglings. The brother usually constructs yurts; he says he's worked for other artists but talks about "energy." She's had to warn him not to mention it in front of her father. He keeps ringing Leah to ask where the pictures are.

"I told you. We're hanging them ourselves. Probably on the day."

"Why so last min?" he asked. "That's nuts."

13

Lucia approaches from the other direction: a piñata of hope, or a battering-ram.

She has made a huge mistake.

What was she thinking? The moment she opens the front door to Priya, everyone will be able to tell. Of all the nights to choose for spontaneity. She should be terrified of what she's done, what she still intends to do.

Yet she can't stop grinning. Slowly past the clematis with its leathery leaves like offal, the front of 74, trying too hard with its lavenders and verbena and standard olive. She's jumpy, like horses scenting smoke. In a few seconds she'll be home. Like a revolutionary with a bomb under her coat, she is bringing disaster in.

The air is vodka, light and cold. On the doormat remnant, she gives her hair a cursory smoothing, pulls off her mismatched gloves. Is it unfair to hope that they might have cleared up? Ray's heavy-pocketed donkey-jacket is under the hatstand; sartorially the eighties were good to him. There's a smell of burned toast. Usually, the moment she lets herself into the front hall, she's holding her breath, braced for the blackness. Even if Ray's many daily phone calls have been relatively calm, during her journey home anything could have upset him. *She* could have.

Lately she's been letting his crises rush past her, like the tide parting around a rock. He always insists on her ringing him, leaving notes explaining her whereabouts and ETA, thorough debriefings about every meeting. It used to feel like loving closeness.

The hallway is painted a dense blue-green. Sometimes it's like pushing up through an enormous weight of seawater, or running up a down escalator to face Ray's latest catastrophe. Tonight, at least, he'll be excited, so she needs to be alert yet apparently relaxed: coffee then one glass of wine. She pinches the pale papyrus skin of her inner elbow. You can do this. You can fake it for a few hours, tonight of all nights.

Her second encounter with Priya Menon, MP, was an accident. A fortnight had passed and Lucia had barely thought of her since the party, not felt a thrill, not sensed the germination of chaos. But, perhaps, she was ready.

She had been fiddling about all week with *Dead Helot*, *Spines* and *Green Night*; nothing was working. She needed the windy rural walks other artists mention in interviews; a coastal garret; a murmuration. But this is her life, so, instead, she nipped down to the National Gallery: late closing.

The cool stony scent of the Sainsbury Wing has always soothed her. She sat in front of the *Wilton Diptych*; her favorite, for its monochrome wing-tips; the texture of the gold leaf, like the air in a miracle; the fierce deep lapis robes and the face of the kneeling king, a reverential undertaker. Carmel used to bring them here and let her sit. It made her an artist and so, at the beginning of their coupledom, she shyly led Ray to pay homage, or tell her if she was wrong. And Ray . . .

Ray claimed it. He'd always loved it too, he said; knew more about the oak and gilding, was inspired by the profiles. Later he claimed she'd nicked the saint's crown for one of her *Queen Beelzebubs*, would tell her that angels were off limits, because he was already painting them. It became his, only his.

So the *Wilton* slowly lost its power and, this time, it failed her completely. It was almost December: a black rainy evening, kebab-shop lighting in the puddles, every bus packed with irritable women lugging home wrapping paper. She was not at her best but, these days, who is? The Tufnell Park lifts were down so she trudged up the windy Kentish Town elevator, noticed it had started to pour, sighed unkindly as a man fussed at the turnstiles, caught the eye of the woman beside her.

They frowned in vague recognition and then Priya had said: "I know who you are" and they'd started chatting as they waited for the torrent to pass. By the time she'd put up her umbrella they were laughing and Lucia thought: Oh, she's not so scary.

"I'm this way," Lucia said, gesturing right.

"I'm down there. Oh well. Tell you what, come for a drink," said Priya.

"What, now?"

"Why not? Rare I'm out so early, time on my hands."

"I should . . ."

"Come on. I'm bored easily."

"OK, I think," said Lucia. "I'll just send a . . . a text," and Priya smirked.

She led her, talking, all the way down Prince of Wales Road, under the railway bridge and down a narrow lane, picturesquely ashy London brickwork at odd angles, closed-up workshops, a sign saying G&D IRON SMELTING SCRAP. "Reminds me of the places I grew up," Priya said. "I didn't know anyone in London, then I saw Queen's Crescent and felt at home. For what that's worth."

"I know," said Lucia.

Her house was shut and still. Big multi-paned windows glinting in the street lights like a little factory; not the usual dull shrubs at the front but, mostly, banana-plant. Lucia smiled.

"Like it?" said Priya.

"Oh, yes. Very much."

"Let's get you inside, then," said Priya, and she unlocked the heavy door.

What did Lucia expect? A dim messy living room not unlike her own, wine, confidences, pools of light as they semi-reclined on one of those corner sofas. When she saw Priya Menon's glossy white kitchen table and yellow tulips, smelled clean air, she knew coming here was a mistake. Priya Menon can talk to anyone; she'd soon realize Lucia was nothing special. Already Lucia felt dense with clumsiness: all the usual earnest enthusiasms, her lack of coolness about anything, and also for her hubristic, unjustified, imaginary version of the evening in which they would have: what? Become friends?

It was nothing like that.

They drank tea; "I have," Priya said, "nothing but old mayonnaise and vodka. And a kettle."

"That's not good. Don't . . . don't you eat? I eat."

"Christ. Loads."

"I'm very greedy," said Lucia, and Priya lifted her eyebrows.

"Well, me too, but I'm either out for dinner or staggering back at midnight. It's a takeaway or nothing. Although I am strangely drawn to a sandwich toaster."

Lucia watched herself gesturing, trying to brush off the clay-handprint on her trousers, expecting the warmth to dissolve into an awkward exchange of personal experiences, like unsuccessful tribal negotiations. But Priya answered every question, asked even more back. She gossiped, swore, discovered a hole in her woolen tights and before Lucia's very eyes darned it.

"Of course I can sew," she said. "MPs are like sailors; it's all about emergency repairs. Sewing-kits and plasters and shoes in every cupboard. Obviously the good ones swap with each other."

"Are you friends with any . . . Tories?" asked Lucia.

"Of course! To a point. Don't you sew for your work?"

"A bit," Lucia said cautiously.

"But it's not needlepoint."

"Christ, no. Massive Frankenstein stitches. But only sometimes. It's mostly wax and rubbish and sticks."

"Of course," Priya said, "I know your work."

"Do you?"

"You look amazed. But not your husband's."

"Oh. That's not the usual . . . I mean, it's complicated."

"Hmm," said Priya. "Well. I've been hoping to spot you."

She had the sort of brain one wants to fall inside. The laughing and the openness were what Lucia remembered, afterward. Aren't MPs supposed to be discreet? They discussed the point at which prime ministers go mad; the curvature of the earth; rigor mortis; Midlands Hindus versus London Hindus ("ve-ry different. But the Midlands are treated poorer in everything, you must know that?"); if lavender is edible; cultural signifiers of status ("for us it was plastic-covered furniture and unaffordable cars"); Priya's mother ("difficult. Horrible past") and grandmother ("still did all our cooking at ninety-eight, that's why I can't") but not her father, who had been, Lucia deduced, an engineering student from Gujarat. "Died young, they all do. But Keralan women live forever." Her language was very precise; she used her hands. She was fiercer than she had expected, more piratical. She told Lucia about the closing of domestic-abuse shelters, abortion-clinic security, running away from home at sixteen, the impossibility of getting changed in her Westminster office because the blind covered only half of the overlooked window, "but I do it anyway. It's only other MPs. Perks them up."

Lucia was expecting to find her cold, was thinking of this as a research trip: that marvelous triangular nose, the Joan of Arc warrior halo. Perhaps, she'd thought, I'll be able to use her. She kept an eye on her lovely skull.

But Priya asked direct questions: did her parents meet at the Galty in Cricklewood? Did she know about Weaver's Lung? Who in her family believed in God? What did she read? She wanted to know about the act of art itself. And she seemed surprised that Lucia was not, like her, an only child. "So what do you have?"

"I . . . I . . ."

"Well?"

"I have a lost brother."

"As in dead?"

"As in lost. He . . . We're not in touch. He's younger, a bit. After Dad died . . ."

"Does he still see your mam?"

"Barely," said Lucia and Priya nodded once, and started telling her about urinary infections among female MPs, upper-arm squeezes from male MPs, invitations to hospital bedsides and wakes. "Weekends at home it can be three or four Asian weddings."

"Are they friends, some of them? Your . . . constituents?"

"Of course. But there's a veil. They want you to be perfect. They'll say: 'Ooh get you, Mrs. Menon, you're in the shop!' and I'll say, 'MPs need bin-liners too.' Mostly, everyone wants you to come to their events and launches and special dinners. My diary is . . . mental. I get twenty invites a week, just at home. Loads more in London."

"So London's not home?"

"Christ, no. Although it's just mine, so I love it for that. I mean, not Sid's."

"Oh. I see."

"Do you?" said Priya, grinning. "Anyway," she said strictly, "the invitations are an honor. It all matters. It's a privilege to help them."

"Of c—"

"It's because I believe in things," she said. "Women, immigrants, schooling, you know, the absolute basics, so everyone asks. It sounds awful, but they're just so desperate for someone to help them, to be seen. The forms are . . . so if I can sort benefits, ring someone in housing, it changes their lives. Or just listen to the poor sods. They send me . . . items. You should see my office, it's awash."

"With . . . ?"

"Every time I do something, even local radio, there are millions of thank-you cards. Padded granny ones, primary-school kids—oh my God—but also presents. Books, handmade jewelry, boxes of caramelized nuts . . . the other day on *Newsnight* I said I liked marmalade, and eleven different people brought Seville oranges and jam jars to the office."

"In Parliament?"

"No, you muggins. The shop. Back in Coventry."

"What's it like?" Lucia asked, cleverly. "Where you work?"

Priya shrugged. "The constituency office? Not interesting. Bigger than my Westminster one, which is all neat and smart, identical to everyone else's, very close-fitting doors and ergonomic deskage. The Coventry one's just a big pile of boxes, crap, campaigning leaflets. Outside a bus stop. Next to a laundrette. Lots of grannies looking in and shaking their heads."

Later, when they were talking about their childhoods, Priya said her mum, mam, was "angry." Then she said, changing the subject, "it helps to have a spouse who's good at the local meet and greet back home. And Sid is."

She said that being stuck in the Chamber or the Strangers' bar, socializing for work until midnight, all the unhealthy food, booze, being wired all the time, made it hard to sleep.

"What do you do?"

"Listen to the radio. Text my friends. Worry. Plot. Winding down is . . . well. Now, I need a real drink, so you'd better go before the fun begins."

And later still, pulling on her coat in the doorway, Lucia found herself wanting to discuss sandwich toasters, the pros and cons. She wanted to say, "I'd love a vodka," but she wasn't that sort of person. Instead, she found herself accidentally telling Priya that, three years ago this coming February, something horrible happened.

She indicated the general area. Priya looked her in the eye. She didn't make a stupid joke, or appear disgusted, or seem to see Lucia as a woman under a death-cloud, pathetic and doomed.

She said: "After that kind of trauma, shock, some sort of PTSD would be normal. Physical, psychological . . . Did you get depressed?"

And Lucia, who has rarely said that word even to herself, hesitates.

"Did you?"

"I suppose . . . Ray says I was horrible. So maybe. Although he thinks he was brilliantly supportive, etcetera. That he nursed me. He did try. Maybe I was traumatized, I haven't thought . . . My role was to be the sad patient."

"Surprise. And are you . . . reconciled?"

"With him?"

"No, with—" and she looked down, below Lucia's chin, her throat, her chest, her, say it, breastbone. "With what happened."

"Oh."

"Are you?"

"No," Lucia said, swallowing. "We're not reconciled."

14

Dragging his wheelie-case, Martyn, Jess's virtually fiancé, huffs up Brixham Hill.

What makes a man? Courage. Courage, and chest hair. Shouldn't he be able to plan for himself and Jess unilaterally? If they lived down here he could work at a little school, not toil all day through Higher special access requirements and piano-hire accountability committees.

"No way," Jess always says.

"But your family are desperate for us, you, to move to London."

"You don't believe that? Just because Dad says it's a phase, living up here, doesn't mean he wants me back. And Leah loves pretending she's street, you know, 'going Camden' and 'the ginger line,' but it's all front. They're like monks; they think that beyond the borough you'd just . . . fall off the world."

"That's not fair."

"It is. Leah says she's fine, but does she have a choice? And Patrick . . . it's awful. He needs help. Have you noticed he's getting shyer? Maybe he's agoraphobic. Or depressed; don't boys get schizophrenic?"

"You have to stop trying to rescue them."

"Why?"

"Because they're fine. You're meddling. Just leave them. Don't you want *us* to be happy?"

So far, his hopes for a healing of the Great Rift have been dashed. If, instead of obsessing over her father's imaginary crimes, she allowed herself to grow closer, they could ditch their rented tenement flat in gray Edinburgh, where he does his marking in industrial ear-protectors, thanks to an infestation of students, and find a pretty London terraced house close by. He could invite his old friends and show them what a man he has become.

Better still, almost too wonderful to contemplate, they could be installed in Patrick's old bedroom, steering the Hanrahans back into happiness. This warmth could be theirs, full-time, and he knows how to achieve it. Nothing will make them more delighted than if he brings Jess permanently home.

When will she appreciate what she has? He is ever more awash in nostalgia for Jess's upbringing, not his own. There must be a German word for that.

Take the cellar; the first time he saw it, he felt an almost erotic thrill. The single bulb, swinging at head-height, revealed a gloriously filthy world: solid wooden boxes carelessly dumped in a corner; rusted bottle-racks, the cells irregularly filled, like honeycomb. It made his mouth water. The floor appeared to be actual dirt, like in a forest. An armchair-sized wire hedgehog stood by the door, its prongs covered in empty bottles: Ray apparently once had a scheme to sell sloe gin.

Martyn still can't get over his refusal to recycle, despite the council's jazzy flyers. Ray doesn't believe in the environment; "I refuse," he says, "to join this charade." Lately, in Edinburgh, Martyn has been throwing old newspapers into the general rubbish bin and, as Ray points out, the world twirls on.

And Martyn isn't an outdoors man, but the part that most

haunts him is the garden. He drifts down the rills and inlets of his favorite daydream; becoming a gentleman farmer in the Hanrahans' back garden. Imagine inviting friends for drinks. Imagine growing up here, in this secure wildness, encircled by hedges tamed by Patrick's terrifying electric saw. The Hanrahans' garden, really several stuck together, is outrageous: ridiculously wide and long and overgrown, an accident of haphazard planning, protected ash trees, encroachment on adjoining land. They have many neighbors, mostly furious. One night, allegedly, Ray made Patrick move an entire fence.

There are stretches of crumbly walls and ragged hedgerow; at least two sheds; Patrick's caravan; a homemade pergola draped with rotten unripened grapes. It's so vast that even in late winter, shorn of leafage, from the caravan one can't see the plum tree; from the bay and rosemary one can't see the house. It smells of fermenting windfalls, wet leaves, mortality.

Jess is childishly furious about the neglect. Yet, when he suggests the obvious solution, she overreacts. She's upset that her childhood bedroom has been "requisitioned" as her father's office, box-files everywhere, a napping chair, a drafting-table, Paisley's eviscerated toys. She disapproves of her father's old friends, cartoonists and so forth, who come over for booze, leaving drips round the toilet. To Martyn it seems relaxed, and isn't that a jewel to be prized? The untidiness is funny, the creative dramas exciting, and the invisible rules, like museum lasers, keep him on an adrenalized high.

Like Achilles rounding the walls of Troy, crimson hands and lust in his heart, he is picking up speed. As he passes through the Tufnell Park ticket-gate, nodding at the tough-looking TFL man, there's a curl of excitement in his chest. He has always wanted to swing down from the vines, to be tested. Every man needs a quest.

Lately Jess has been possessive about time to herself. It's ridiculous; they are a couple, she shouldn't be having long baths in silence. If he so much as pops in to sit on the loo and update her with the day's news, she turns grumpy. It's all down to that awful skinny woman, Astrid Pringle. She's where the rot set in.

Martyn is a man now, with white hairs in distressing places. Isn't it time he took charge?

Which brings to mind the last time he and Jess, etc. He'd been having a conversation about it, in his mind, for weeks beforehand. Fat little kiddies, grandchildren for the in-laws; Ray would welcome him much more warmly. They'd all be excited to have Jess close by. And, although Martyn rarely shirks his spousal responsibilities, sometimes his, well, focus, seems to lapse. He needs a certain amount of imagination. Others, he's sure, do the same; although not, obviously, Jess. She's a tricky girl but he knows her mind; he's definitely all she wants.

Afterward, pleasingly sweaty, having attempted to repay her in kind but slightly nodding off more than once, he again thought: no, don't mention it now. Talk about it in the morning, when she's fresh. He was smiling into his pillow at the thought of Ray's gratitude; Leah's respect; even, perhaps, the joy of Patrick.

And his thoughts drift, as they do more than perhaps they ought, to poor old Patrick, Patch, tinkering away in self-imposed caravan isolation. Jess once mentioned a bad fight with Ray. Patch is only a stepson but grew up with Ray, in this warm, welcoming house; what a waste of a perfect childhood. He is, Ray says, not streetwise: no sense of humor. Sharp-profiled as a doomed wartime pilot, clean-shaven, very tightly wound, he has never married; no known girlfriends. He once said: "I don't do touch."

What does this mean, precisely? Martyn would give money to know.

Fathers, too, are not something Martyn's qualified to handle. On first sighting Martyn, Ray turned his head like a disgusted eagle and Martyn, who had been reading up on his reputation, his bracing irascibility, genuinely thought he might faint. Ray sat on the edge of the sofa, coaxing wax from his ear with an unbent paperclip, wearing the grin that, Martyn now knows, signifies triumph over lesser life-forms.

But Martyn was sleeping with this man's sweet hazelnutty daughter; at least, he probably would that very night. And he was runty, with mad-professor hair and *Beano* knees; not tall and well shaped like the rest of them, but a prawn of a man. With her lashy green-and-blue eyes and heavy hair, the tentative way she holds her head forward, like a camel, Jess was out of his league, visually. Even his clothes were wrong. Jess had warned him not to be smart but he'd worn a jacket anyway, in defiance, with Marcus Aurelius's *Meditations* poking from the pocket. He hadn't known how Ray dislikes academic striving, overeducation; teachers, in fact.

Ray looked him over through his big black-framed glasses, lingered on his lapels, and Martyn knew that he had erred. Ray Hanrahan could sling him downstairs with one hand; his expression suggested: I know you, and I don't like what I see.

Now that he understands Ray's struggle, it's moving how his adult children, exes, brothers, still gather around him, like a family of attractive gorillas around a silverback. He'd expected Ray to be gaunt and dry and English; Jess has a touching politeness, which he assumed was the family way. So imagine his surprise to be insulted, repeatedly: "Thingy," "you idiot," or, twice, "that wee tartan arse." It took him some time to realize that Ray Hanrahan may appear like an impatient Anglo-Saxon despot—that scowling bonhomie, the voice—but he's all heart. Martyn learned to bring him tales of others' misfortune, like a cat laying torn mice at his feet. The comments about Martyn's lack of a father, the fact that he is deaf in one ear, are all affection. Patrick's big mistake is showing fear.

And still, whenever Martyn thinks he's identified his level in Ray's mysterious hierarchy, a dubious friend will drop by and Martyn becomes invisible. Only Patrick is lower. But he's guessing that a bit of decisive manliness, some emphatic family values, as demonstrated this weekend, will turn it around.

Lucia was daunting, too, for about an hour: the gray streaks, the pale, squarish face and soulful eyes, distracted, presumably, by her Art. She lives so much in her studio, and in her head, but Martyn is sure he has her blessing. He tries to be sensitive about her illness, not to be seen looking. Jess was still distraught about it when they met, most of a year afterward. To Martyn she was just another girl, sitting near his table at a raucous leaving do at the Star of Leith, December 2007; young at twenty-eightish, not a drinker then, so quite flirty. She was just starting at Dalziel's, with a sweet freshly hatched yolkiness after struggling through her PGCE. He'd had a difficult week, a series of upsetting misunderstandings now buried in the past, and had thought: I might find comfort here. And once they'd got together, him well established in Edinburgh, a confident sophisticated Head of Geography, well, deputy, at St. Jerome's and ready to move on, he'd been so pleased to have a girlfriend that he hadn't even considered her parents, much, but they sounded like horrible hippies. Jess claimed her father hadn't spoken to her during teacher training, not once; she cried about it occasionally.

"How could he possibly mind?"

"He thinks I betrayed him."

"Oh, come on. By getting an education?"

She frowned at him. "You can't imagine how bad it was," she said, as if there'd been a war.

"He just missed you."

"He says I'm . . . a snob. And other things."

"But he's a sophisticated man. London, bohemians, doesn't that . . . ?"

"Believe me. Don't even mention your degree unless . . . You'll understand, if you come?"

"Maybe," he'd said. He knows all about sand-kicked-in faces. And what kind of son would spend that train fare on visiting someone else's family, while his mother sits alone at home in Dalry, Ayrshire?

Jess hadn't yet decided that Ray had let her mother down; she was still warm about him, hoping for closeness. "We eat," she said. "Endlessly," and Martyn thought of his mother, cling-filmer of single sausages, diluter of tinned soup; the microwave disinfected to its eyeteeth. Hers is not a house in which a man can relax.

Then Jess confided about her artist father. "You must have seen *Screw*?"

"I . . . maybe."

"Though he's more abstract now. Much more. He was a bit famous once; he might be again. If he worked. But he can't." And Martyn had chosen not to pry.

Then, as they labored up Brixham Hill the first time, Jess said, "I warn you, it's a madhouse. Maybe you should have gone to the barber. We should have brought a better bottle. Remember not to kiss me in front of them, Dad says it's not fair on Leah. Though he's . . . oh God. This is probably a mistake."

But, within hours, he knew he was home. His sticky soul was nourished by the sight of the hallway, the wide floorboards whose sheeny grain remind him of mighty oaks, the original Ark. He couldn't get over the size of the television; the fridge, big as a mortician's but in a desperate state, rammed with luxury: Bakewell tarts, miniature pork pies, pre-grated cheese. The noise was exhilarating, as far removed from his knife-scraping childhood silence as life on the ocean floor. There was limitless alcohol, reclining on the sofa like a pasha, swaddling central heating, not a light turned off, not a coaster used, and a mighty chunk of next door's lilac blazing in the illegal fireplace.

"Don't the neighbors mind?" he'd asked.

"He wears brown socks. Probably a perv," said Ray.

Jess says the house makes her feel sick, that if they weren't so middle-class it would be condemned. She claims that without Patrick's repairs it would slither down Brixham Hill. Maybe this weekend he'll see more of Patrick. Patch looks up to Ray, yet persists in annoying him with acts of cussedness: vegetarianism, longish hair, the caravan. Ray calls him the Wild Toddler of the Woods. When Patrick sneezes, Ray rolls his eyes, makes that trill of disgust. "God's sake!" he'll growl. He must be, thinks Martyn with an ache of older-brotherly feeling, an unhappy man. Ray likes commenting on his absent-mindedness, his distraction: "Look at him. He doesn't live in the real world."

Jess disagrees. She says her brother is serene, as still waters are serene. When she and Martyn first met, she'd try to drum up cookery jobs for him; a pizza place in Highgate, a Nepalese in Acton, a prison kitchen. When she began to coax him toward Edinburgh, Martyn drew the line. The first time they met, Patrick had a new black toilet seat looped over his arm like a tribal bracelet, his army-surplus satchel bouncing on his hip. What if this clearly unstable young man wanted to stay with them? Who was she to play God, to force change? People are entitled to their private thoughts.

And Leah: "Of course she's not fulfilled," Jess says. "How could she be?"

"But your dad is her vocation. She says so."

"Bollocks. He does. He calls her May Morris, but she's Dorothea Casaubon." Martyn's always meant to look that up. "Dad says she's the talented one, swears she's an artist too, all that guff about 'the family business.' Doesn't occur to him she might not want to be. And how about romance?"

"What about it?"

"She's not going to find true love, is she, looking after him? She needs to go abroad, miles. Australia. I could kill him."

"You mean true love like ours? She says she doesn't mind."

"You believe her? She cries at babies. Buys secondhand Mills and Boon at that spooky donkey-charity shop at the roundabout. Last time I asked Leah, she said, 'I couldn't abandon him.' As if he's alone. Ha! Do you realize she's never h—"

"What?"

"Forget it."

Thanks to Leah, Martyn understands Ray's torments better now. He knows not to ask the nature of Ray's affliction: definitely not a birth defect, because he's talked about his energetic youth. He often comments sadly on runners and cyclists: "Look at them, so fit. Life isn't fair." If Jess mutters that he, too, could exercise, Ray withdraws, deeply hurt.

Could it be a tragic wasting disease? What does polio look like? Parts of London are probably still hotbeds of TB; whenever Martyn's sent on one of the Hanrahans' mysterious missions, the pharmacists' counters feel unsafe. Thanks to his own upbringing, gleaming with bleach and moist towelettes, he still can't quite tell what's an acceptable level of dirt.

No: he's concluded that it must have been an accident. Poor, poor Ray. The man's so clearly a hero; uncomplainingly bearing the countless house-visits of the family doctor, although Jess claims that Dr. Brian McLaren, unsuccessful Independent candidate in the recent Camden Council by-elections, is the worst GP in London. She says that he is in her father's thrall, or is it the other way round? That Ray's bond with his tame quack grows ever tighter. Dr. Mac's openhanded approach to prescriptions will be the death of Ray.

But Ray surely knows what's right for him, and Dr. McLaren agrees.

Jess says that his pain isn't straightforward. He's definitely suffering; he sometimes jokes about sending Leah down to the Cally Road to score for him and Martyn has to hide the shock. Obviously Leah would never do that. Once, after dinner, when like a tiger he was full of meat, he mentioned oxysomething: oxygen is a natural element.

And it's not fair to compare Ray, an artist, to, say, Martyn's own mother. Marion's easily seventy but still fit as a barrel, arranging chinchilla cages and fake rocks for snakes. Or her creepingly racist friends; they'll all live to be a hundred, without benefiting humanity in any way. So, if someone has to drive to an out-of-the-way pharmacy, late at night, rather the worse for wear themselves, to collect a bag of medication like a diplomatic pouch, better not to probe.

Almost there, like the cavalry. The Hanrahans need a firm hand on the tiller, rudder, whatever you call it. Ray will be delighted; Patrick, in his quiet way, too. Although he is perfectly innocent, Martyn feels himself grow hard.

15

Oh God. She needs to tell Ray who's coming to dinner.

"Finally, she bothers to drop in," he's yelling. "I'm slaving down here. Could you possibly give me a hand, for the most important weekend of my tragic life?"

Through the thicket of raincoats and acrylic Arsenal scarves; foothills of unopened gallery magazines, pizza flyers. Only fear keeps her spirits up. The hall carpet is worn, corduroyish; trapped in its fibers is the particular Hanrahan house smell of cardboard, roast chicken, the brow-bands of aged hats. The old desk they use as a hall table, the chair and watering-can and boxes beside it, are lost in a slither of mess. At least in the living room she's shoved slippers into hiding places, straightened books, but the guests will still have to pass the hall outside her bedroom, where the clutter intensifies. And the kitchen. Shit, think, shit, think, she tells herself, flexing her stiff fingers. What have I done?

Ray is kneeling to swear at the oven, surrounded by spent matches. Two huge chunks of raw lamb, bones glistening pearly violet as a gland, wait quietly on the countertop. "I shouldn't be surprised," he's saying, "that I have to do everything. It's been flat out all day, getting this place ready. I just hoped for a bit of help."

"Sorry I'm late," she says. "Sorry," but his deep sigh promises trouble ahead.

He is wearing his most disreputable jumper, slamming pans around. "Stop fannying around. Do something."

She covers her eyes with a hand, breathing quickly through her nose like a panicked beast. Ray begins his daily rosary of complaints and woundings; she responds, reassuring, justifying while looking around at what there is to do.

OK. Do not cry.

A knife stands erect in a jar of Heinz Sandwich Spread; the table is fanned with crumbs and satsuma peel. She'd like to clear it with a sweep of her arm, tip the whole lot over. The lamb was meant to be Ray's field but all he's done is oversalt it, as if gritting a path. She sets to, squashing the pink skins off garlic cloves, stabbing the lamb's greasy hide with kitchen scissors to push them in, while he grumbles and has a long pee with the downstairs toilet door open. He says he's in charge but never takes stirring seriously: garlic scorches, tomatoes stick.

"Get out of the fridge. There's no time for one of your sandwiches," he says. Nowhere in the literature of inappropriate adult longing, not *The Awakening*, even unsexy *Madame Bovary*, is anyone as hungry as she is. "And Vivienne's been banging on about duvets to Leah, which I'd assumed you'd sorted out. She's invited herself tomorrow. God knows I don't want her. Can't keep her away, though, poor lonely thing."

Might Vivienne be one of those women who manage this successfully: the plate-spinning, the secret meetings? She definitely had a man on the cards when Ray met Lucia; Ray's heartbreak was part of the appeal. He has forgotten this.

It's as if a blindfold has come undone. The kitchen units, once daringly apple-green, are too stuffed to close: old instant noodles, blooming chocolate. Ray is furious whenever anything he likes is thrown out. He hates her bags of soup beans, complains there was no room for her "apocalypse rations," but she still sneaks tomato paste and sardines in at the back. Nothing has been replaced or modernized: the kettle on the hob (Ray says electric is bourgeois), which rumbles and clanks so loudly that all conversation has to stop; the fluorescent strip-lighting like a hospital; the scuffed swing-bin; the rusted drying-rack. When did it all tip from bohemian to simply squalid? Each socket serves too many appliances; the spindly aloe vera and Kellogg's Corn Flakes commemorative egg cup still sit on the deep windowsill above the sink, dotted with dead basil leaves. And, like chicken-pox scars, family history lingers: torn kitten-stickers; glitter-pens down the side of the fridge; wobbly fork-scratches on the table; a tiny jelly commando, his parachute tangled in the corner light. How had she imagined Priya here?

My God, thinks Lucia, dread washing over her as if a freezer has been opened, I need to cancel, at least warn her. And she doesn't really know about Ray, whose state isn't easily described. But Priya will ignore her messages until the last possible moment, when she is already outside the front door.

And what if Marie-Claude rings again?

The sink looks blocked; she gets on her knees for the plunger and is hit by the clean reek of disinfectant. Her sinuses burn with a three-year-old memory, the pink meatiness of what lay beneath her dressing in the dark. She can feel, almost, blisters from the adhesive that held the drains to her side, the weight that sat on her chest, a blind lump like solidified porridge shot through with pain.

"It's infected," she'd insisted to the night nurse and the SHO, reluctantly summoned, like a woken child. Every detail bursts back into lurid life, like dogs snapping their teeth behind a screen: the five hospital mornings, afternoons and midnights, tears sinking itchily into her pillowcase, sunlight dragging its way across the floor, an oxygen tube coolly breathing into her nostrils, like a discreet mustache. Ray's two visits, one in tears, the screaming fight that followed the other (her own voice very small with morphine, Leah blazing in his defense). Beside the tannined sink, she slips back to the beginning.

Here was the roller for covering examination-beds with blue paper and the foam blocks to hold tender parts in place; the pressed cardboard bowler-hats for vomit. The magical language of medicine: suture; cannula; discomfort; fluid. The many varieties of biopsy: the staple-gun, the wire, the needle so thick that extra nurses were needed to hold her down, or was it to push it in, while Maura, her favorite, held her hand.

It was like descending a ladder into a well. The horror grew in increments; it stretched to three weeks, another fortnight, and months began to pile up unnoticed while Lucia sat in waiting rooms. The plastic surgeon opened his glossy album of reconstruction photographs; those blind nippleless mounds she was supposed to admire, and his little phrases as, with manicured fingernails, he fondled his desk-ornaments: "dog-ear scar"; "nipple-origami"; "conservation"; "coring out the breast." She made herself a list of women who'd gone through the same thing: an eighties singer, an elderly American actress and Fanny Burney, famous for being Byron's wife or sister, perhaps both, who'd had it without anesthetic, just a leather strap to bite on.

So, Lucia thought, I ought to be able to cope.

Each new test was meant to be merely double-checking, belt and braces; everyone, from her husband to the exhausted doctor, was confident the next results would be fine.

It turned out that one could be both safe and sorry.

Soon she sat weeping before kindly women offering choices: between different types of destruction, different risks of death.

"What would you tell your mother to do?" she'd ask them. "How can I decide?"

And, when it eventually happened, the narrowing of the television picture to a cathode dot, she awoke and noticed that her face was bulging and rippling, sick with opiates, before the pain began, and the morphine pump for visitors, and the white noise of nursing and the hot frightening nights.

She no longer checks herself. What would be the point? If there's something in there spreading its tendrils, its center fattening, she'll be one of those women who pretend not to feel it. She could not possibly endure even the smallest edge, a rind, of what she went through before: the mammogram's crush, the MRI roar, the icy ultrasound wand revealing her new doom, like a jellyfish in a bag of sand.

At the Whittington she'd talked to a sweet volunteer, Judy, who had had both sides done, ten years apart, and apparently could bear it. Lucia thinks: if it happens again, I won't be able to.

Except, lately, things have changed.

Firmly she turns off the tap: saving every drop of London water. It's almost seven, too late to do anything. There's no time to explain to Priya. The invitation was stupid, a babyish yielding to this constant hunger. And what about the others? She'd persuaded herself that Ray, preoccupied, would notice nothing; that she could pull off a glancing introduction to Jess, at least. Now she thinks, sitting shakily on the edge of the kitchen table: what if there's a confrontation? Or if Priya sees how disgusting the house is, and it finishes us once and for all?

Besides, she's put down her phone somewhere, because of Marie-Claude. And Patrick's looking anxious, which makes her jumpy, and there's still no sign of Jess but now Martyn's arrived, following her around the kitchen, offering to "sous-chef" while picking at the salad. Larry from the exhibition space drops in, muttering about a small leak and why aren't the pieces hung already?

"Could you," begins Lucia. "Ray's in the living room. Can you, I don't know, praise him as much as you possibly can? Imply you had to fight off someone else to show his work, even?"

"I don't—"

"Please. It's important. He needs . . . encouragement," she says and Larry, bellowing convivially to Ray, finally goes up.

She keeps letting tiny private smiles escape but it's not funny; this is a disaster. Everything's shot to shit; the house looks revolting, she's behind with all of dinner. Nevertheless, she holds on to her secret hunger like a bag of crumbs.

Priya is coming, and a bubble of thrill pops underneath Lucia's sternum. If she changes her outfit, Ray will comment. It's her indecisiveness, her anxiety, that always messes things up, even before the children; the midnights of their infancies, sitting awake, heavy damp child drowsing on her lap, terror gently lapping as she began to understand that she would ruin them.

But hadn't it already gone wrong for Patrick: cortisol pouring into his tiny blood cells when she grew him? Even when she still was at art school, and hopeful, he was always a nervous baby. The colic, the wakefulness that kept him in her bed, until Ray booted him out of there.

Lucia's kids are not OK. Maybe Ray's right and it's her fault, how they are: Patrick too quiet out in the garden, Leah full of rage. It makes no sense: she was the first baby of her and Ray's glorious union. How could all that love curdle in that sweet illogical child-mind into such loathing of her mother? Did it begin when she was thirteen, fourteen, and Ray began mourning, in advance, the empty nest? Leah only had a tiny bit of time to spare for her parents; Ray was bereft at the mere idea of losing her. Because he loved his elder daughter so, it seemed kinder, to both of them, for Lucia to stand back. Her love was so scrambled that she gave her to him.

And now Jess, who was such a worry at school, is distant but fine, and Leah's not, and Patrick never was. Every time she hears sirens, she fears they are for him. Ray confidently traces the roots of their undoing to Lucia's own parents although, if he ever found out about what Lucia's done, he'd say it was that. But she is sure, almost completely, that what happened in November is not behind their ruin; that it has not shaken things loose. They were always like this.

She loves, no, adores them but now she, too, needs to survive.

Ten past, and Lucia hears the doorbell. As a bouncy ball seems to float at the top of its rebound, hanging for a perfect demi-second before falling back to earth, her heart pauses.

"No one's bloody organized," she hears Ray bellow as she races downstairs. Anger flares up her arms. She's done so many dinners for him; for his nasty friends, his women, but, when she invites someone new, Ray declares them self-absorbed, uninterested in his work. Once they'd have asked Marie-Claude tonight, or another dealer on the off-chance. Lucia would try to make them happy for Ray's sake, yet he'd still feel overlooked. Her heart would fall as the last guest said goodbye.

Now joy is breaking out all over. She wrenches open the door.

"Hiiiiii," says a tanned, narrow-eyed, very blond man, with a tall glamorous case like a portable crypt, a leather hold-all, a tennis racket and a velour neck-cushion. "Eric Nakamura."

Lucia gapes.

"Are you OK?"

"Christ. You're not, I was exp—never mind."

"You're Lu-*see*-a? *Lu*-cha? I looked online; Lu-*chee*-a? None of your interviews say."

She glances over her shoulder, lowers her voice. "*Lu*-seea. Emphasis on the first syl—"

"I am so excited to meet with you!"

He doesn't mean her personally. "You are here for Ray, though," she reminds him.

Eric Nakamura pauses. "Yes, but I was wondering if you and I could—"

"Sorry, I'm in the middle of a—cooking. Leave your cases," she says. "Ray? Ray! Eric is here—oh, Leah! Brilliant. Come and help," and she legs it back to the kitchen, to hide her face.

16

Priya's kisses are not as Lucia remembers women's kisses were, in the chemical era of art-school love. Hers are calmer, more precise yet also much, much more effective. The least touch and Lucia is swooning, beyond thought or sense or conscience. They're an unvanquishable force.

"Why," Lucia has asked her, "are you so incredible at this? Seriously. Please explain."

And Priya, smiling, kissed her again.

But, although it's sex in miniature, Priya's views of sex itself have tight parameters. She doesn't like, or want, or approve, of certain actions. There was an incident in her past. Even when stupid with lust, Lucia has to self-edit, avoid spooking Priya or disgusting her with her body or her need. Logistics constrain them even more. There have been moments of incredible lenience; against a mirror in Priya's own bathroom; her fingers in Priya's mouth; something she said in the heat that Lucia thinks of at least once a day, on purpose, to feel herself melt. But what they can do, in person, to each other, is limited.

No wonder she's losing her mind.

Every household object is laden with power. Will Priya spot

the trapped fluff in an amateurishly framed Tate poster, the tea-drips on the blue cushion and now think: this is not the woman for me?

Priya's house is extremely clean. She's rigorous, exacting. Lucia is wild for information: how much she sees Siddhartha, her husband; what she eats when alone. Despite her bouts of eighties pop, of color, of tenderness, she is not relaxing. She lightly mocks Lucia about everything, from her Circle Line confusions to the stasis in her work. Thanks to her mysterious but definitely testing childhood, Priya believes in self-control, tenacity. When Lucia casts around for connections, proof of how much they have in common after all, Priya will have none of it: "Oh, I like the sea too. We should be friends," she'll say with an edge, and it hurts Lucia's heart.

Her mind is swift and sharp. She says Lucia's is soft, that she should push herself more, and she's right.

There is no future; Lucia does know this. Her heart is breaking slowly, by the hour. But, every time they meet, barely or not even touching, the air between them charged, Lucia discreetly breathing in Priya's hair and, watching her mouth, she knows she is powerless. She cannot give her up.

But she should.

While Lucia is steady and constant, Priya's affection is thin as ice. No, not ice; an unpredictable fire. It can be enormous, or suddenly vanish. They can be holding hands under a corner table in an old-fashioned Greek restaurant, sending each other joltingly ardent messages deep into the night, but then Lucia will admit she's never read Dickens, or defend her love of funk, and Priya's amusement tips into scorn. As a teenager Lucia would dress every day in her limited finery, in case her blond god and his friends passed her after school. Now, because MPs' hours are long and prone to sudden changes, and their occasional decisions to ditch everything and meet in a pub, a freezing park, cannot be forecast or controlled, she lives in trembling desperate hope all over again.

No woman she knows has done this. Marriages do end, but slowly, not in a bonfire.

Her brakes are off. She can't decide whether to make herself or the house look decent first, so she races around shoeless, hair dripping, while trying to sweep up ash and make vinaigrette for fifteen. She can smell her own body.

She had been certain that she could never take off her clothes in front of anyone new again. Ray was used to it; he'd say, "Well, I don't care, so why's it matter? Just me and you now, poor girl," gently, as if to a disfigured child. And she knew she was lucky, to have escaped chemo, to have had the reconstruction straight away. Her grotesqueness was irrelevant: eyes averted from reflections, the bathroom door thoroughly locked. It would have been a form of vanity to think it mattered.

Without a minute to spare, she gazes so deeply into the past that her eyes ache. She pulls off her work jeans, faces the mirror in her knickers. She's become expert at not glimpsing herself below the neck. The suppliers of camisole-effect lace modesty panels, discreetly ruched viscose leisurewear, all advertised by brave real women, don't cater for those who hate even the catalogues' envelopes, still weep quietly at every scan, tears rolling into their hair. Women like Lucia don't need an Annabelle Soft Touch Half-Support Pocketed Tankini, because swimming shows how the misplaced back-muscle leaps and twitches at her chest, and she'll never do it in public again. She needs other accessories: blinkers to prevent accidental sightings of one's mutilated body, those lovely morphine pumps to blunt the sorrow.

At right angles to the mirror, arm carefully positioned, an observer wouldn't know she's numb from ribs to shoulder blade, ugly as it's possible for a woman to be. Her upper left quadrant feels wooden, no more hers than a false tooth. If she turns toward her reflection, she sees the long, curved silver shark-scar below her shoulder blade, its ends hideously pursed. Turn away: reveal, very slowly, the horror of what she has been left with, not real warm flesh or a convincing substitute, but a deflating beach ball, a raisin: silicone in a flesh bag, distorted, pinched, however it catches the light.

And the rest of her is looking saggy and worried and old. Priya is forty-six, still a thing of beauty.

Even now, the merest edge of recollection makes her swoop inside. Should she change her knickers, in case they find a moment in the kitchen . . .

It's past seven; this is ridiculous. This morning she'd decided on black trousers and a navy top because Ray once said she looked good in it. She can't wear her old favorites anymore, or what she thinks of as her fol-de-rol shirt, because he'll notice, and keep on about it: "Well, it's not what I'd choose" or "Ooh look, someone's making an effort," like a neon arrow.

Ray calls her Scruff, Wurzel. He says: "Straighten that sweater over your hump." It's a joke, but he does it in public. It makes her hot with self-disgust. But clothes must be worn and, eventually, she chooses, or submits to, a long tubular red and gray subtly tartan skirt, and a tight but camouflaging black jumper, soon to reek of lamb fat. The skirt once seemed vaguely Sex Pistols/neo-tweed but already she's sweaty, ashamed, like a sturdy country-woman. Her supportive tights clutch her like a new exoskeleton. She pulls at the fabric, trying to aerate.

Why would anyone court disaster? She and Priya are hardly going to run off together, risk either of their marriages, their careers; Priya is clear as diamonds about that. Lucia needs to stop this breathless hoping. But what about the journalists who orbit the Central Lobby, begging for something quotable? Any observant passerby could expose them, bring ruin.

It's like striding off across a frozen lake, tender ice barely holding. You would need such strength, if it were for yourself. You'd have to have started to imagine, after so long in the wilderness, that you could be loved. You would need to trust that you might not disintegrate, that your work could even flourish, however much your lungs hurt.

You would only dare to do it to save a life: your children's, or your own.

"Seen Patrick?" asks Martyn in the hall.

Lucia pokes her head round the living room door but Ray's still deep in chat with Eric Nakamura. The back door bangs shut behind Martyn as she reenters the kitchen; he's in a hurry.

She keeps checking the kitchen clock but not making sense of the time. "He's getting hungry," she hears Leah call. "Everything under control?"

She has the instincts of a piranha whiffling through the muddy Orinoco. Lucia hadn't even heard her on the stairs. Hold it together. Be alert.

The garden is calling to her, black and delicious. Even when she was convalescing, Ray would hate it when she disappeared.

"It," he'd say, "is a mania," and she denied it, while her fingers twitched for the secateurs. She'd often creep out into the cold private night with a torch when he'd had people over until ruinously late, opening amusing liqueurs. It was peace and joy and her alone; it fed her soul. They all know that nothing would keep her from her snail-hunting, her weed-pulling, which is why, since November, they have been a perfect excuse to disappear into the deepest corners, phone glowing in her pocket, and begin the chains of texting that feed her through the days.

In the process of burying her libido, Lucia had forgotten ever wanting women. Nowadays, apparently, queerness, gayness, whatever it was, is fine, not a big drama for certain young people. But not everyone is relaxed about it. Not even in her world.

And she was embarrassingly monogamous for three decades. Even to think of another person as attractive felt treacherous; on the street, let alone in bed, so a lid was soldered over the thought of women's soft mouths, their smooth planes and curves, the shock of discovery. Life was easier without.

Then, somewhere south of King's Cross, on a December night so cold her eyeballs had felt like peeled grapes, Priya prized the lid open.

It was Monday; she was, as usual, chopping carrots. She was wiped out; Ray still insists on all the family Christmas traditions. He was upstairs, so her phone was on the kitchen table, in case he needed her. Or Patrick might send her a message from the caravan, or Archway Bridge.

"Stop making allowances," Ray says.

Might the gentle ache in her chest be the usual sadness, or could it be the tuning fork, the first reverberations of an idea? Was it a thought about India?

Lately, India kept popping up. She was becoming curious. She wanted to try puffed chickpeas, goat tikka; tired old Bombay Nights on Holloway Road can't quench her interest. She began—and she told herself that this was purely for inspiration—to search for photographs of Gujarat; to attempt, very tentatively, to read an old and ungripping history of the Raj.

On Thursday Ray would be out until late, at a PV for his racist pal Philip.

"I'm not going," Lucia had said.

"Not important enough for you," said Ray. "I get it." He has always hated Philip, but hides it now that his creepy oils are selling. "He says you're snotty. Others agree."

When her phone peeped and she grabbed it, her heart was already racing for the gory disaster, the blue light. But it was Priya, with an invitation.

Thursday eve, I need fun, are you around? Chinese?

17

The Hanrahans are on edge. Lucia keeps checking her watch, biting her lower lip. She must be wound up about the exhibition; whatever is bothering her, Martyn thinks, will vanish in the joy of my decision. Ours. They need us back here, even if they don't know it yet.

He folds the feeling safely away, like a tooth.

Ray in his chair is surrounded by small bowls of crisps, like a bear. Enormous shadows flare over the bookcases; the house smells of garlic and illegal wood smoke. The living room is filling up but Martyn manages to pass Ray the better peanuts; the man is insatiable for salt. When Martyn knocks into the table, Leah urgently hushes him, then apologizes to Ray, as if he's disturbed a sacred rite.

"People can simply come to me," he says, "if they have questions. I mean, I know the place. Oh, hello, Graeme."

Uncle Graeme ignores him, bumbling across the hall with two bursting carrier bags in each hand like pantomime paws.

"I thought," murmurs Martyn to Leah, "he lives down the road?"

"He does."

"In the big flats?"

"Yes," says Leah. "Though don't go over. Ever." Martyn opens his mouth, closes it.

"Anyway, he's staying here tonight. Maybe tomorrow too."

"Um, why?"

"Because," Leah explains, as if to a dunce, "he's family. The brothers need to be together."

With an oomph of relief, he sits on the squashier sofa in the living room, drink in hand, cushion feathers flying, and starts casually leafing through an old Argos catalog. Patrick materializes, fleetingly. Ray's stubble glitters like sand. However familiar his stories, you always laugh; it's his delivery, the edge of shock. His eyes are perpetually upon you; also you're generally standing, which makes you nervous. Ray says it strengthens the legs.

"Will Jess be here soon?" asks Lucia sotto voce.

"Definitely," Martyn reassures her.

Even without Jess, he is in the bosom, although Ray won't answer when he asks about how the exhibition's shaping up. Leah said it wasn't ready; Patrick, looking antsy, said Leah was in charge. There's a surprising amount of anger inside her, like Lady Macbeth. Honestly, from the way those girls behave, you'd think they hated each other.

Jess told him that they'll have spent a fortune on sorting out the Hall for this show. She once claimed that, as insects in hotter, hungrier countries race toward sugar, the dodgy tradespersons of North London gravitate to Ray.

"He laps it up. Thinks they're friends, or he's their sort of . . . patron? God, you should hear his builder-charming voice."

Leah keeps him in sight, like an eyelid tremor, even when she's being the hostess, listening to Uncle Graeme's painstaking exposé of traffic-calming corruption. Everyone's asking about the show, commenting tactlessly on how late Jess is. And her mother seems tenser than usual, a cable pulled too tightly.

Patrick's AWOL again, Martyn notices. People keep coming in but never him: the shabby gallery owner, trying to conceal balding with an elevated fringe. Gerry something, another of Ray's gang, is standing in the hallway, apparently reading a book he himself has written, and Salvo the wineshop man, a beefy cockney Italian, has arrived with much manly embracing, booming about people Martyn doesn't know. Next is a poet and his distraught-looking critic wife, or is it the other way round? The wife is wearing a furry gilet; "Why's she come as a Flintstone?" Ray says, at normal volume, and after that the wife keeps her face turned from him. Then it's one of Ray's protégés, a youngish artist whom Jess calls the Catamite, and Leah calls his slave. Ray seems to love him, arm round his shoulders. Martyn, as one of the men of the house, begins to fret. It's time to tell Ray that he and Jess are staying: a shiny treasure to bestow. He who hesitates ends up back in Dalry, Ayrshire, where things are not, technically, as Martyn has portrayed them.

It's definitely time to talk to Ray. I need, he thinks, a chance to catch up man to man, *mano a mano*. I'm family now. Gradually, respectfully, he moves nearer. There's a gap on the wall where one of Ray's pieces must have been taken for the show.

"I'll show you some of Leah's photographs later," he is promising the Catamite and Eric Nakamura. "She gets her talent from me. And her gorgeousness. And her hair."

Leah's relationship with her father is what Jess's could be, if she was nicer to him. When Martyn sees Leah encouraging him, sitting on his knee, it moves him in a number of confusing ways.

"Don't you think it's weird?" Jess says that Ray has an unseemly fascination with his elder daughter's love-life, that he was too interested in Leah's old school friends, pouring more wine, extracting tales of their horrible parents, crowing that they "love hanging out here." He'd boast about the condoms and bongs.

"It's not . . . you know, though . . ." says Martyn. "Bad?"

" 'Course not! At least . . . no. I'd know."

"Then you're just jealous. Envious. Jealous. Whichever. Anyway. They're really close; it's sweet. And you always say you're the lucky one, not being entangled like she is. You can't have it both ways."

"I am. Definitely. It's just I'd have liked the chance."

If Ray does self-medicate, who could blame him? Jess won't discuss it, but clearly something is going on. Martyn's shoved it to the side. He's hoping it will disappear, like a couple of other matters.

He's about to touch his imminently father-in-law's arm, ask him for a private and, well, exciting word, when the poet says: "I hear you've something lined up. A show, is it? At Camden Arts?"

"No, no," Martyn steps in. "At a Hall. St. John's Guild, Almoners . . . something. Lectures, events; very illustrious."

"Interesting features," claims the Catamite. "Tucked away off the roundabout, that big Gothic . . . famous garden, apparently. Like, a fern collection. But won't it, you know, be a strain?"

"My father's not weak," says Leah sternly.

"Are we invited?" says the wife, hopefully, leaning down to stroke the cat. "You're a handsome"—she says, peering underneath—"fellow." She looks startled; Paisley, Ray frequently proclaims, is all man. "What's your name?"

"Paisley," Martyn says, and he sees the corner of Ray's grin.

"Oh. That's . . . unusual. As in the pattern?"

"As in," says Leah, "the politician."

"Of course. Are you . . . Irish?"

"Just Mum," Leah replies as Ray says: "Only Lucia, thankfully."

There is a small, not unfamiliar, hesitation. "But I thought, Hanrahan must b—"

Ray cuts across her. "Fully English, thank you very much."

"I see," the wife says, frowning.

"Leave it," says Leah abruptly.

She doesn't hear. "So . . . sorry, your mother, Lucia, must be a Protestant?"

"No."

"But then, Ian Paisl—Isn't that quite inflammatory?"

"It's a joke," says Leah, sighing.

"I'll fetch you a drink," Martyn offers in the pause but, when he returns, single ice cube, just how Ray likes it, the Catamite had barged in and is sitting on the arm of his chair. Annoying boy: everything about him, from his mighty knees to the golden back of his neck, his milk-fed femurs, riles Martyn. He can't stop looking at him, just to be irritated.

So, swift as a careful arrow, he goes to help Leah count the RSVPs.

The first floor is Ray's and Lucia's domain. On either side of the door to Vivienne's flat are hung stormy woodcuts by the notorious George Gregory Pye, one of Ray's friends since art college, until the final falling-out. Some have AUCTION scrawled on the backs; Leah's bagsied most of the others. Ray knows how much Jess loves the GG Pyes. He once promised her the second one along but, last time they were here, she checked and it was labeled LEAH.

On every stair stand pillars of old newspapers, which must remain in precisely the order they were once placed. The corridor is a perilous ravine, with only a bumpy gully through which to move, goose-stepping over fleetingly steady places. He takes a breath, taps on the door of Ray's office.

In the slithering landslide of ignored paperwork in the corner, on Jess's old single bed, he spots two boxes of unused invitations, embossed on thick green card. The floor is a cascade of curly envelopes and crumbling rubber bands. A slab of unopened letters serves as a table; on a cat-treat advent calendar lies a bowl containing grapes at every life-stage, two forks, a fluffy wax earplug and a jumbo pack of painkillers.

He starts trying to tally the numbers for tomorrow, but tactfully, because Leah's getting very defensive about her long paper list of Nos and Possibles.

"Liggers," she's muttering. "Lightweights." With each new name an ancient grudge is exposed. "Bruce Spender? He should be so lucky. And, seriously, the Jessups?"

There seem to be over fifty Yeses. "That is," he says lightly, "a hell of a lot of vol-au-vents."

"It's fine," says Leah. "The catering's all sorted."

"Excellent," says Martyn. "Um, so what banqueting have you got planned?"

There's something in her eyes that might be panic. She starts twisting a strand of hair; "That's going to be the really amazing part," she says. "We've . . . There's a brilliant guy, who, maybe you've heard of him, Pablo Nathaniel?"

"What, that gallery man?"

"His son. He's a complete genius. Restaurant person. Cook. He's said he'll do it as a huge favor to Dad."

"Not for free?"

"Well, no. But mates' rates."

"Oh, so he's a friend of your father's?"

"Of mine," says Leah, and she stands up energetically, starts fiddling with the computer cable.

"Great. Great! What exactly is he cooking?"

"It is," says Leah, "all still a bit up in the air."

Martyn frowns. "But should—"

"It's going to be spectacular," interrupts Leah. "And worth it. I'm sure there were more . . . hang on."

Martyn's looking discreetly at receipts. "How much," he asks, "does it cost to have a picture framed?"

"Hundred, hundred and fifty. Depends on the glass. That's not professional level even. But there's that bloke on Junction Road near the pet shop, he loves Dad so it's virtually free. Dad's handling all that, didn't want me to worry. He's very protective."

"Mmm. Wow," he says appreciatively. "And he, Ray, is showing how many pictures?"

But Leah doesn't hear. He's desperate to know how much the art will sell for—£500? £10,000?—but she says it's private. He's only seen the odd example, a couple of self-portraits from his more figurative years, a landscape hanging in the living room, and even those were hard to navigate; is that a nose? What do the thick painty drips signify? Leah won't discuss the sizes, or how people will get the paintings home. Martyn needs a crib sheet; how will he explain the work to inquirers if he doesn't know what they're meant to be of?

He's suspecting that usually professional exhibition organizers are involved. Like Sir Leonard Woolley at Troy, he keeps making extraordinary discoveries: is this a laminator? He's poking around for some sort of price list but keeps turning up steep invoices instead: for D-rings, color printing, polishing cloths, rolls of bubble wrap; specialist light bulbs; two dozen sheets of twenty-eight acid-free archive-quality Sold stickers from Sothern's Fine Arts Services of Piccadilly, each an ordinary-looking red dot costing seventy-nine pence.

"Are we really sure about these?"

"Why not?"

"Will he . . . they're quite pricey, and will he realisticall—"

"We're not using Lidl freezer labels," says Leah. "Are you

insane?" Everything enrages her, despite her reputation as the mild one. "He's an international artist!"

"Of course. Only the best, b—"

"And *if* any are left, we'll just use them next time. It's not," she adds, "really any of your business."

He hesitates. There's an atmosphere. "No, of course not. I hadn't realized that exhibitions needed so much . . . stuff."

"Mm."

Some of the invoices, the ones Ray calls "red and inflamed," are from last year, the year before. "We're getting there," she keeps saying. "Dave Austerberry'd better be coming."

"Who?"

"From the *Highgate Gazette*. They're obsessed with Dad. Don't tell me you haven't heard of him."

"By the way," Martyn says, rubber-banding a stack of postcards printed with Ray's quite famous *Portrait of the artist on the edge*, "I can't wait to see the . . . art. God, it's so exciting; you know I've only ever seen the ones in the house? Are any affordable by . . . me?"

She scrunches up her pretty face, like a martyr suffering for her Lord. "Don't be stupid," she says.

"Right. Yes. Well, does he paint you lot? Patrick? Hard to imagine him sitting sti—"

Leah closes her eyes. She takes a breath. "Me. He paints me."

There's a touch of Patrick around her brow and temples, Martyn's thinking, when Leah says: "You know she doesn't get it."

"Who?"

"She thinks," says Leah, "that I . . . indulge him."

"I . . . oh, Jess?"

"But that's . . . how can she imagine," she says, "what it's like, being important to someone who needs you so much? He tells me everything. He's so funny, and so intelligent, much more than I am, so it's kind of a . . . a . . ."

"Duty?"

"Honor: making him feel able to work. And *Lucia* won't, and Jess won't, but someone has to. You wouldn't believe some of the awful stuff he's gone through, but he can totally rely on me. Anyway, where else would I live? What would I do? I'm lucky," she says.

Martyn falters. If he and Jess moved in, would Leah abandon them? But, before he can prod her, she's straight back to the Yeses. "Ugh, Penny Cable? She can't even *paint*. People are outrageous; they just want booze and a bit of his glamor."

"I must admit I'm pretty excit—"

"Poor Dad. If you're one of the greatest living British artists, everybody wants a piece."

Martyn's still wondering if catering was necessary. And live music? The Hanrahans will be ruined.

"Have you done one, a show, before?"

Leah's back is turned, but she says, after a moment, "Yes."

"How do you make sure people buy the work? Apart from reviews, do you advertise?" but Leah's suddenly much more interested in the neighbors (but not the bastards at 32. Or 19–25, actually. Or the flats). She passingly mentions having ordered fifteen pairs of glass tea-light holders, from a friend of the caterer's.

"Lush ones. Sort of bubbly."

"You mean handmade?"

"'Course. The man sent a drawing."

"OK. Are you allowed candles in a place like that?"

"Stop worrying. Anyway, we're being scrifty. Thrifty. Guess who's taking the photos?"

"Who?"

"Me! I've got Dad's old Canon; he's a brilliant photographer."

"Oh," says Martyn. "I mean, that's great."

Leah lifts her chin. "You don't think I can do it."

"No, I do," says Martyn. "Absolutely. It's good to be supporting him," he says. "It's such a pity," he adds cunningly, "that we're so far away. If we lived closer, there'd be so much I, Jess and I, could do to help."

"Yeah, right," says Leah. "But she'd nev—"

"Actually, don't tell Jess I said so, but we're . . . there are plans." He lowers his voice. "In the pipeline."

Leah's eyes fill; in her blink, her anxious hands, there's something Martyn doesn't want to see. "Wow," she says. "Would you?"

"You, you'd want us to move back?"

"'Course!" The tears escape; they roll down her cheeks to her mouth and she licks them up. "Right now, if you can. He's not well. Of course she should be here. I need . . . it's a great idea. Get your stuff sent over from Scotland, and—"

"Hang on," says Martyn. "We'd have to plan. It'll take time, and it's . . . Our whole, well, not lives, but our jobs are out there," and a silence begins to thicken. What has he said wrong? "But I'm sure we will. Why are you crying? There's loads of room, and if—"

"You what? What do you mean?" says Leah. "Room where?"

18

Lucia has a plan and she executes it perfectly. She lures Eric Nakamura to the critic and then, one hand on Ray's shoulder, the other replenishing his special violently spicy rice crackers, she says airily: "We've acquired a couple of extra guests to celebrate with."

She never had boldness like that, before. Pretending to adjust the curtains, she's remembering how, on the way to that Chinese restaurant on an icy night like this, she had tried to squash her pride that Priya Menon apparently wanted her company. She must, Lucia had decided, be included in a bigger dinner: a friendly social gesture to someone you don't really want to see. Or it would be for brain-picking: you conceitedly believe the person wants your company but actually it's to assess their son's A-level art coursework, or give a sketch to a school auction. Her tentatively puffed ego began to deflate. Ray does always say she takes herself too seriously.

The restaurant was a former pub, a corner Szechuan; steamy windows in the frozen air. She'd told Ray she was meeting an art-school friend, Suze; he says Suze is provincial. Suze has started saying that Lucia needs to stand up to him. She once told her: "I'd kill for you. And clean up afterward. Remember that."

Lucia pushed open the door.

The vowel sounds were like Chinatown but it wasn't the bright clatter she'd expected. There was a fug of rum and star anise, an orchestral version of "Let's Face the Music and Dance"; the room was darkly slatted, red-and-gold as a bordello. What was she doing here? She couldn't even quite remember Priya's voice. Then she looked again.

There she was. She sat at a table for four, candlelit beneath a plastic bas-relief of storks and pagodas and a shimmering peach-and-sapphire sky. She was in profile, typing hurriedly to, presumably, cabinet ministers. She didn't look up until Lucia loomed over her, and then she grinned.

Nobody else joined them. Priya made her laugh and laugh and over-order: sea-tasting aubergine, morning glory with sesame oil, laminated pork, a ferocious soup of tiny mushrooms that they agreed was like spicy cat-piss. Lucia watched her: that firm chin, those diamond-cut lips and, when Priya caught her looking, heat spread like cream over her breastbone and up her neck. She had become fifteen again, encountering a boy in the wild, aglow.

They drank plum wine, like deadly bubble gum. Under the table, her hand began to take the moldable shape of Priya's head, cradling the occipital bone. She kept her eyes from Priya's blouse. Priya's blouse, although buttoned right up to its sensible collar, appeared to be silk: a dark rosy matte pink. It was meant to be looked at, as was, presumably, what lay beneath it, under the softness: something softer still. Lucia, usually, would have minded. She can't bear the sight of women in fabric that clings to them.

But Priya didn't know her, before. She is allowed.

"Let's have some cognac," she said, and the waiter appeared at her side.

"Is that wise? It's late already, and—"

"It'll be fine," said Priya. "Trust me." And, knowing that Ray would be back much later, full of snubs and grievance, Lucia let it happen.

They drank the cognac; she looked at Priya's jaw, her lids, her hands: strong-looking, clean squarish nails, beautiful and nothing like Lucia's. There was a ring on her right, a flat black stone; a gold necklace. This was a woman, Lucia thought, who chooses to take care of herself.

Lucia tried to look knowledgeable about select committees, *Newsnight*, Prime Minister's Questions. Priya prodded her: "What's your next show? What do your gallery say?" The fan of tendons on the back of her hand quivered; the pearly muscles, the tiny nets.

"Hello?" said Priya. "Are you in a fugue state?"

"What?"

"You odd woman. You seem . . . elsewhere."

So Lucia asked questions and gradually extracted a little about how Priya grew. While Lucia was spending her pocket money on hair slides from Dagenham market, or drinking cider in Valentines Park, Priya was hiding from her mother's rages in public libraries, long winter weekends of track practice, brass ensembles ("though they wouldn't sit with me; said my coat smelt of curry"), math club in youth centers, chess with her quiet father who worked nights in a newsagent's to put her through private school. Priya's mother hit her with a vacuum-cleaner pipe when she cut her hair, with a hand when she came second in a gymnastics contest. "It wasn't her fault," Priya said. "She deserved a better life. All the constant assessment about were we as good as her friends, crappy council flat, desperate car. Keralans are very competitive. She was working in a care home because they didn't want a Paki midwife."

"Oh!"

"Mmmhm. Whereas, apparently, I was both Paki and coconut. And she'd cry at the thought of her family, who looked down on her for marrying a Gujarati man. But she, she wanted me to be the best."

"Were you?"

"Mostly, yes. And at least I got married when all my cousins did. Major issue. And a Hindu."

"Oh. Really? Tell—"

Priya went on: "Though, God, she hated me being in politics. Embarrassing at temple."

"But surel—"

"No, no. Civil servant. Consultant. Not . . . furious about everything, and knocking on doors begging for people's votes."

Everything she said had a cutting intimacy; it was like being excitingly flayed. "Does he even work?" she asked about Ray.

"Of course! He's much more . . . he's very successful," Lucia said, and Priya pursed her lips.

"But his time's been and gone, hasn't it?"

"No!"

"It's true. You know it."

"I've never, he . . . it's peculiar talking about it like this. I don't usually . . ." and Priya merely smirked. "That's definitely not . . . how things are seen."

Lucia didn't dare look at her watch. She'd meant to be home by now but this was much too interesting, and she was possibly too drunk, to stop.

Then Priya said:

"Do you know Hellie Brook?"

"The artist?"

"Is there more than one?"

"I do a bit. We've done shows together, but she—Why? How do you . . . ?"

"We used to live together at college."

"Live?" said Lucia. Hellie Brook is unsmiling, flat, tall. She's successful enough for Ray to hate her so Lucia always avoided her, out of loyalty. "Oh, was that when she was with Malcolm Gunner?"

"I certainly hope not," said Priya. "No, she was with me."

"With you?"

"With me."

"With as in . . . with?"

"Yes," said Priya, and held her gaze.

Ray takes the news of their extra guests strangely well.

Lucia emphasizes the husband. "Remember you met him at an opening, I think? Last year? You really got on. He's a doctor, or something, isn't he? Hands? I—I bumped into him on the way home. This evening. He asked all about you."

"Oh yes, Stan, Sid . . . whatever, he did take a shine," and everyone begins to relax. "Husband of that Minim, Menom woman, the politician, isn't he? Poor bastard; he did look hag-ridden."

"Well, anyway, he asked why I had so much parsley and I told him about tonight and tomorrow, your big show, and he was so excited that, accid—"

"You didn't invite him to the show?" Leah says.

"I . . ." She tries to keep looking straight at Ray, to read him but remain unread. Has he guessed? The longer one is married, the harder truth becomes. "I, actually, I did mention that he could drop by. Later."

"Oh did you?"

"I . . . yes."

"Sorry, who's coming?" asks the Catamite. "Do we approve?"

"Which politician?"

"God, not that woman. The shouty one?" says Larry. "Asian? That's his wife?"

"She might," says Lucia passingly, "come too. Is she a politician? I suppose."

Now Ray goes to the window. He hoicks the lower frame open with one hairy arm. "Where are they, then?" he says, leaning out into the rain. "More liggers. Christ, everyone wants a piece."

"Oh, they—he didn't say. Maybe they won't make it after all," she tells him.

He glances at her over his shoulder, looks back outside: a wolf, waiting. "She's only MP for Sheffield or Birmingham, somewhere like that, isn't she? Not even in the actual government. She'd better be Labour, though, or she's not setting foot inside my house."

Usually, Lucia would mouth "our house" if his back was turned. Now Priya really is coming, will be exposed to Ray, like a big crazy lion nosing its prey. She'll see the cluttered photos up the stairs: furious Jess throwing ice cream, glops of sunlit strawberry glinting like a fountain; Pat and Leah in a paddling pool filled with dead leaves, both platinum-haired, scowling like little padded Furies, a sadness in Patrick's face because the previous moment, uncaptured on Kodak, Leah had whacked him with her bucket. There's one of Lucia herself in her only ever bikini, grinning shyly on a Dorset beach. It makes her sad for so many reasons but, whenever she takes the picture down, Ray reattaches it. It's nailed there now with so many brass hooks and entangled wires that she's given up.

"I mean, she might not come," she says. "Or he."

"I could tell her a thing or two about local government," says Gerry, a jazz-album reviewer.

"If they think they're too posh for us," Ray declares, "they can shove it. It's late and I'm starving. We're not waiting for them, I'll tell you that much."

"Nope," says Leah.

"Anyway," Ray says indignantly, "what do we pay them for? They can't be voting constantly, can they? There aren't enough . . . laws." Lucia presses her lips together. "And that poor bloke. Stan. Sid? Imagine being married to such an an—Well," he adds, pausing significantly, "let's not get into that."

Sid: she tries not to think about him, without success. If Ray found out, would the husbands fight? A battle on the patio, like elephant seals clashing their blubbery chests? Not that Ray can ever find out.

What does Sid know about Priya's London life? "I mean, I could always cancel," she says, and holds her breath.

I'd burst into flames. Short of killing my children, there is nothing I would not do to see her. Lucia used to set herself tests: how far she'd go to spare her babies pain. Swimming rivers, walking stony perilous paths, losing an arm, and/or leg? Left? Definitely. Right? Yes: anything. Make me prove my love.

But it was a lie, even then. She should have stood up for Patrick and didn't. There were so many times they could have stopped for hot chocolate after school, but she had hurried back so Ray wouldn't feel rejected. She could have lain beside her sweet boy on his little bed and properly assessed the risks posed by:

Poltergeists
Bears
Mummies
Vampires and pigeons
Doomsday
Wolves and other wild dogs
Robbers

Poisoners
Clowns, obviously
Fire
Spies
Aslan
Ghosts
Whales
Tiny sharks
Giants
Caves and cavemen
Struwwelpeter
Knives

until he was reassured and could sleep, not lie terrified for hours with his big eyes glinting in the dark, listening out for the creak of her feet on the stairs: "Mum? Mum?"

"Leave him!" Ray would say, every time she peeped through the crack in the door and so, to her secret shame, she did and he grew up like this.

Given a chance, would she abandon them now?

"No, don't cancel them," says Ray. "It'll be amusing."

It's so late and the lamb's nowhere near ready but, because an MP is coming, everyone's perked up. Even Gerry isn't pretending to be unimpressed. "Isn't she the one from Nottingham?"

"No, that's . . . the young one," Lucia says uncertainly.

Leah is staring at her: she is a noticer, the family's sentry, and Lucia is blazing.

There's plenty of wine but they're chomping through the crisps. Ray keeps saying "Priya whatever," disdainfully, as if the party selectors failed in their duty to check prospective MPs with him.

"I have terribly low blood sugar," says the thin critic's wife and

Lucia, not glancing at Ray, says: "I'll see if there are any more tortilla chips."

She turns on the kitchen radio, leans her head against *The Sainsbury Book of Wholemeal Home Baking.* Her chest feels as if it will burst with longing; she's so nervous that her tongue stings.

Priya is about to arrive.

Now?

Now, surely.

The seconds ripen, fall. She hasn't thought this through, any of it: the awkwardness of delivering a guest to him, like presenting a tender fruit to a tyrant. Priya won't charm and soothe him, be flirted with. And she must remember not to mention having met Lucia; Ray won't like the idea of a new independent friend.

What if, under the pressure of not saying anything, Lucia starts crying, or laughing? Adulterous wives must be everywhere. Has Gillian ever? And Ray's ex, the sacred Vivienne? They should be recognizable by their glowing skin, their shining hair.

Her chest is wet with sweat. Once, gingerly, she'd entered an online forum for women who had experiences like hers, straight into a thread about sternum cancer. She touches the hot bone.

"No, you know," she hears the thin critic's wife say, "she's quite ordinary. I mean, socially. She's Wolverhampton? Somewhere like that. Pakistani. Single parent, tower block, blah?"

"Used to be a dinner-lady, didn't she?" asks Gerry. "Or illiterate. The mother?"

"Well," says the thin critic's wife.

Priya made herself. She is fearlessness and determination and grit and what, thinks Lucia, are all of you?

After the Chinese restaurant, Lucia would take out the facts and marvel over them from every angle, like a miser.

"We need an agenda," Lucia had said. "There's too much to discuss," and Priya grinned.

Then she said: "Your eyes are beautiful."

The restaurant was trying to close around them. Lucia asked: "Is it true that so many MPs cheat on their wives? Are secret gamblers, drinkers, God knows?"

Priya smiled. "You can't imagine. It's power. MPs do have to be risk-takers. We stake so much on getting here, every election. Family, money, time, and the volunteers—last year was insane. And also, well, it's interesting work, so people are drawn to you. And helping people makes us feel privileged; it can go to your head. But mainly it's . . ."

"What?"

"Power. People love power. Having it and being near it."

"Really," said Lucia.

Later, Priya said: "You'd be amazed what a mandate does for some people. Gives them even more confidence."

"Are you confident?" Lucia asked.

"What do you think?" said Priya, and her eyes held Lucia's steadily: that slow look between women, which Lucia had thought she'd never see again.

19

"Has anyone seen Patrick?" Martyn asks, again.

Leah sighs. "Apparently heard foxes."

"Oh, Pat, Patch and his beasts," he says fondly. "Has he gone to observe them? Should I check on—"

"It's disrespectful," says their father. "Maybe he's peeping at us through a little hole. Or off dogging."

"Dad!" says Leah proudly.

"Someone," Ray says, "go and fetch him."

"I will," Martyn says.

It's cold out here, and shadowy; it smells of violence. He hurries through the warped gate; down the side return, fashioned by Patrick into a homemade cloister. It is roofed with corrugated plastic jaundiced by sunlight, gray and green with dirt. He squeezes past deceased bike frames and cracked chimney pots, the rusted skeleton of a roof rack, weed killer, faded skittles, a lichenous cool-box, logs so mossy and sodden they could be used as fire extinguishers. Raindrops darken his shirt, making it tricky to look casual; still, at least it's not sweat.

Where is Patrick?

Of course he's not over interested, whatever Jess claims. Patrick *is* interesting, one of those fascinatingly talented yet vocationless men. Apparently, he can paint and draw; he is, or was, an amazing swimmer, which Martyn would give money to see. With that pure profile, and narrow considering eyes, the height, he could have been anything he wanted.

Will he, Martyn wonders, let him into his caravan?

"Patrick?"

Martyn edges closer.

The roar of nature is all around him; even in winter, it creeps with life. There's a stink of moss and rust. The lawn glistens, crowded with trees; black branches, reckless fresh young leaves.

Leah and Ray are convinced that Patrick needs a girlfriend. They urge him to look up Leah's old school friends, most of whom live only streets away from, if not actually in, their childhood home. He must long for coupledom.

"If not, why not?" Ray always says. "What's wrong with him? I don't believe in a sexless man."

But Patrick is so blinky and twitchy, so hypervigilant, observes Martyn, who has always suspected he'd be a good doctor. And, as he'll explain once again to Jess, dragging her brother to Edinburgh would be destructive, not only for him but for the family, the organism that is the Hanrahans. Much, much better if the Edinburgh faction move down here.

Because of the cold, he's trembling. He can't call loudly, lest he scare off the foxes. It's moving to think of Patrick at night in his, presumably, narrow bed, alert to nature.

There's a sound behind him and Martyn jumps. Buck up, he tells himself, peering into bosky undergrowth, the impenetrable shrubbery. He retucks his shirt. No sign of Patrick; the caravan looks dark and still; not, in close up, quite so tempting. Could Patch have nipped out? Would he be on the Heath, alone? He and Martyn have so much to chat about.

"Anyone out here?" he calls softly, just to be sure.

A dead leaf falls wetly against his hand. Patrick is on all fours in his improvised knee-protectors, head-torch on, reattaching a vine eye. The dogtooth border of the herb bed, an ill-judged birthday present for Ray last year, digs painfully into his thigh. Even now he scrabbles for ways to please Ray, telling him about repairs he's done and savings made, as if his stepfather's disdain could be staunched. He has spent his life doing this, growing more irritating, like grit in a shoe.

He hears something.

Too much blood thumps in his ears. He dropped something in the dark dank must of twigs and mold by the side return, but even the thought of trudging back makes him emit little moans; being met again by whatever it was that he sensed last night. He's too white and weak for them, like a root under a stone. He cannot do it. Like a failed hide-and-seeker he sits on his heels, waiting.

Then, somewhere behind him, he hears a movement, or sees a sound and he's about to lose control of his most dignity-preserving muscles when he realizes it's Martyn.

Martyn feels weightless. "Christ," he says. "It's freezing out here. How are you doing, er, mate?"

Patrick, looking extremely flustered, makes a small sound of welcome.

"I thought you'd nipped over to the Gallery. I could help right now," says Martyn. He'd hoped that this evening, everything sorted for tomorrow, they could be standing around drinking tea from big mugs, befriending the carpenters and chatting about Patrick's early life. "How's . . . work?"

"Oh! I'm doing one on the Avenue, lawyers," says Patrick, wiping his hands on his hips. "They want a knot . . . thing."

"Uh oh."

"Yes. And my old judo teacher. He's getting on and their garden's mad."

"As mad as this?"

"Well, no." Patrick gives an amused snuffle.

"You must have been snowed under. The exhibition, I mean. But what a relief that it's all under control. I bet . . . Ray isn't . . . it needs to be just right, doesn't it." Now they're knee-deep in revelation, all the wrong emotions are surging up: curiosity, the urge to confess. "You still in the caravan?"

"Yep."

"I've never seen inside it."

"Right."

"So . . ."

"Can I?" he asks brightly.

"What?"

"See inside?"

The scrumpling in Patrick's chest, the sense of holding himself small and still inside a faulty container, grips him even here, outside. He's starting to feel sick. He never knows how to extricate himself from talking; only Martyn can cut them free. But Martyn won't stop. What does he want? His task is to make Jess happy, keep her away from here.

The soil is clotted with beautiful worm-casts. Patrick's fingers paddle in the soil; he used to find bits of starfish, pounded into fertilizer. He's never been alone with Martyn before, close enough to punch.

"Are you," Martyn says suddenly, as if someone's behind him, pushing, "still cooking?"

"What?"

"I just happened to remember you're interested. Didn't you do a what-are-they-called, City and . . ."

"A bit," says Patrick. The old unworthiness unfurls. "At the Vincent Rooms."

"Jess says you almost completed. That you were really good. I'm sure she . . ."

"I wanted to do Patisserie," he blurts out, "but that wasn't . . . Ray said it wasn't. Financially viable." He swallows. "I think."

"I see." Martyn leans closer, squats down. He's staring at Patrick's big knees. "Did you not have some kind of, ah, crisis?"

"A breakdown," Patrick says, to end this. He eyes the cherry tree hopefully; he hasn't survived this family without a deep acquaintance with the garden, its undergrowth and damp corners. "I had a nervous breakdown. They said."

Martyn frowns, moves his mouth, flushes. "Who's they?"

"The team."

"Oh. Hmm. But you still cook, don't you?"

"Well. It's not . . . I made the cake."

"Which looks delicious!" Martyn says. "Really . . . zesty."

"I'd better go."

"Of course," says Martyn. " 'Course." This is almost the end of the conversation. Then the air ripples, as if they've both glanced down and found themselves on the brink of a precipice.

"Sometimes . . ." Martyn says.

"What?"

"Your . . . old Ray, he can be a bit . . . you know. Unencouraging."

Patrick's mouth dries. Three decades and he has never discussed his stepfather; it's barely crossed his mind that he could.

Ray's power, the fear of upsetting him, is like an unbreakable spell. He takes a deep breath. He nods. "It's . . ."

"You should stand up for yourself," says Martyn. "Say what you want. What's the worst he could do?"

20

Jess loves this house. No, she hates it. Lurking on the pavement feels like adolescence: light glinting from the living room upstairs through the fat yew-hedge, the laughter. If he's cheerful, you can always hear her father. Her head throbs with the effort of listening.

Like a small animal scuttling toward destruction, she's breathing too quickly, clenching her hands. No wonder she's so tired. At Dalziel's she strides down the corridors, dodges the Head's guiding hand, keeps the shoutier boys in check. But her father paralyzes her.

The garden gate hangs by a single hinge, bleeding rust. There is a smear of stars, a moon like ice. Her skull is heavy. Parakeets scream past on their way to the reservoir; the Overground train screeches toward Upper Holloway. Dear God, please let Martyn not have pissed Dad off already, or be too happy. Lord, make him just miserable enough . . .

For what?

To decide that something must change.

The front door has been left on the latch, like it's 1950. Inside the hall is worse than she'd remembered: stuff piled everywhere, people clattering about upstairs, a smell of cigs and burning meat. Motes of madness fall through the air. She's holding her breath, almost daring to run for it, when she sees her sister looking up from the kitchen stairs.

"Oho," says Leah. "It's Stinky."

"God! Didn't see you. Nearly had a heart attack," says Jess, taking off her backpack as if she was about to anyway. "Were you lurking at the spy hole?"

"Ha," says Leah. "No. Too busy. And don't expect a smile. If you'd bloody come yesterday . . ."

"Don't start," Jess says.

"Not starting anything. No time."

"Good. It's weird to be . . . How is he?"

"Well. Obviously he misses you."

"Really?"

"Come on, then," says Leah. "Let's try to find a use for you," and Jess scowls. She mustn't talk about her job, because hearing about people's careers makes Leah feel bad; relationships, ditto. Anything could cause a sinking into despair. "How's Mum?"

"Your fucking mother doesn't think. She's totally vague, even more than usual. She's just announced yet another person's invited tonight, some MP. What about how Dad would feel?"

Their hug backfires; Leah's scratchy wool embrace goes from loose to tight, like a trap. Despite everything, Jess closes her eyes and breathes in. She is beautiful, Jess's sister, with her small mouth, small head, hair curled around her ears pointing to the neatness of her jawline. The Virgin Queen. It would be easy to hate her.

"How are you?" Jess, held like a wrestler, waits for her chance to pull free.

"Fine. Fine. Are you coming to see Dad? He's drowning in sucker-uppers."

Jess says: "There must be stuff to organize. Are you on track?"

Leah'd had hopes. She'd been sure that, up there in Scotland, her sister would quickly remember how lucky she is, unlike those she'd left behind, and want to help them.

"Everything's fine," Leah tells her. "So aren't you coming to talk to Dad? What's the matter with you? Aren't you desperate to?"

Jess shrugs. She was a great child shrugger: plenty of shoulder action, hands twirling in the air like a New Yorker. Now she seems subdued. It's like with their dad, all over again; she turns against them.

She doesn't look happy, Leah thinks, and she should be. She needs to understand that it's getting urgent. I can't wait. "I still can't believe he's really doing a show," says Jess tentatively. Leah already has that heart-sinking aggrieved look. Her small arched brows are drawn together. "Do you think he's . . . It will be good, won't it?"

Leah dodges. She's a pro. "You didn't let Paise out, did you?"

Allegedly Paisley has emotional difficulties. He was rescued from a wicked shopkeeper. He's afraid of snow, mice, men: "Asian men," Ray says, "particularly. Sorry, my cat's a racist."

Jess always tells him, "Dad, you can't say that," and he claims he doesn't understand why.

He insists Leah has a gift for feline communication. "She should have been a telly vet. If not a model."

"I'm handling the whole thing," Leah tells Jess, "for him. It's going to be major. OK? Life does go on without you."

"Fine." Jess glances at the stairs, delays a moment longer. "I'll help, though, if you need, if . . ."

"Dad did say you'd make it all about you. Don't trip on the step."

"I know," Jess says, gritting her teeth so hard her molars creak. "I did live here."

"You still do," says Leah. "In your soul."

Jess takes a deep breath through her nose. Martyn says she should shrug off Leah's digs, her father's put-downs. He thinks it's funny that Jess cannot bear to be teased, that she cannot endure these childish things.

Should she leave her bag? She takes off her damp coat. "Is Martyn . . . ?"

"Martyn's so good with him," says Leah. "You're very lucky."

The living room is heaving. For a second, two, their father feigns not noticing her in the doorway.

Then he turns. "And you are?"

Everyone else laughs. Her eyes feel dusty; the sockets itch. They behave as if squalor is normal; the broken picture frames balanced against the skirting board, the dying yucca, grotty bookshelves like museums of junk: keys, icons, chess pieces, impossibly small pencil stubs, what her father calls his artifacts, mostly corks with needle legs. When someone drops a book, the Hanrahans inhale sharply. But Ray is grinning, opening his arms like a head waiter, although he does his trick of pretending he can't quite pronounce her name: "Yessica!"

"Hi, Dad."

"Here she is," he says. "The wee prodigal."

"I'm not—"

"What do you think of my haircut?"

"It's very . . ." she stops herself saying handsome. This is life as Ray's other daughter; the meting out of his pleasures, denying his ego its nasty thrills. "Neat," and, instantly, his welcome cools.

"So get me a drink," he says. "Can't believe that a daughter of mine would buy green shoes. They look like gherkins."

"Actually—" she begins. She changed at the last minute, from boots her mother bought her, which he had objected to on Leah's behalf. These are Portuguese and made of bamboo fiber, but that will give him more amusement than he deserves.

"Where's that elderly boyfriend of yours?"

"I said not to, Dad."

"Well, he is ancient. Unlike me."

"Oh hello!" says Martyn, hurrying in from somewhere, red-cheeked and excited-looking. "Girlfriend!" He gives her a hello-kiss. "Where were you?"

They're separated from Ray by a wall of admirers. Her brother's come in behind him, smelling of cold. He seems fraught; his senses are on the outside, like a pioneering surgical experiment. He gives her a little nervous grin, but Ray will feel left out if they make a song and dance of their reunion.

"It just seems odd to put himself through an exhibition," says Jess quietly to Martyn. She points at Ray with her chin, as if their eyes aren't all on him already; you're always gauging his mood, knowing exactly where he is in the room. "Why is he doing it? I'm worried."

"Isn't she always?" says Martyn to Leah.

"I didn't make him do it," Leah replies hotly. "Our father is an *artist.* Since before you were born. Just because he wasn't in fashion, didn't cheapen himse—"

"But I thought the whole point was he can't work much. His energy . . . Has he done many? What has he shown you?"

"You're very tough on him," Martyn tells her. "Your sister's right. Anyone else starving?"

"That's all Mum needs," says Jess. "Looking after him, then cooking for twenty."

"Shh," hisses Leah. "She gets all the attention. Why shouldn't Dad have a ch—"

"It's not a competition. They could both . . ."

"Don't be naive." Paisley the cat jumps on the table among Ray's private ice cubes, swishing his puffy ginger tail from side to side. "What is it, Paisley?" murmurs Leah, as to a lover, picking the cat up and cradling it like an inflated furious baby. Jess averts her eyes. "Picklington? Paise?"

Leah's thoughts are unknowable. Maybe she has been missing Jess, despite her opacity, the dark threads. Maybe, like Jess, she is haunted by their coolness, the rows they have about their father, the fear about their mother, and longs to repair it. She could have done. She should have. It was her move.

"Come on, sis. It isn't Mum's fault that h—"

"And he's been working really hard for months. So we thought we'd strike while the iron's, you know."

"Hot," offers Martyn.

"OK. OK. Where is Mum, anyway?"

"He deserves an exhibition," Leah continues, lowering her voice to a fierce whisper. "He's doing, you know," she says, "despite everything, amazingly well."

"Ha."

"Don't," says Leah. "You know it's not easy."

"Well, only because . . ." They both glance at Martyn. "Can you get Dad another drink?"

Jess follows her into the corridor. They stand on shoe boxes and forgotten floppy disks as if it's perfectly normal. "You promised you'd talk to Dr. Mac."

Leah's face is blank with denial. Even the new little lines on her forehead disappear. She says: "He's in pain. How can I . . . How can anyone tell him . . ." Her eyes fill with tears, again, or natural sparkle.

"But it's dange—"

"He *needs* it. It's not for you to deprive him of his medicine. He's an ill man," Leah says. "And a genius."

"Not exactly ill."

"Girls," says Martyn, sidling out to join them. His mad hair and wonky collar should move her. "He's asking after you."

"Anyway," Leah says smoothly, "better find glasses for this stupid extra guest, or her husband."

"Politicians," Martyn says. "They're all the same. It's OK, though, Ray knows her, she's a fan."

Jess's heart crunches in her chest, hard and small and lonely. She needs her mother. Leah always says, "Jess and Lucia: a love story." She claims their love is selfish, that it leaves their father out. Since the operation Jess has been too scared to visit often, because she can't say "Don't die." Will it be her father's cigs that kill Lucia? The stress of living with him? Jess can't understand the genetics; her mind seals up when she tries. She's waited months to see her mother, be pressed to her bobbly jumper-bosom; Lucia once said she was the light of her life.

Leah and Martyn are whispering and grinning as if she's not there.

"I'm going to find Mum," she says, and Leah, who has survived their parents, stares back at her like a stranger.

21

Dreamily, Lucia touches the side of her face and discovers she's wearing the spiraly studs Priya gave her.

"Mum?" she hears Leah yelling, but she's already running upstairs.

She closes the door, opens it again, re-drapes her mother's precious blue scarf over the dressing-table mirror, beside the graveyard of belts from when she still had a waist. It no longer smells of the past; it smells of nothing. It's unthinkable that Priya may never meet her mother. Not for the violet depth of her eyelids, the strength of her arthritic and spotted hand, which Lucia needs to draw constantly, but because Carmel Brophy, while absolutely disgusted, would appreciate Priya's grit, her resolve.

Priya's mother seems to have died when she was a teenager. Every time Lucia glimpses Priya's past pain she falls deeper; faster, even, than at the sight of the cut of her triceps, her temples, the tiny gold hoop in her uppermost ear-edge, completely hidden under that swoosh of shining hair.

Was that the phone? Definitely not the doorbell. Oh God; should she quickly change back into trousers?

This morning an urge began to creep over her: to touch the depths. Recklessly, she'd sent a message: *What's happening to us?*

Quite quickly, Priya texted back: *Are you scared? I am. A bit. Are you?*

Of course Priya didn't reply.

It's an irresistible drip of adrenaline, this permanent not-knowing. Racing around the bedroom like a rogue spaniel at Crufts, picking up ugly tops, half getting into alternative tights, she feels an edge of panic. There's a sound in her throat, a suppressed excited scream. It's the opposite of vertigo; she is unmoored. Any moment now, she'll hear the diesel chug of a taxi and there will be Priya, fresh from the Chamber.

Lucia holds herself still but there's only self-conscious laughter, creaking floorboards, the clink of glass from the living room. And then, almost before it starts, like a predator's footstep, she hears the landline begin to ring.

She's so sure it will be Priya, canceling, that Marie-Claude's accent is a relief. "Hello?" she says, very quietly. "Oh! Please, I can't now. I can't, he's here." The chambers of her heart are draining, like caves at low tide. "I will ring as soon as the weekend's over, but I . . . sorry. What?"

"I think you are ignoring me. Sit down," says Marie-Claude, possibly smiling, and something like an arrow is let loose.

"Sorry. Sorry, sorry. I—it was difficult. I was working, amazingly, and then there's this quite—for—you know, I told you Ray's having this show, tomorrow; there's a big party, food. I think you're invited. Anyway, I couldn't . . . OK, I'm sitting. Are you going to tell me what's up?"

"He is there? With you?"

Everything feels monumental: cherubs tootling through trumpets, the sky gone black. "Not exactly. Downstairs, with some . . . Listen, I know we need a catch-up, but there's a lot going on. I'm a bit frazzled. Can't I ring on Monday?"

Marie-Claude has always been intensely diplomatic about

Ray. Now she says: "I do not care about his show, Lutsia. Listen to me. Breathe, and listen."

Lucia tried a casual breath out. "I'm already—Is it something bad?"

"Stupid," says Marie-Claude. "I want you to guess who telephoned me."

"Oh, I can't. I should really . . ."

"Guess."

"I've no idea! Whatever it is, is it really so urg—"

There is an important pause. "I wait," said Marie-Claude.

"OK. I really ought to go. Um. The Pope."

"Don't be silly."

"OK. Um. The . . . what's exciting? A magazine?"

"Bigger."

"I haven't got . . . Bobbie?"

"Big-ger."

"Another collector?"

"James Duguid."

"Why," Lucia asks carefully, "would James Duguid ring?" She leans against the bed; her chest is light.

"So you know what it means. Yes?"

"I do . . . I know . . . but why, why would he . . . ?" And she thinks: Priya. I need to tell her whatever this is.

"I know. I know. It is incredible. But completely correct."

"I don't . . ."

"They want you. Venice! It is so exciting, the most exciting. The biggest honor. It is what we dreamed of, your Dolly and now I. You in the pavilion, darling, making whatever you want, however big. Representing your country. This is the most—the greatest—accolade of all."

"So have you seen my lesser daughter?" Jess hears from the living room. It's her father's convivial voice; it makes her teeth clench. "Probably looking for something to correct," and she imagines walking in there, telling him how he makes people feel. She could peel him to his sheeny bones, if he hadn't raised her.

"What," he says, "are you wittering on about?" and she can tell he's speaking to Martyn. She waits to hear what will happen to her next.

"Formally," Martyn's saying. There's a feeling of something about to drop. Then she hears: "I know I should speak to her."

She thinks: I'm going to be sick. Her hand grips the bannister, as if she can make courage bleed from the wood. She could run in and distract Martyn, pretend not to realize what he's asking her father. She thought they wanted the same future: far from home and Ray. A floorboard creaks under her ugly green shoe. Is that what he wants?

She thinks: I want Mum.

Quiet foot on the bottom stair as she creeps upstairs, nicking a phone charger on the way. Lucia is murmuring in the darkness on the other side of her bedroom. Jess squints; is she lying down? Sitting on the carpet? That, or the tone of her voice, makes Jess pause with her hand on the door, listening.

"No. Not seriously," Lucia says again.

"Yes."

"No. You are joking. This is a—a trick."

"Not at all."

Apparently, it began at Frieze. Donna Magorian, one of the British Council's panel for the Biennale, had visited the Hertz-Chamaut booth. As luck would have it, they were showing a version of *Grim*: they'd paid to have it fabricated but on the small side, easily dismantled.

"Sorry, when was this?" says Lucia.

"I told you! Zero-six."

"Oh. Then. I see." Lucia had been there but only in body, drifting around the huge tent on the West Side piers like a ghost. A few weeks before, hand on the door after visiting her GP for advice about Patrick, she had asked a casual question. The GP frowned. She referred Lucia for a scan, then another; the new year, in increments, turned dark. And then, although everyone said it wouldn't, the worst did happen, a sledgehammer spinning slowly from the sky, and she stopped caring. It was like struggling to one's feet in a rough sea, for another wave to smack one over the head.

Lucia had thought, before and afterward, that she was over.

She had rung Marie-Claude to tell her, from a bus on Piccadilly, and Marie-Claude ran down from the gallery to meet her, with actual tears. She has a history of kindness; once at the Armory, when Lucia and Ray had a particularly horrible row in public, about how it demeaned Ray to hold her hand when they entered the tent, Marie-Claude ignored everyone else and made herself a human shield until Lucia had semi-recovered.

So, when Julian Hertz spotted Donna Magorian looking thoughtful near the Frieze booth, he told Marie-Claude, who *pronto* rang Lucia, who immediately wiped it from her mind.

"So," Lucia is whispering into the phone, "hang on." With every piece she proves to herself that she's both a genius and a moron but she has always suspected that *Grim* has a sort of strength. "You definitely told me? It was me?"

"Naturally."

"What did I say?"

"It is not relevant, now," says Marie-Claude. "The point is

she—*she*—must have recommended you. On the basis of that piece."

"You *are* joking?"

"When ever do I joke?"

"True. But you can't . . . it can't be . . . I'm not even old. This is ridiculous."

"They have offered you a show. Not a retrospective."

"No."

"Of course I am completely serious. It is happening."

"You, you're saying it's . . . me? They've chosen me. My God."

"You represent Britain now. In that funny little hilltop palace; all the materials, the assistance, you could wish for. Let it sink into your mind."

But it won't. It can't. Maybe it's a test, devised by Ray. Then Lucia thinks: any minute Priya will arrive, and I can tell her.

"And," says Marie-Claude, who sounds a bit champagney already, "I didn't say to you but she also came to the stand at List."

"What? Last year?"

"Yes. She greeted me. Looked for some time."

"Why didn't you tell me? Jesus, this is too m—"

Marie-Claude snorts. "Don't be ridiculous. You think, what, I should stop fainting in the middle of the gallery and send you a message? And what do I say: 'Lucia, it is I, this has happened, it will definitely not lead anywhere but here's a thing to make you hope,' while you are having all that trouble with Patrique . . ."

"But you cou—"

"Of course I do not tell you. But I had a good feeling. They asked us for your CV, your documentation, you know."

"I didn't know. How could I have, if you hadn't . . ."

"Well," says Marie-Claude, "there was no point. You'd be excited. Wouldn't you?"

"I . . ."

"Or perhaps not. I know you and your . . . self-destruction." Marie-Claude pauses and, for a horrible moment, Lucia wonders if she could possibly mean Priya. No: there are other incidents, never discussed, degrading but only professionally. "But you understand."

"What?" Lucia asks her.

"From today everything changes. You tell Ray immediately, and start thinking of ideas. And they want us to visit next week, for meeting and feasting, and then as much time as you will. The work must be done there, as much as possible, what a hardship, so they set it up. Even somewhere for you to stay, a per diem for pleasure. Oh, I could kill you; Venice is the most beautiful. Did I not always say you could do it, be on top of the others?"

"I—I assumed you said that to everyone." Lucia's eyes feel blocky, as if she's forgotten how to blink.

"Now it all begins. I accepted anyway," Marie-Claude tells her. "On Behalf of the Artist. You don't have time to bother with these things."

"Jesus. When? You didn't ask me?"

"Don't be silly," says Marie-Claude.

"Hang on, though," says Lucia. "I need to think," as if they don't both already know what her answer will be.

Then, from the other side of the room, Lucia hears a voice.

"Mum?"

She whips round, pushes herself up to look over the mattress. Silhouetted in the hall light is her lovely Monkey, her girl. What has she heard?

Shit.

"It's you!" she says joyously, then whispers back at Marie-Claude, "*Could you hang on, sorry. Sorry. I'm not alone. Don't—*"

"What's happening?" says Jess, and the overhead light flicks on. "Who are you talking to?"

Lucia squints, stands, adjusts her face. "I need to, oh . . . just finishing this silly work thing," she says with a big smile. "One sec . . . *I'll ring you tomorrow. OK?*"

She hangs up, billows around the bed to the door. She is too astonished to breathe.

"What did you . . . what's up?" says Jess.

She gazes at her daughter like a cod. "Nothing! Why? It's so late, isn't your . . . ?" Her new secret is scattered all over the bedroom. She needs to get Jess out of here. No time to let it sink in; it isn't going to. Her mind pulls away to Priya, she hasn't thought about her for maybe a full minute. Shouldn't she be here already? What if she's already in there, with Ray?

A little moan of anticipation escapes her. Forgetting to change earrings, top, shoes, she hurries past Jess, saying: "There's so much to do, in fact. Wow. Yes. Bloody, um, students. Come and help me with dinner," and, craning her neck to make sure there's no Priya in the living room, glancing hungrily toward the spy hole, she herds Jess down to the kitchen.

Something's different; not only her mother's hair, although it's less dusty and twiggy than normal, and she's tucking it behind one ear. And, when she stood, Jess saw she was dressed as if she'd noticed skirts suit her, which Jess has told her a million times. But there's more; she seems not quite herself.

"Mum. Are you honestly OK?"

"Me? Of course. Totally. I mean, nothing new but . . . Are you? God, I have missed you, it's been ages," her mother says, but she sounds insincere. "Not that it's not great you're making a new life. Here." Lucia passes her the appalling oven glove. "Tell me how everything, um, is."

"Let me," says Jess. She picks up a pot of plain yogurt, grimaces at the date. The rice is under a dishcloth, steaming; roast carrots and garlicky greens and chickpeas. "Do we have lemons?"

"Your father will . . ." her mother starts saying, but she's patting her pocket, looking for her phone.

"Shall I take this up in the pan? Can't believe you've managed to cook so much. He doesn't deserve you."

"Mmm? Don't be silly. Yes, yes, do, with this spoon. I'll . . . hang on," she says, but Jess can see she's looking at the clock, counting on her fingers.

Something's up. No doubt about it. She looks almost good, like she's remade.

No, that's not it. The change is in her face.

Jess, who can't stop wanting excitement, choosing rather than being chosen, a deep new equal love, feels the beating of her heart and thinks: why not me too?

Lucia untucks her phone from her jumper armpit without even meaning to, because why would there be a message?

But there is one, from Priya.

The lamb should have rested. It sizzles and pops in its slick of fat; she doesn't take care. She wants to be burned.

22

This time eight weeks ago, they were outside the Chinese restaurant, breathless in the cold and not sober. The air was so icy that her nostrils felt scorched. Priya was laughing like a seagull, so loudly that anyone in the flats above them might look out, but Lucia didn't care. Urgency made her bold. "I need to know, how you, why you . . . how did you guess about me? That it was OK. To tell me. About Hellie."

"I didn't," said Priya.

"Then why did you . . . I mean, it's such a risk. You must have known. Subconsciously. About me, my former . . ."

"Nope."

"Oh."

"But I do now," Priya said, and she smiled.

Buffered by Szechuan peppercorns and cognac, tucked into the alleyway, there seemed no rush to catch the night bus. When Priya produced a cig ("another vice I don't admit to"), Lucia decided she wanted one too. Or, at least, to share it.

"Seriously?" said Priya. "You seem too wholesome for that."

Lucia swallowed and leaned toward Priya, whose chin was illuminated by the lighter-flame, watched her take a puff.

"Aren't these about a pound each nowadays?"

"Minimum."

"I really am quite drunk," Lucia said. "I mean, properly." She was trying to balance on a mansion-block doorstep, a cave in a thicket of laurel. The soles of her boots would not hold the edge. "And I'm so square this'll give me a head rush."

"We are old people."

"I'm much older than you. What are you, forty-f—?"

"Forty-six," says Priya.

Lucia frowned.

"Hurry up, woman," said Priya, and Lucia put it to her lips.

"Those brown glazed tiles look like chocolate. Burned caramel," and Priya made a wry face, all eyebrows and cheekbones. "What?"

"Get you, all artistic. They do look lickable. Do you feel . . . thirsty?"

"Desiccated," said Lucia, and Priya smirked.

Lucia pretended not to notice. "Is this some kind of, you know. Peabody Estate? I could live here," she said wildly. "By myself, I mean."

"Yes, early social housing; loads of it round St. Pancras. I am ratted." Then she was quiet.

"What? OK, drunk. You don't seem it."

"Well," said Priya, "I am. It's very bad."

Her hand was outstretched. It neared Lucia's coat, her collar. Lucia thought, oh, she wants the cig back, but it wasn't that, not at all.

PART THREE

SATURDAY MORNING

23

A stream of water twists like a drill bit from the tap. It is thick with limescale. Only yesterday morning Lucia had tried to scrape it off, as if Priya would enter her kitchen, notice the minor leavings of minerals, and end it.

She has wondered, in the past, about compressing the powder into stone for a small piece; something to do with reverse aqueducts. She'd put the idea aside, because it would enrage Ray.

She could do it for Venice, but of course that isn't going to happen.

Priya has done this before, let her down so casually.

Hearts are elastic, but only to a point.

Jess steps, waits, listens. She has crept down the loft ladder, clothes draped over her arms, shoes clutched like castanets, and then past the bedrooms to the hall. No one has called out. No time for a bath; barely toothbrushing, because she needs to escape before Martyn wakes and the house fills again. She pees, flushes, dresses, heart in mouth; nothing. Amazing that, today of all days, no one's about.

But, just before she can slip out of the front door, she hears someone in the kitchen. She peers down; her mother is at the sink, hands pressed to her face. Oh, thank God.

Jess has been bred in silence, but mothers and daughters should dare to be honest.

Last night, when Jess returned to the living room, her father was tellingly bright. Dr. Mac, his GP, accompanied him proudly, like a jockey leading in his winning horse. Leah seemed fixated on the least important detail of tomorrow, the catering; it's like she had mentionitis, constantly dropping Larry Nathaniel's son Pablo into the conversation, as if they all should be honored that he's being paid to feed them stupid-sounding tapas. Who could she tell that her mother seemed, even by her usual vague standards, off-balance?

"Mum?"

It's like a moment in a play, when intimacies can be swapped and foundations strengthened. She wants to know about being pregnant, hear her mother's liberating confession of art-school lost love, ask if she thinks Martyn is her best chance. Do families have a tipping point? But Jess loves her mother. She never sees her. This is not the time.

Or is it? Fuck it. She opens her mouth to confess. But her mother looks different, sad and tired. Something's wrong. Wronger than usual: fire down below.

"Will it be a success?" she'd asked last night, in the kitchen. "Have you actually seen what Dad's done?"

"No," said Lucia. "Have you?"

"He wouldn't show *me*."

Her mother rose above it. "I'm sure it'll be fine," she said distractedly. "You look lovely. Very pink."

Jess pretended to pick a feather off her mother's shoulder. Lucia gave her a crinkly eye smile.

"It's so lovely that you're here," she said, rubbing tiredly at her cheek, which was lightly garnished with thyme leaves, and Jess forgot to ask her who'd been on the phone.

"Mum?" she says now. Should she go to her? "Is everything . . . OK?"

An odd expression crosses Lucia's face: fear, or excitement, swiftly checked, like an Etch A Sketch twiddled clean. "Oh yes," she says. "Absolutely normal. Nothing special. You?"

She smiles at Jess. Jess looks back, into the sad, soft eyes that shone right through her childhood, the truest love she knows. Here, at the end of something, a spark of self-salvation flickers. Do what you need to save yourself, it whispers to her.

"Perfectly fine," she says and picks up her bag, and goes.

"So," says Uncle David, "what delights do we have in store?"

Gillian, his wife, puts down her laptop case, looks through her purse. Her kids, the Gillians, are trailing back and forth from their Peugeot with pillows, cool-bags, dangling iPods, falling textbooks. They're both medical students; "More socially inadequate swots," Ray says. "Exactly what this country needs."

"If anyone has a minute," Lucia begins, "I'd love a hand w—" but Uncle David walks straight past her. Ray's family, after three decades, are still waiting for his young wife to settle down. Uncle David, a famously good husband who encourages Gillian's success, enjoys asking Lucia about Balzac, Grieg, and marveling at her ignorance. Ray joins in; it bonds them, despite David having been to university. It's a fine line, which only Ray can navigate.

The Gillians mill about complaining: the bread, the height of the stair-treads, the boiler, long overdue the service that Ray's friend Norris said he'd do on the cheap. The daughter, Becca, twenty-ish but seems younger, looks about to cry.

"Oh sweetheart, what do you need?" asks Lucia.

"She's absolutely fine," says Gillian firmly, as Becca wanders off. "Just give her a task." Lucia can't quite meet her eye. "Unless everything's already in hand. You don't seem," she says, looking Lucia up and down, "terribly relaxed." Her arthritis must be bad; she's using a stick. "It is today, isn't it? What time is kickoff?"

"Six. Well, five for us. The welcoming committee."

"So it's all ready? Just waiting for the hordes?"

"Well . . ."

"Hmm."

"Hello, yeah, morning," says Leah, heading straight for the kettle. "Everything's under control."

"Good. Good," says Gillian. "So, presumably, he's doing well, for them to want a show? We're all agog. Will Ray be raking it in?" and she gives David a very obvious nudge.

"It's not actually like that," Leah begins.

"Because," says Gillian. "In terms of—"

Becca plucks at her mother's garment. "Mum? Mum?"

"All OK, love?" says Gillian, not looking up.

Becca wavers like an anxious toddler; her pasty Sheffield forehead shines. She looks stricken. "Where's Jess?"

Aunt Gillian is famous, apparently, in giant-tortoise circles. She shows no clemency; once, in a casual conversation, she corrected Martyn's grammar. I bet, he thinks, she'd flout the Geneva Convention.

Ray would enjoy that. But he's bickering with his brother, David the scientist. There's an unease Martyn recognizes from class; someone will trespass on their neighbor's leg-space, or lightly insult their pet, and it all kicks off.

"This is nice. Who's it by?" Gillian says, as she wanders around the house.

———

By ten, everyone is up to something. Leah takes Ray to the exhibition space, with a celebratory bacon sandwich in double foil. Martyn comes too, with an enormous picnicky breakfast to share with Patrick; "The meat's obviously for me," he says, tucking another sausage roll into his pocket. Leah is wrapped up like a sanatorium nurse, arm in arm with Ray the brave soldier. They are being secretive.

Gillian's on a step ladder changing the light bulbs in the sitting room. She seems restless, wanting to chat; Lucia is keeping clear. Uncle David's taken their medical children to the Wellcome, like Mormons paying homage to the Golden Plates, and Eric Nakamura is on the way to the White Cube, which hasn't gone down well.

But the main problem is Lucia's face. Marie-Claude has left another message; Priya has not. It makes her body hurt. It's like being drunk: the desperation, the thrill. Her arm skin looks like seawater brushed by a fast wind. You are old, she tells herself. Wanted, but old. All your joy should be over.

Last night, lying beside Ray, small tears pooling in what she thinks of as her "nostrilatrium," she tried to accept her future life: Venice refused, Priya surrendered, maybe a new commission from Germany or more teaching, whatever would keep them afloat and Ray unenraged. She should be able to live on the fact that Venice wanted her, at least. It ought to be enough.

Jess is striding through waves of anger, slower and slower. Her face seems doughy, as if she could fall asleep mid-step. By the time she's reached the chemist's, she's almost let herself forget why she's here.

A bell dings operatically when she steps on the doormat and everyone turns, like crows disturbed. There are three grannies waiting on fold-out chairs, a right-angled old man by the retractable walking sticks. She inspects the cuticle-slicers, the 99p bubble bath, waiting for the queue to recede, but the assistant is slow and her rivals are patient as cattle. The sitters watch with interest as she edges toward the till, behind a shivery person who discusses in detail their need for fig syrup. Then every pendulous ear strains to listen; they see the packet she pays for, shoves deep in her bag. One of them will be the aunt of a Ray-friend. There is no private life here. With the valor of ten young women, she walks back toward the doormat, staring defiantly in the direction of what may be trusses. She is almost crushing the narrow box, trying to remember suitable toilets. In twenty-four hours she can leave London, knowing whatever it is she will know.

Gillian has her own troubles. She has been cultivating David, making sure the dinner table looks welcoming every single evening, seven o'clock on the dot, all his favorite snacks permanently on hand; in bed too, if necessary. And all so that, this weekend, he'll confront his brother about the house.

Given David's recent news, they need to be strategic.

It isn't rightfully Ray's; the Hanrahans know this. The fact that Ray is irrational, dubiously medicated, that his children are too weird for tertiary education (did the elder two even finish A levels?), shouldn't mean that Gillian's own offspring must go without. This rotting house: Ray and Lucia should downsize and release a fortune. Besides, most of the art and china was left to all three brothers by their father, nasty old Gordon Hanrahan, and some of it looks quite valuable. Graeme is a write-off; their mother used to say he's never got over being an only surviving twin. Gillian suspects the truth is more psychiatric.

Perhaps she should raise it herself with Lucia, not that Lucia notices anything. Besides, knowing Ray's family's weird code of honor, poor old Lucia will feel she should inform him and there will be hell to pay.

And, because David cannot bear the thought of Ray knowing, she can't tell Lucia that, on Thursday, he's having a stent put in.

So she's protected him, so far. When Leah rang about this special weekend of Ray-celebration, which she needs like a hole in the head, David had been at a gestational diabetes conference in Windsor.

"We can't stay with you, though," Gillian said quickly, visualizing her brother-in-law's unwholesome habitat, versus a hygienic suburban bed and breakfast. Could she allege her arthritis is too bad for stairs? "There's no room, surely, you still there, and now your poor brother's moved back in . . ."

Leah interrupted: "Dad needs me. Anyway, Patch's not in the actual house, remember? He's in the caravan."

"That grotty caravan? I thought it was abandoned by some friend of your f—"

"Yup," said Leah.

"It'll be too much for you, though, surely," Gillian pressed. "All four of us. Your mother has no time to feed ext—"

"She loves it," Leah said. "Anyway, Dad's the real cook. She's more, you know, basics."

Ray is one of the great bad cooks; on this, David and Gillian are united. His patchy reheating, DEFRA-level overconfidence about sell-by dates, heavy hand with seasoning, mean that, while everyone makes an enormous fuss about his roasts and stews, she'll have to bring cereal bars, apples, oatcakes. David likes to know what he's eating. Gillian's life is a battleground in which greed and not letting herself go, ever, ceaselessly skirmish.

Her mind began filling with the difficulties of the weekend:

how to obtain salad, civilized baths, all the details that make life semi-bearable.

"Is," she asked, wondering how to get on to the subject of bedding, "the exhibition only him? Or with another artist? Your mother, isn't she—?"

"No," Leah replied, sounding as if she was swallowing an ice cube. "It's . . . well, it isn't huge. But a big deal, in . . . in art terms. Whatever anyone thinks, he's still a major figure," and Gillian began to wonder.

Patrick hides.

First he dodges into the shadowed phone booth at the back of the hallway, with its metal shelf and hanging pencil string. The thought of Ray roaring at him, which he can usually endure, sends his blood racing around his body, too quick to let oxygen in. What if someone else is here, hears Patrick's humiliation? If Ray publicly says something horrible, final, it would be the end of him.

Ray and Leah complain loudly; they know he's in the building, which makes it harder to undo. Indecision coagulates in his stomach. He slips past the bleachy toilet and through the door of the dark main room. His lungs are roaring but he's managing to be silent, almost; only the occasional squeak of fear. Sweat is pouring off his neck; his hands shake. He hears their footsteps, distant as they cross the Gallery, then louder, coming out into the open and downstairs to the ground floor. Don't let them find me.

But he needs to tell Ray about the job; he has never wanted anything so much. His dread is pulling Ray closer. He has to make him say yes.

There's a glint by his foot: a big staple, nearly new. Something brutal is required; more serious bloodletting to make change begin. He presses his fingertip to lift it, begins to drive the sharp end into the callused skin of his palm.

There's a point, with Leah's father, where you just have to have faith.

He won't talk about the work. The upstairs space is all set up, looking quite good, quite professional, if you ignore the many non-RSVPs and the selfish refusal of Larry Nathaniel to allow smoking indoors, which obviously they'll ignore, and Patrick not here when they need him, and Pablo not answering his phone.

When Ray agreed that Pablo's guys could do the catering, she'd been fine to communicate only by text, to accept "yass" or "k" in response. Pablo is too busy and creative for chat. But then some stupid woman complained that his restaurant's organic chicken pie was Morrison's, and a different council department kicked off about immigrants, or was it hygiene, so he's been stressed. He hasn't always answered. She heard something about site visits, then that the full Mediterrfusion tasting menu might be tricky, but nothing for a day. Or two. It should be all right; she's waited for him so many times before, hanging about opposite the pub for an accidental bumping-into, lurking near the newsagent's on Junction Road where she once spotted him buying tobacco. It definitely isn't that he's avoiding her.

She gives her father an encouraging hug, hoping he hasn't noticed the splintery floorboards, how cheap the printed biog looks, the crappy fabric draped over the trestles. No one is helping; she's done all this for him. He just needs to let the pictures out of his studio. Patrick swears the car's full of petrol, the tires are pumped; she wants to believe there's enough time to hang them, but she's starting to feel furious at everyone who doesn't believe in him. There's no more she can do, except keep ringing Pablo.

Sukie Blackstock is invited tonight.

Leah's proud of keeping the current RSVPs on her person, on the back of a huge Costco receipt; she pulls it out like a herald and narrates it at meals. But, as she left this morning, she handed it to Gillian.

"You're a grown-up," she'd said. "Don't let it out of your sight."

Obviously Gillian doesn't know about Sukie Blackstock; none of Lucia's friends do. She wanted them still to think well of him. But she'd asked Gillian to see the list and Gillian pointed out that she looked pale. So Lucia admitted the reason she needed to check the names. Gillian did not, as she'd expected, lightly say: "Oh I know, David's done the same" or "best to grin and bear it."

She cradled the spent light bulb under her chin, grabbed the ladder-top with her free hand and slowly lowered herself onto the little platform, her eyes on Lucia's.

"I'm sorry, what? That absolute sod."

For so long, Lucia's hidden it; she can't tell how it looks to the naked eye anymore. Aren't all marriages unhappy quite often? "It's not such an—I mean, who knows exactly wh—"

"That bastard," Gillian says, and Lucia makes a hushing gesture. "Slow down. Tell me everything. Why didn't you say?"

Lucia looks out of the window. The brick in the February sunlight is apricot, edible. "I was protecting him. From what you might think of . . . Is that mad? And he—he always said it wasn't fair to tell people about it, on her or him. That they wouldn't understand. You won't tell David, will you? You mustn't. Please. Ray would b—"

"But, you peculiar woman, why? I mean, it's your business.

But it's a big deal. Now. Let me be clear. How long after your operation did this happen?"

Lucia blinks, breathes in the clarity. "I—I can't be sure. I knew in my heart, but he kept kept kept denying it. But he was so excitable, you know how he gets, sort of feverishly hilarious, and I remember on Patrick's birthday I was so . . . scorchingly sad and worried all the time, the closed-door phone calls, the mysteriously late dinners in town. But he just said I was being paranoid, and controlling. Which I really am, often. Usually. He's right."

"That's his story, when you don't fall in with what he wants," says Gillian, and Lucia inhales sharply. "So, you're vague about the dates?"

Lucia hasn't dared ask anyone about neurological damage. Might there have been a faint whiff of oxygen-deprivation, a distracted anesthetist, during surgery number two, or three? The drains beside her bed had kept filling with blood; they couldn't understand why, so returned to reoperate that evening, through her scar. A few hours later, deep in the night, it happened again; her signature on the consent form looked like a false eyelash. Eight hours of surgery, four dark pints of a stranger's blood, or the shock, or the medication; some, or all, have blunted her.

This had seemed helpful: smudging certain horrors of the time. The operation was 27 February 2007; the third anniversary is racing toward her. She's kept whatever did happen between Ray and Sukie Blackstock as a block of nastiness, frozen at some point after, not technically during, the months she'd spent derailed, destroyed.

But now something unwanted is nudging into place. She remembers that, in the winter of 2006, Ray had begged and cajoled and insisted on introducing them: his wife and his osteopath ("healer, really," he'd say. "It's incredible, the laying-on of hands"). They'd been walking past the pain clinic; Lucia has always assumed it was coincidence, but how did Ray know Sukie Blackstock would be there? And exactly where?

Behind the fire door on the concrete staircase—had he her mobile number, already? Was that allowed, in the NHS?—Sukie Blackstock and Lucia smiled at each other. Sukie teased Ray. Lucia, already at least one biopsy down, had tried, despite her grief, to behave like a sophisticated woman. Why had he steamrollered her into doing this?

And was it when Ray and Sukie were still straightforwardly practitioner and patient, before the weird era of friendship? Ray was so deeply excited when Sukie Blackstock declared that they could be friends, insisting it was allowed, no boundaries crossed, although obviously she mustn't tell anyone, a friend, a nurse. "It might get her into trouble." He said that Lucia was unreasonably suspicious and Sukie Blackstock was trustworthy. Lucia could tell she was a wiggling manipulative force for harm. It was as if he was showing off a sparkling stick of dynamite and expecting her to rejoice for him.

And then, edging closer to the stink of thawing shame, she slots in the rough date of that dinner with the korma and My Partner Gareth; then, a full year later, having to go to a French film with her and Ray.

"We're friends," he said. "That's what friends do." And refusing would have led to such upset, distress.

The next month was when he finally confessed.

She'd been so certain that something was up, had begged him for the truth for weeks. One night, sitting on the edge of the bath looking down at her nakedness, he said he'd tell her, if she really wanted to know.

"What kind of something?" she had asked, almost calmly.

"Well."

"Say it."

"We didn't have full sex."

"Oh. God. I knew! I knew, you—"

"You realize," he said, "that technically it was abuse. She was my clinician. I'm the victim here."

"You had an affair!"

"No! Absolutely not. How could you say that?"

And round and round and round.

So, logically, something was in train before her operation. And, without question, just afterward; within weeks, days. She'd written a blurry diary, to keep track of consultations and results, but it had ended up being full of how overwhelmed Ray said he was, her miserable certainty he was lying. Lately she's reread a page or two.

In the darkest time of Lucia's life, he had absolutely and totally betrayed her.

"Christ," she tells Gillian, "and then six months after was when he admitted it. 'It.' Whatever they'd . . . So it must have been very in the wake. You remember, I could hardly leave the house for months, no work for a year. It was very . . . fresh," she says, and dips back for a moment into the wound, the dimness in her bedroom while the sun slowly set and he told her she was too upset, too much.

What a sucker.

"Tell me," she says to Gillian, "is it weird that I'm only working out the timings now?"

"No."

"Why not?"

"Shock, I suppose. Self-protection. Being so trodden on."

"Ow. OK. So, when that woman came to ours for his birthd—"

"She came to your house?"

"You know that. Don't you? Several times. He—he said it mattered to him that I accept his . . . friends."

"Christ."

"Oh my God. I married a narcissist."

"Well, yes."

After a pause, Lucia goes on: "Anyway, so that evening it was definitely going on. My God. As I went to all those appointments, or when I was in hospital, or, or convalescing . . . it was happening then?"

"Is there anything else?" asks Gillian, a little later.

"That he did?"

"I meant . . . going on. Consequently. Currently. With you."

"Oh! Why, well, no, absolutely not," says Lucia, glancing like a weak spy at the phone. Marie-Claude has been prowling round the edge of her mind all morning. Lucia will not let her into the castle. Success is the last thing they need.

"You're not . . . seeing anyone?"

"What?"

"Well, why not? After what he did. It would end some marriages. Most."

Lucia shuts down her face. "Who," she says, "would want me?"

24

In mid-January, Priya told her: "Let's not take it slow. I've done this before; you have too, distantly, you grandma, in your ancient past."

"True," said Lucia. "But I h—"

"Thank God you're not an innocent, with women. It's so boring," and visions of naked innocents, softer, firmer, filled Lucia's mind, for solitary suffering.

Even for the right woman (despite what she has implied in the heat, at least once), Priya will never leave her husband. Lucia has tried to tease out the truth like gravel in a child's plump palm, but still hasn't established whether the issue is the public eye, which obviously would be reason enough, or being Hindu, whatever that involves or . . . that she simply doesn't want to. That she doesn't want Lucia enough.

They had done much, primarily in the mews round the back of the Dove in Pimlico but also, before then, among God knows what in the shrubbery of a scrappy Holborn square. But, since it—"it"—began, they had never been alone in a room. If one has snogged extensively in side streets, discussed everything in the intervals of simply looking, or by text, in secret midnight phone calls, one knows so much yet almost nothing. She has never seen

Priya's back. They have felt each other almost everywhere and yet the idea of an expanse of skin, of access to the joints and folds, is dumbfounding. The greatest thing of all would be nakedness.

She had survived the thirty-two days since the Chinese restaurant on three meetings, encounters; she would recollect them while washing spinach and want to submerge her face so she could scream. When Priya mentioned a spare evening, Lucia's stupid heart tolled in her chest. The strain of trying not to beg has changed her cells. She is light with hunger, singing to herself like a lunatic; every color and object is associated with hope, the pain of love.

Priya herself has said the word. What else could it be?

Once before, on the cobbles in Pimlico, her legs shook, hard, like a dog. Priya laughed, then moaned; it seemed to fuel her. Lucia has not yet made Priya's legs shake.

"Come to mine after nine-ten," so, of course, she did.

Ray flicks the switches and the Guildworkers' Hall lights up. "There he is. Pissing about. We've been here since the crack, waiting for you."

Patrick, dazzled, says: "Sorry, I was . . ." and Ray gives his dragon snort.

"So," says Leah, "got everything sorted?"

"I think," ventures Patrick, "it is all under con-control."

"Hah."

"It's just . . ." Life is a series of tests. He must force his way through this, to start the next conversation. "Your pictures," he says. "I can't hang them if they're not . . ."

"Well, they're on their way," says Leah. "I'm handling it, aren't I, Dad," she says. "It's confidential, this bit. I'll do whatever it needs."

"But moving them . . ."

"I can do it," says Leah, more firmly. "I'll get a cab."

"You'll need mo—"

"A fucking fleet of taxis, then. OK? Leave it," says Ray.

A shallow triangle: Ray and Leah just inside the main room, Patrick in the corner, back to the wall. If either of them moves, he cannot do it. But they stand in their places, Leah looking worriedly over her shoulder, fiddling with the keys, Ray's head back, chin up, eyeing the gallery like a fighter.

"Sorry," says Patrick, trying to feel the present infusing his bones, which he's practiced in the caravan with a Tibetan tape from Mrs. R. "I need to ask, tell, say . . ."

"Oh for God's sake," says Leah. "What do you want to know? Is it urgent, because I need to speak to the cateri—"

"I . . ." begins Patrick. "They . . . I—"

"Will he spit it out," says Ray.

"They want me to help in the kitchen at a pub and I can live upstairs."

Ray and Leah exchange glances. "What," she says, "in the name of fuck are you talking about?"

"It's . . . I . . . it's starting Monday. The manager said. It's a good thing. A job."

"This," says Leah, "is Dad's special day."

Ray sighs. "Was."

"No, no," says Patrick. "That's not . . . it isn't negative, it's work! I mean I'd have to move my stuff out, but . . ."

"It's fine," Ray says, his voice dead. "Let's cancel my show. Let's make today a celebration of Patrick's baking."

"No, sorry, I . . . I didn't—"

"I am not," says Ray, "going to think about this selfishness now. I don't have the energy." He turns and stalks off, through the front door.

Patrick looks at his shoes.

"Right, you, listen to me," says Leah.

"What? Sorry, I can exp—" Patrick begins. "I didn't mean to upset him. But this is what I've been, I assumed I'd never . . . Mrs. R says they'll pay better than she can, and I get a room. And I'd come back whenever anything needs to be fix—"

"Shut up," says Leah.

"Sorry?"

"Shut it. OK? Listen to me. We have a problem and the least you can do, now, is fix it."

"So," says Lucia lightly, "what's up? Where are you?"

Priya never rings "just for a chat." She hasn't mentioned last night's non-visit; why should she? Government business.

"On my way to a school United Nations conferencey thing. Ever been to Clapton?"

"No. Are . . . are you eating?"

"Breakfast," Priya says crunchily, "a bagel. Sesame."

She doesn't say: come and meet me. Or: I'm sorry about yesterday. Chalk Farm isn't far. I'd have walked out of this garden barefoot and over there, thinks Lucia. Or on my knees, like a pathetic old pilgrim. Even my passion has no class.

Then she remembers last night's craziness. She could blurt out about Venice, make Priya marvel. No; absolutely not.

"Guess who left a message?"

"The Prime Minister?"

"Plonker," says Priya. "It was Hellie."

Whenever Lucia's prodded, wondering if Priya and Hellie still meet, Priya snaps shut like a mousetrap: not the humane kind. If only she'd tell Lucia there's nothing to worry about. Her throat tightens. She thinks: be cool.

"*The* Hellie?" she asks.

Priya, involved with her bagel, merely laughs through her nose, breathily, as if she were right up against Lucia's ear. Lucia understands that the risk isn't that she'll lose her to Sid, or to the next interesting woman, but that Priya will go back to strong, humorless Hellie, who is everything Lucia fails to be.

The future fans out before her; she's a gambler with one chance.

"By the way," she says. She grabs a sprig of rosemary, breathes in the resin of hillsides, goddesses. "I had a phone call last night too. Are you ready to hear something amazing?"

In the name of all that's holy, let no one be home.

There is still pee on Jess's fingers from the toilet at the Black Ball. She'd tried to conceal herself with her coat but she's bound to be on a Dark Web porn site now. Until they see what she was peeing on. It's in her pocket; the bin was stuffed and foetid, swampy with other women's secrets. She'd have felt criminal leaving it in that place of drunken ruin, like abandoning a baby where it would be unfound.

If she sees her mother, she will cry. Patrick: she might tell him. Martyn will suspect that something is up. She and her father are raring for a bust-up; when are they ever not? But the worst person, she thinks, pushing through the front door, would be . . .

Leah, standing on the bottom step, looking fresh and beautiful: "Oh. Hi."

"Hi."

"Where've you been? Christ, wait until you hear what your idiot brother has . . . come and help me smoke a ciggie," she says, as Jess hears a male footstep on the stairs. It might be Martyn.

"OK."

The back door bangs behind them; they both wait for their father's shout.

"Go on, have one, you loon, it won't kill you." Leah's holding out her Rothmans. Jess looks hard at the pear tree. The thought of her sister's pink lungs clogged with tar makes her feel quite violent.

"You know that's stupid," she says. "Given Mum's hi—"

"Don't," Leah says, hands over her ears. "I can't bear it."

Leah, Jess tries to remember, is a good dear person; she's just been infected by their father. There is what passes for a companionable silence, except that Leah is dragging the life out of her cigarette, while Jess clenches her fists to stop herself gnawing her thumb. It feels like a chance to say something important. A piebald cat, possibly a relation of Paisley, swaggers along the path. Please, no, thinks Jess, as it leaps with heavy grace onto her lap.

"Ow." She shifts her knees. After all these years away, she's more daring. Fibers must have been broken, the force field weakened. Surely? "So," she begins, putting a hand on her sister's back. "Where are we with . . . him? I mean, generally."

"You wouldn't understand," says Leah, and Jess takes her hand away. "Even just getting him his, you know, stuff, it's a full-time . . ."

"Well, yes," said Jess, over the sound of the walls closing in, the slosh of unknown fins beneath dark water. "It's upsetting. Seeing him like this, and Mum." The cat is purring, its eyes on Jess. It looks like it might bite. "And, well, we could be titrating his dosage, if we make a plan."

"Don't start on all that again."

"You can buy special placebo pills online, I've read about it. You j—"

"Can you stop? I've got enough on my . . . All your 'Shouldn't Dad see another doctor? Shouldn't we wean him off' crap," says Leah in her special Jess-voice, high and posh and warbley like a Morningside duchess. "Dr. Mac is in charge and if he says—"

Jess flops her knees; the cat thumps to the ground. The blind rage of siblinghood is upon her. "He's a poisoner! God. I'm . . . I want to help."

"I am sick," Leah says, "of being the only one who does anything. Your brother is worse than useless, it breaks Dad's heart. His latest . . . forget it. But you . . . you've been protected from reality for long enough."

"*I* have been? Are you serious? *You* . . ." and then she remembers what's in her pocket, and weariness overcomes her. "Oh, forget it."

"Fine."

"Fine. So."

"Mum's being crap. Since you didn't ask."

"I did notice. Does she n—"

"But the main thing is, after the opening," Leah says, "Dad might feel a bit flat."

"Is there a, a problem, with it?"

"No! But anyone would. It's unavoidable. So you need to stay at least a week. Distract him."

"You know we can't," Jess says. "How—"

"But you have to." Leah's lowered her voice; they could be plotting an assassination. Tears begin to escape; they roll down her cheeks and to her mouth and she licks them away. "You can't just bail."

"Sis," says Jess hopelessly, "we really do have to get back. Our whole, well, jobs are out there, and . . ."

Leah shrugs, clutches her elbow across her chest, drags again on her cigarette like a woman who's dodged disaster. They watch a blackbird screaming out of a tree; somewhere a motor dies. "Yeah," she says. "Your life. Well, Martyn loves it down here."

"OK. Yes. But he doesn't un—"

"It's not right, sacrificing someone else's happiness. You can't do that to him."

Jess frowns; somewhere she has made a huge mistake. "Martyn? But he . . ."

"Not Martyn," says Leah, with elder-sibling scorn. "Dad."

"Wow," Priya keeps saying. "You absolute knockout."

She's tenderer than usual on the phone; she calls Lucia girl, which, for her, is practically love. She repeats "Biennale" with emphasis on different syllables, and Lucia laughs and shushes her and doesn't know how to confess that she is going to refuse it. How can she, when Priya's so delighted with her?

Priya whispers, "And think of the party. The opening, or private . . . whatd'youcallit. View. I'll be there. Didn't I say we'll go abroad together?"

Lucia catches her breath. "Will you wear your green dress?"

"The one I told you about? With the zip?"

"Yes. The zip. Help."

"Or maybe a sari. Now I can finally bear them. Give your fans something to ogle. And *you,*" says Priya, "in something fabulous I will have bought you. Like a wrapping. And at some point, after the speeches . . ."

"The thing i—"

"Shh, I will take you off through a service door past the kitchens, a cool private corridor where no one, probably, will see us, and into a cypressy garden at the back . . ."

"Ohhh. But actu—"

"You know," Priya says, "talent should always be rewarded. We must practice."

"Meaning?"

"I told you I have a trip tomorrow. Two or three nights in Bristol. Know anyone in Bristol?"

"No."

"Neither do I. It's perfect. So. Why don't you?"

"What?"

"Come away with me."

"Seriously?"

"Maybe. Let me think," says Priya.

That's not enough. Lucia's going for broke. "Let *me* think," she says. "Although . . . here's a thought. Come to the opening tonight. Seriously. No one will think it's weird. Because I've got to see you. I do really have to explain something."

25

Jess needs to ransack. Any minute Martyn will find her, complaining about neglect. Who wouldn't want a little kick before that?

She hasn't been down in the basement for years. Every time there's a condiment crisis, she's elsewhere until the ketchup has been retrieved, increasingly by Martyn, who still believes that cellar-access is a rare honor.

Her father is so proud of the deep jungly green of the corridor, the absence of beige good taste, but the damp is exposing itself. The paint-blisters have miniature blisters of their own, glaucous blooms like the skin of a plum. Opening the door, thickly painted as a ship's, sounds like killing pigs; you'd think no one ever comes down here. Martyn says that the stony air could kill you, happily: botrytis and ancient cork, wine-salts, history. No: it's the stink of decay.

Down four steps, whose walls are lined with, if not technically toadstools, then fungal blisters, a toxic crust. The main room has ramparts of stained Tupperware and jam jars; discolored candles; cash-and-carry pallets of macaroni and silver foil; restaurant tubs of peppercorns; forgotten Christmas teas. Some of the rusty tins are fermented-looking, like dead heroes' Antarctic stores. All along the back wall are red cupboards with doors akimbo, stuffed with teapots and fax machines, redundant printers like segments of elephant, gritty from ceiling dust and whitewash crumbs. Machines hum and chirrup; a huge chest-freezer, an ex-fridge, bags of old knitwear through which moths stickily tunnel. She makes herself see the torn lampshades and boxes of yellowing thrillers, the damp, the filth, letting it settle on her skin and sink into her bloodstream: inoculation. She needs to be cured; she needs to go. There is nothing for her here.

The air's cold, cheesy tang could be refreshing, were it not for the feeling of being inside an irretrievably broken mind. There are spiders' webs everywhere, furry cathedrals of them, dotted with tiny bandaged corpses: folded mayflies, daddy longlegs. She ducks to avoid a dried wasp, rotating at the end of a thread, and almost falls against a cardboard box that is half-rotted, flaking—oh Christ, no, gnawed. A bubble of vomit eases up her oesophagus: a feeling of sickness, without and within. Her body itches: the grime, the aversion to reason. She's trying to look at it as a stranger might, without sentiment or rage, but it's worse than she has ever seen it. They're past saving, all of them.

"Oh, hello, sweetheart," says Lucia. "All OK?"

"No," whispers Becca, prodding at the fireplace with a poker and waiting for Uncle Ray to shout. Her eyes are continually pooling with tears; she will claim hay fever if anybody asks, but no one will. Oh God, they're spilling over again.

Uncle Ray acted like their arrival was an astonishing surprise. Maybe it's because of the weird standoff between him and her dad, but he's even scarier than she remembered, swearing at her when she tripped over the rug. Patrick, on whom she had an embarrassing crush when she was young, has barely noticed her. All the cousins are on edge, as if a surprise is about to burst out too soon.

Earlier a sweaty doctor came by for a home visit, like Uncle Ray was a heifer needing James Herriot, and Becca's dad followed him upstairs. Five minutes later he stormed back down and now he and Uncle Ray are already not speaking. Her father sits harrumphing in the living room, loudly recording letters for his secretary and ignoring Becca, as though she is nothing to do with him.

Then there's a whole weird nonargument about where Becca and her brother will sleep. The main bit of the house is, apparently, full, which makes her father furious, and after endless awkwardness it's decided that "the kids" should stay in the other part of the house, lined up on the floor of Ray's old wife's sitting room like cannon fodder.

Her mum keeps getting up to check her plenteous eye shadow in the mirror above the mantelpiece. Her father, who usually prides himself on his grayhoundy physique, has gobbled handfuls of peanuts. Becca is staring at the top of his bald head, willing him to look up, which he does not. He's not a bad man. But he isn't the kind of father you'd ask for comfort, except in an emergency.

She is no way sharing a room with her brother. And she's scared to eat because of botulism and by now a certain kind and engaged friend of her brother's, like him a promising biologist, etc., who's been friendly to her, will have found her letter. It was hard to write but it might work. You have to be willing to do anything for love. Boys do like you to be daring. And it might not be horrible. It might not hurt.

Asking Priya to the show was unhinged. If Lucia wasn't a coward she'd risk driving to meet her, but coming back home she would crash, no question, and then it would all emerge. Today can't get much worse, she thinks, and then Ray bursts in, with the rage of hell upon him.

Then he's silent, which, given the timing, is very bad. She puts out a hand toward his general atmosphere.

"Don't touch me!" he says. He is yellowish with wrath, like double cream.

"What's happened? Seen Patch?"

Ray mutters, his jaw coming up: "Oh, what a surprise that he's a priority. Obvious where he gets his selfishness, that little turd."

"Well," says Lucia hurriedly, "that's not exactly fair—"

"And even bloody Leah's left me. Why am I surprised?"

"Oh," asks Lucia, "you came back by yourself? That's good. That's pro—"

"It's abandonment," he says. "As if I care where the caterer is. You'd have thought that for one day everyone could pretend I still matter, but no. So, presumably, you knew?" he asks.

"Knew what?"

"What your son has done to me. Screwed me over completely. Presumably you think that's OK?"

Lucia's still wading through the confusing story—a real job but, oh that sweet boy and his bad timing—when Patrick quietly comes home.

This is when Lucia makes her mistake. The job's a good sign, a small shoot of the self-confidence she's tried to foster (but, Ray says, has instead destroyed with her helicoptering overprotection, her favoring) for years, and she misses it. Why does she fail him, not look back? Because she is trying to wipe away her stupid, joyous smile, the Priya hopes and Venice thrill. Because she doesn't yet know all the facts, is trying to keep everyone cheerful.

None of this explains it. Admit it, Lucia.

What happens is that Lucia says, "Honestly, Patch, couldn't you have waited?" and sees his poor face go still and white because she's done it again. She put Ray first.

Someone calls from the front hallway: "Anyone spotted mine host?"

Martyn's never seen Dr. Mac this close up, like a celebrity. Jess says he has the face he deserves, puffed up with mistaken self-belief. He's pink yet unwrinkled, like an old cherub, although his hair, still dark, still thickish, has abandoned his crown neatly, leaving a tonsure effect. It must be invisible to him, but it shines like a snooker ball from above. As Martyn watches him barreling off to Ray's bedroom with his unprofessional-looking sports bag, he feels something like fear.

Luckily, when the phone starts ringing, Leah's just back. She legs it upstairs but her father won't look at her. "Tell whoever it is to fuck off," he says. He won't even let her help him to his room to rest. But Dr. Mac works wonders. In the golden time, when her father's medicine and blood sugar and pain align, she will try to be forgiven. She picks up the phone. The accent is French; she is instantly on guard. "Hi, yes. It's Leah. No, Mum's not around. Why?"

Marie-Claude is a cow. She hasn't offered any help with Leah's father's exhibition, even though he put her on the guest list. Leah's mother keeps saying, "there's really no need for her to come"; last night she gave a little speech about it and Ray commented loudly, "the thing about your childhood is you never learned to share."

The French cow is giving instructions.

"What? Look, I don't know if you realize, but we've a major sh—"

"Darling," says Marie-Claude, "stop talking. Please, find her for me."

"Her?"

"Yes."

"Why not Ray?"

M-C speaks again, maybe in French this time, who cares, and Leah yells, upstairs, outside, barely bothering to hold the phone away. Like a cat, you never know where her mother will appear from. She comes in, looking knackered, which jogs Leah's heart for a moment. Then she thinks: typical, on Dad's day.

She holds out the phone. "For some reason," she says, "M-C urrrrgently needs to talk to you. What's going on?"

Lucia emits a tiny gurgle. Leah raises her eyebrows. Gillian looks interested; Jess has her look of childhood distress, gray with the effort of not releasing tears.

"Who's that?" says Martyn cheerfully, knocking over the salt. "What have I missed?"

Lucia takes the phone, waits for Leah to leave but she's sorting out the fridge door and Lucia, who is so very tired, thinks: at least it's not Priya, ringing to cancel tonight. I can deal with this.

"Hi," she says, turning casually. "Marie-Claude? Yes, lovely. Sorry, we've been . . ."

"So you are having celebrations?"

"Not at all!" murmurs Lucia, watching Leah's suspicious shoulders. "How are you, anyway?" she asks, lowering her voice but trying to sound normal. Normal is the thing.

"*Cherie*," says Marie-Claude, "this is not reasonable." Lucia makes a stupid nervous sound in her nose.

"Do not fucking tell me we're out of butter," says Leah, who has never accepted the primacy of phone calls. "Mum?"

"It is Saturday," Marie-Claude says.

"I know."

"And? What is it I shall say to them? At the . . ." Her voice seems to boom out of the receiver like a sports-day megaphone. "Biennale."

Lucia gasps, coughs. Marie-Claude says, over the spluttering: "No, do not run away."

Leah is staring hard at her mother; the red laser dot holds steady and true. Did she hear? Lucia smiles reassuringly, like a maniac, shakes her head, rolls her eyes.

"They need you to confirm," says Marie-Claude.

Leah says: "Tell her we're busy."

"Lucia."

Venice wants her; it's a conversation she has barely let herself dream of, more than the Turner, even the Tate. Which proves Ray's premise: she is arrogant. And she realizes now that her plan, to tell him one day of a great loving sacrifice, was stupid. There could never be a right time; even if she did it on her death bed, with her absolutely final breath, he'd be sobbing and yelling about being ignored by the press: the last image as her brain folds into nothingness.

Ray, who wouldn't refuse anything for her. Who deserted her, at such a time of darkness.

"If," says Marie-Claude, "you say no, again, then I arrive at his little show today and I tell him everything."

"You can't, no, pl—"

"Tell him what?" says Leah, right at her elbow.

She looks her daughter straight in the eye and says to Marie-Claude: "Never mind. OK, come tonight and find me. Please. We will talk then."

26

Something is growing inside Jess. It is doubt.

Martyn's being peculiar, smiling hard, looking around like a politician about to give a speech. Can he have guessed? She's avoided being alone with him all afternoon, changed upstairs when he was talking to Eric Nakamura and Ray, but he catches her in the end.

"Why are you running away?" he asks. "Don't you want to hang out with me?"

Astrid Pringle believes he must be able to sense that her heart's not in it. "You're waiting for him to give you permission to dump him," she says. "Not going to happen. He's already talked you out of it, what, twice?"

"Three times. Look, I want to behave decently, to other people. Not be like you know who. Splitting up with Martyn would feel . . . *violent*."

"Well, you might have to be violent then," says Astrid blithely, before heading off to teach thirteen-year-olds to hire cars in Spanish.

"I'm not running away," Jess tells him weakly. "You look smart." He has been planning his outfit for weeks, discussing it loudly in the staff room: his Parents-Evening jacket, the patterned shirt Ray once told him was "natty."

"Do you like it?"

"How does Dad seem? He's already told me off for eating one of Leah's, apparently, special biscuits. Like she's a baby . . . So was he OK?"

"Yes," he says, nodding, like someone making a decision, "and we were catching up."

"On what?"

"What? Oh, so you're wearing *that* dress. I thought you said your dad hates it. Never mind. Have you talked to Leah? Patch around?"

"Isn't he over at the Hall? If the pictures aren't all up by now, it'll be bedlam."

"Don't think so. Leah's in a flap. Do you know this catering fellow? Pablo."

But Jess is thinking about her brother. Patrick needs to be OK. She can't save him.

Christ, she thinks. What if I need to rescue Leah too?

At long long last, it's almost time to leave. Martyn drifts into the kitchen, feeling handsome, looking for provisions. Funny to be so nervous; I suppose, he thinks, that's being part of the team.

"Let's open the wine," says young Jake, as if it's a question, corkscrew already in hand, and Martyn grabs a glass. Gillian pretends not to hear but she is always alert, assessing. Martyn is scratched by Paisley but tries to be brave as, with a weird electronic swishing, Ray begins to descend the staircase; not on foot, or even with a stick, but strapped into a chairlift, like a game Hollywood star for her final curtain.

27

"I'm still shaking," says Martyn, which is true, internally.

Jess clearly hadn't trusted him to understand, which makes him angrier. His shock was so obvious; Ray and Leah and even the Gillians laughed at him.

"But how didn't you notice the track?" asks Jess. "You must have seen him do this before."

"Never. I swear on my life." Even as Leah came forward to ease him into the wheelchair at the bottom, maneuvering it awkwardly between the book piles in the hall to steer him into the living room, what Martyn was witnessing still did not quite sink in. Then he saw Ray's bony hands pushing down on the wheel rims.

The wheelchair isn't even a proper one, just a rickety reject with: PROPERTY OF NHS WHITTINGTON HOSPITAL CASUALTY DO NOT REMOVE stencilled on the canvas back. "Shouldn't he be electric?" he whispers to Gillian, who merely raises her eyebrows. She seems not to understand the gravity of the situation. "This is appalling. Isn't it? If I'd known he was this bad, I—"

"You'd have done what, precisely?" asks Gillian.

He's avoiding her; unpleasant woman. Now he and Jess are strolling to the Gallery, past the reservoir, an uninviting pub, a long, curved street of peeling council mansion flats with improbable names, Cantalowe and Ribblescar. Bus drivers leaving their shift trudge from the depot toward the lights of Archway. Jess is quiet while he talks through it; the ignominy of having been kept in the dark is beginning to ebb. Anyway, he thinks, it's not as if the bloody Hanrahans know everything about my family.

That is a path down which he is definitely not going to head.

"I can't," says Patrick, which Leah ignores. She hands him the money; hurries back into the living room.

"How are you doing, Pa?" he hears her say. "Another few minutes and we'll head off. You look so handsome in that shirt."

She told Patrick there was no time to walk. The number 4 bus used to feel like part of the house. Now he shifts on the itchy seat, checks again over his shoulder, at the CCTV as it flicks between the upper deck, the back, Patrick hunched in his corner, looking like the criminal. The money is loud in his pocket. His bandaged hand, ribbed with brown, throbs on his lap.

Even he, as Leah put it, knows the money won't go far in Waitrose, but Ray will be demeaned by anywhere cheaper.

"Are you sure I need to?" he kept saying. Although Leah said she'd hang the pictures herself, she's still angry. "Maybe the catering man's a bit delayed?"

Leah palely compressed her lips. "Forget it. He's . . . no. Definitely not. We need snacks. And seriously, you have to get a sodding cab back. Don't be weird about it. This is a bloody emergency."

It's years since he was in a huge supermarket; the orange and purple plastic, the crashing baskets. Nothing is where he'd expect; he wanders past melons and gins and mops, unable to ask. Would Ray accept oatcakes? Chocolates? Head down, he returns for a trolley, gathers jumbo bags of ready-salted crisps, grapes, cheap pitted olives, chocolate orange peel to please him, crispbread, the largest-size blocks of Cheddar, six marked-down Family Farmhouse loaves. Hula Hoops? This is not a children's party. Ray will notice that it's all vegetarian; he reaches for cocktail sausages, but cannot do it. He hurries through Meat, averting his eyes.

In the alcove by Baby and Pet he recounts the notes. Whatever Leah says, there must be a way to transport this trolleyful on the bus. Never mind sharing a car with a stranger; just ringing the cab office will finish him.

A tiny old woman, squinting, hair a platinum wave, scrapes the corner of her trolley against his bad knuckles as they pass, scowls unapologetically as if he is to blame. The pain is a tunnel; he grips the child-cage so as not to fall. Luckily, he hasn't eaten, but he's almost too dizzy to queue to pay. Outside, three bags per hand, he tries to catch a bus. The minutes pass. His breathing is shaky; sweat dampens his back. Ray will be furious. Ray, who says he can't take the pub job.

Patrick starts to walk.

Lucia, ready to pass out, is waiting for her lover.

It's gone six o'clock. She is wearing, after several desperate costume changes, the close-fitting hot black wool dress she has worn for almost every opening and party for the last fifteen years, with the pink lightning-bolt earrings Leah gave her for her birthday, and yellow shoes. Priya will say she looks like a Gothic Battenberg but once, when she saw a photo of Lucia being runner-up at the Kent Prize, in this very dress, she said she fancied her.

The entrance is tiled with sub-Minton encaustic; a lavish pattern of buff and rust with some lovely turquoise corners, like a staircase at the V&A, but the rosy color is wearing away, and they're dulled with salt crystals, linseed, paint. Lucia thinks: aren't we all. There's some spirit soap in the studio; she wouldn't mind getting down on her knees with a dish-sponge and losing herself there: an act of service. She is turned on to the point of fear, or perhaps it's the other way round. One of the little blue squares is loose; then it's in her hand.

The plan is, or was: the Hanrahan entourage arrives at five, "less interesting" guests start to show an hour later, with Ray rolling up at five to six on the dot because, as he put it, "I'm not hanging around like an old whore."

Until he's here they're forbidden to go up to the mezzanine, let alone enter the Gallery, so everyone's milling about in the main area. There's no sign of food but a stunning quantity of booze; Ray's new friend Salvo has impressive luck at auctions after mysterious fires. He's done Ray proud, his motivation, as ever, uncertain. Smokers huddle in the famous garden; Lucia's already had to rush home for the spare corkscrew. Patrick's still not arrived; Ray is ignoring him because of the pub job. He's not speaking to Jess either, or to Lucia. Will, she thinks uneasily, this famous show of his be up to scratch? Marie-Claude is imminent. And stupid Lucia hasn't seized her chance to hug and snuggle and interrogate her girl, her Jess, because she's an addict with one consuming interest: the arrival of Priya.

Shouldn't Ray be here by now? Her stomach's rumbling, but it's better out here in the cold hallway than in there, visible. Leah has been watching her, as if she heard Marie-Claude perfectly well. At the back of Lucia's mind, unease flicks its muscular tail.

Priya said she'd be early: a flying visit. When Lucia's children were younger, the least delay of Tube or bus after a meeting would generate this same twisting franticness to be with them. Now Lucia thinks: let us escape somewhere, only to whisper, to touch her bare shoulder. I would do anything.

There's a shuffling sound on the path up to the door; it is ajar but the knocker clanks. Her heart flips like a fish. The door swings open and behold: it's Sukie fucking Blackstock.

"I need a drink," says Jess, grabbing a bottle of red by the neck.

On the way here she remembered what she'd left in her coat pocket; too late to hide it with Martyn at her side. She's bundled the coat up, pocket innermost, stuffed it deep under a bench with her bag and other bag. Everyone waits for Ray to arrive; their heads twitch round at the slightest noise, like nervy woodland creatures.

"Isn't this fun?" says Martyn.

Because it's Ray's show, there's already a feeling of end-of-term misrule: his beardy long-ago flatmate leaning over a young arty woman, loud laughing, a glass smashed. People she's never seen before, or has forgotten, or would like to, stream in; just not her father. Martyn, talking to a woman with lady-novelist hair and what Ray calls menopause jewelry, is waving Jess over as if she's been lost at a funfair. She glugs most of her glassful, wipes wine from her chin. Of course she shouldn't be drinking. Oh God, don't cry.

Martyn's assessing her. Lately he's been giving feedback on her appearance: too much black, try a more feminine shape. He's said twice that Leah looks fantastic; Leah, in a long narrow darkly floral dress, like an artistic vampire, grinned at Jess both times.

"When's the food?" he asks Leah, looking around for somewhere to leave his anorak. He thinks that wearing it every visit endears him to their father, as if rebellion, taken slowly, will eventually win him over. He straightens his now-crumpled jacket. "Everyone's going to drink too much. Did you ask for mini-burgers?" He murmurs something else to her, too quietly for Jess to hear.

"You two," she says, trying to sound jokey. "You're like secret advisers."

"Calm down," says Martyn. "We're just making plans. It's a good thing. Our future."

"Don't you think it's a bit strange to do it without me?" Jess starts to say, with a little laugh, when she realizes he's stuffing his anorak into the deep gap where she pushed her own coat.

"Mart—"

"What?" he snaps, and it occurs to her that he too is anxious.

"Can we maybe focus this once on our father," says Leah, each word a spondee of dislike. "We'll tell you later."

It might be the wine, or the Whiskey Mac she downed at the Black Ball before she could face the pub toilet, that has jolted her from the path of righteousness, but Jess thinks: absolutely no way. "Are you joking? What is it?"

And Leah whispers again in Martyn's ear. They bend into each other like a couple with a secret.

With a *whump* like a gas fire catching, Lucia is alert. She shimmers with vestigial rage; never mind her own crimes, let's fight this little bitch, this thief, this entrapper of idiot men.

Sukie Blackstock, inevitably, is wearing very high heels, a pencil skirt. Such a cliché; Ray should be ashamed. Under her dramatic waisted coat and stupid fur hat, Sukie's black blouse is translucent, balloon-sleeved, like a dubious St. Petersburg governess about to marry money.

"Oh, isn't this lovely," she says with that fake smile: hundreds of teeth, a saccharine shark. She's brought My Partner Gareth, whose suede scalp and knuckly face suggest both romantic pain and too much exercise. He bobs behind her like a squire, discreetly on call.

"Are we late?" she asks innocently, as My Partner Gareth produces a bottle of apple juice from his coat pocket.

Lucia is too furious to smile, too well trained not to.

"Early, actually," she says, which is such a cop-out. "Practically the first."

"Well, it's good to see you," says Sukie Blackstock, almost clamping her ferrety claw onto Lucia's wrist.

Lucia pulls back, points unnecessarily to the last-minute coat rack rigged up by Patrick out of two filing cabinets and a curtain pole. It's as if Ray has muzzled her, pulled out and mounted her tongue. If she were Priya, she'd roar with bloodlust, send these polluters running. But she is mute, merely gives a horrible little smile and pretends to be checking her phone for the only message that could obliterate Sukie Blackstock entirely.

A miracle. Priya has texted. She should defer the pleasure or pain of reading it until these bastards are out of the way, but how can she resist her?

At the sound of her gasp, Sukie Blackstock narrows her eyes.

Ray wheels himself in like a broken hero, and there is a cheer. He's definitely ignoring Jess; later he'll breezily reintroduce her to an old family friend, as if moving to Scotland gave her amnesia. Everyone mills about, as if this bit is the point. Jess dodges her sister, like hostile bacteria on a biology slide. She needs a crisp, anything. Vague smile so no one can corner her as she searches for nourishment; her least favorite Gillian, Jake, is being hostly, sucking up like a page boy. Edging past him, she sees it again: that passing of an understanding between Martyn and Leah.

"What," she gestures, "is going on?"

This seems to decide him. He sidles closer to her father, puts his hand on Ray's wheelchair handle. He gestures Jess to his side and then he's saying, in a voice both louder and more intimate than usual, "Actually we do have some news."

Jess tries to smile. "Do we?"

"We do!" and the Gillians murmur encouragingly and Leah narrows her eyes, as if Jess has forgotten to close the door to her soul. Even her father is smirking, or smiling, but he's looking hard at her.

"We," begins Martyn, "and I'm sorry if this isn't the right moment but, anyway, while we're waiting for the real fun to start . . ."

"Bloody warm-up acts," says Ray.

"I thought I'd share some cheering news."

Jess can feel her face set, so false her teeth hurt. She looks around for her mother.

"We, Jess and I, will be coming back soon, for good."

"Wh—"

"Because . . . we're trying for a baby!"

28

Lucia has managed to stay in the entrance after Ray's arrival.

"Aren't you coming up?" asks practically everyone as the minutes grind by and she pretends to be happy to see them: John Phillips Royal Academician with his halitosis, Caroline something and her late-onset husband. Nobody says, "But you seem to be vibrating." She can't keep track of reality, let alone the invented facts: where she's been on certain evenings, whom she was meant to have met when. For an icy second, she can't even remember what the secret is.

The girls stick their heads into the hallway, respectively plaintive and hostile. They're fine, she tells herself. Jess has Martyn and Leah has, well . . .

And then, at last, unbelievably, Priya arrives in a rush of cold air, perfume, pheromones. She floats down the corridor toward Lucia, stops seven or eight feet away. Space is not emptiness; Ray scoffs at this, says Lucia's trying to be profound, but the gap between them is solid enough to climb.

Some of Ray's cronies follow; they push past to overtake her before anyone thinks to look round. From behind the men's backs Priya holds her gaze with such an ardent private look, mouth compressed to keep the smile in, that Lucia's body seems to thump. She cannot turn her eyes away. Every rustle, the swish of Priya's elbow against her coat, the kiss of her feet on the tiles, is amplified, like Lucia's own breath.

"Let me . . . I'll hang up your coat," Lucia says, and Priya leans nearer, close enough to inhale.

"Oh, it's you," says Duncan Edge loudly. "How do *you* know Ray?"

He's looming over her. Priya lowers her eyes from Lucia's, smiles up at him. Smooth as you like, she says, "Local celebrity," and he nods knowledgeably, delighted to have her full attention.

The guests part before her like Israelites; Lucia watches, aches. Priya is beautiful in a sleeveless silk top tucked into trousers, lilac, black; glossy hair like half a yard of sex pouring down her back. Lucia would kill, go to prison, to have a moment alone with her now, pressed against a beam, either of them doing the pressing. But instead she plays hostess, funneling guests toward Ray and dodging questions. "Still doing your . . . art?" say two of his acolytes, then a third. "Haven't heard from you for a while. Easing off a bit? Nice for Ray to have his time in the spotlight. Still sculpturing?"

"Trying!" she answers. Even though Priya's so impressed about Venice, it's a relief to know Marie-Claude's on her way, that soon she'll understand she must tell the Biennale people to forget it. It isn't worth the Ray-stress. Anything but that.

Their coats are entwined. She needs to rescue hers, but Martyn is shepherding her toward the stairs. He seems dissatisfied, his hand unpleasantly hot on her hip. She can smell his sweat.

"Seen Patrick?" he asks her, then Leah, who turns away impatiently.

Everyone's drinking far too much, except for water. There's no way to ask politely what's happened to the catering, why Leah's constantly checking her phone, muttering about a taxi. Will Ray give a signal when they're all allowed to see the show? He's unconcernedly chatting, like a visiting potentate, not the subject; has Dr. Mac tried something new? Even the guests are anxious. Are there going to be speeches, the ting-tinging of a glass? Jess thinks: I need a pee. She starts biting her fingers and Martyn bats her hand from her mouth as if she's a pet. How could he have said that, here, unilaterally? It takes all her training not to whack his arm away.

An unbelievably long time passes before Leah, hand on her father's shoulder, clears her throat. Everyone's ready; they hush instantly.

"OK," she says. "Up you go."

There is nervous laughter, unsuccessful cheering. What is to be done about Ray? A secret lift is rumored, or four large men hoisting his wheelchair but, after explaining that he doesn't want a palaver, Ray taps his way very slowly up the stairs, his pale walking stick matching his linen jacket.

"Are we ready?" asks Martyn, hot on her heels. Jess's mother, nibbling her lip in the way her father hates, is still faffing about in the entrance hall, as ever forgetting people's names. Did she even hear Martyn? Jess keeps looking behind for her as she trails upstairs next to him, wanting to push.

"Ready as we'll ever be," says Leah up at the top, as if it has nothing to do with her. She looks, thinks Jess, totally knackered. She lifts the clip on the embarrassing red rope across the entrance to the Gallery, takes her place by a pile of little booklets at the doorway: biographies of "the artist Ray Hanrahan," like something at the Tate.

They're filing into the Gallery now. Even from the backs of

their heads, Jess can tell they're automatically adopting the Art Face: knowledgeable reverence.

Then they fall silent.

"That's promising, surely?" says Martyn. "They must love it."

Leah, unsmiling, hands a booklet to the Sorensens. She misses nothing so of course she knows that Jess and Martyn are next in the line, yet she pretends not to register them.

"Do you need one of these?" she says, deadpan, and Martyn says: "*Ha ha ha!*"

Jess thinks: I cannot keep faking it beside him. He's made such a public show of her, of them. She's too hot, almost faint; people are looking at her stomach. Downstairs, bundled under the coat bench, the cold white stick keeps its secret.

And at last she catches a glimpse through the clog of guests at the doorway and into the Gallery: pools of illumination against the walls, oddly clustered tea-light holders on pedestals, extra booklets everywhere and the room dividers, to which her brother has nailed fabric in an unwise peacock blue, hung with . . .

Where are the pictures?

PART FOUR

29

Priya is still downstairs. Everyone wants to give her advice, complain about their neighbors' trellising, amuse her. She's a queen bee being shown around a new hive.

So Lucia needs to stay here just outside the Gallery entrance, greeting people; it's for the common good. Ray will already be angry with her; she might as well loiter where she can look down from the mezzanine, for when Priya reappears.

Has she even made it to the foot of the stairs? It's impossible to see without folding oneself completely over the balcony, and death by falling at Ray's exhibition would be an unforgivable way to go. Lucia tries to keep the thread between them taut by sheer force of will, but Priya spills so much friendliness, bordering on flirtation, on the ground. Handsome men, sensible women, drifty English girls; if she could, Lucia would ban them all.

"Hello! Yes, absolutely," she says, well past making sense. Marie-Claude may rock up at any moment, must be headed off at the pass but, with Priya in the same building, it's impossible to concentrate. Eric Nakamura enters, looking puzzled, in conversation with a very tall fair man who seems to be holding Ray's ex-wife's hand. Lucia leans against the fire extinguisher; it's like a merry-go-round, a swirl of everyone you least want to see. It takes a moment to notice the approach of Sukie Blackstock: the first horsewoman of the Apocalypse.

Loathing rises through her like floodwater. She feels her skin wrinkling as the scrawny crow draws closer. She's never before had a chance to hate her purely; there was too much grief. Maybe Sukie Blackstock could sense it: adultery radar, pinging in the depths to indicate prey.

Now she's reckless: Joan of Arc with her vorpal sword. The taste of murder is so bright that, in any other setting, she'd be grabbing a napkin to make a little sketch, probably lying to Ray that it was a shopping list. Amazing, what one will do for love. But, wedged here between the Gallery and the top of the stairs, acting wifelike, she looks her foe straight in the eye.

Sukie Blackstock beams back. She has the clotted mascara and bright intimacy of a woman who gets through husbands like Tube tickets. Could she conceivably think that they're . . . friends? "Is it wonderful?" she asks.

"What?"

"The show! Oh, I bet it is, I'm so excited," and Lucia, polite even now, waves her in.

Jess is mouthing something. Lucia points to herself, shrugs theatrically. Jess, in the noisy crowd of the Gallery, raises her eyebrows, en-un-ci-ates the words more clear-ly. Like identifying one's newborn's cry in a wristband mix-up, shouldn't a good mother be able to sense what her daughter is saying? It's this that alarms her, not whatever Jess is miming, because it seems absurd.

Leah's still passing out her booklets. She has her mother's spelling problem; Lucia could take one to check, but it's too late. Too late. If what Jess was signing at her were true, surely Leah would have intervened? It can't be possible; the mere thought makes her want to run away. Surely there is a limit, even for Ray.

Leah is as inscrutable as an egg.

"Your father," begins Lucia.

"What about him?"

"He . . ." Someone's trying to say hello, hand on Lucia's back, but she needs to force herself to take a look inside the Gallery. And also find Priya. And intercept Marie-Claude. Leah looks shifty; she is not Lucia's most truthful child.

It cannot be healthy to be permanently braced but something's off: the frequency from the main room. It's like being in a foreign city where, underneath the café merriment, one senses the beginning of a riot.

"You'd have told me, wouldn't you," Lucia asks Leah quickly, "if there was anything wrong?"

30

Gillian and David, back to back, turn slowly, like characters in a rom-com blizzard. This is not romance, although tomorrow night, when they're back in Sheffield and have showered the weekend from their pores, it will bring them together with, she is confident, impressive passion. For all David's faults, the slow saturation of marriage, what keeps them going is: a) bed; b) he's proud of her work; c) when it comes to his family, she knows he knows she knows.

Behind his little bum, she reaches for his hand. Squeeze; squeeze back. She doesn't dare to face him until she's arranged her expression; he is a giggler too. It's why she fell for him. But the noise is too great for whispering, so they edge sideways, as if admiring the same stretch of wall.

"Oh," she says. "My God."

"I know."

"Did you guess, in advance?"

"Of course not. Did you?"

"No! Absolutely. Why, do you think anyone did?"

"Well, Leah, maybe," says David.

"She must have. She's organized everything. There's a lot of work involved in these things, exhibitions, isn't there?"

"Well, not by the artist," and she can feel him beginning to shake.

"Get a grip," she says. They can't lose it now; it happened once at a performance of *The Nutcracker*, Becca galumphing as Bear Two and they were escorted through silent corridors by the deputy head. "Think sad thoughts."

"Right. Right. I'm back," he says.

"It's actually," she reminds him, "quite a shock."

"Isn't it."

"Did you suspect, even?"

"No! They go on about his genius like a . . . like evangelicals. I really assumed . . ."

"I know."

". . . a full show. I believed them. Whatever that would be, twenty pictures? Thirty?"

"Not three."

"Four. At a pinch," he says, the wobble back in his voice.

If anything goes wrong in his stent operation, thinks Gillian, throat suddenly tight, that's it for me. Really, what would be the point? So she releases his hand.

Behind them, she can hear a confident young man booming about negative capability. After a pause for David to contain himself, she murmurs: "Does that one even count, though? It looks like . . . pencil."

"Christ almighty," David says. "What has the poor sod done?"

Even before Lucia turns, she knows her from the strength of her grip. Marie-Claude does not bother to speak. She simply makes a French face, demurring, droll, and holds out her arms. Lucia yields. A hug: if she'd had them more often in the last ten years, maybe none of this would have happened, she thinks, and her eyes immediately fill.

What a sap.

"We have a talk immediately," says Marie-Claude.

Experienced Marie-Claude watchers know her language of dressing up. Black jeans always, because if one has legs like that in one's sixties one shares them with the world but, if she's going all out, it's black biker-boots rather than All Stars, black glasses-frames instead of red, and a smart T-shirt means business.

Tonight it's a full house, including the best top Lucia has ever seen: short and sexy and made of huge black sequins, like a military fish.

It's a tell. Someone here will spot it. They'll say to Ray, "What's the big excitement?"

Lucia tries to see over Marie-Claude's shoulder, but Marie-Claude is tall and very fit, despite the smoking. She often talks to her artists from a rowing machine.

"You should not try to escape me," she says. "That is for babies. Let him do his things," she says, waving her elegant hand toward the exhibition, "and come now with me outside so we can establish our plans."

Lucia pulls away. She needs to prioritize disasters. Marie-Claude must be corralled, downstairs ideally; maybe if Lucia submits to a quick discussion, Marie-Claude will let her go. But the beadier artists will notice. Meanwhile, Ray will be wounded that his wife's gallerist hasn't bothered to attend. And what if Lucia misses Priya? Nothing, not even her career, or Marie-Claude, even Ray, will keep Lucia away from her.

Although, she reminds herself, she's turning down Venice for her marriage.

Making the decision has nothing to do with Priya.

By pretending to check the booklet, Jess has managed to release herself from Martyn's hot hand, but he does not budge. He isn't even hailing acquaintances with his art thoughts.

"Babe," he says, but quietly enough not to hear.

Leah or Patrick have tried to make the lack of pictures seem intentional, dramatic. They've spotlit what there is, as if they're a selection from his oeuvre, but it's still four, barely. Her face burns with Hanrahan shame; sweat drips beneath her bra-wires. The first she knows well; it has been on most of the walls in the house, propped up in every corner, spotted with coffee, its varnish crazed. The card beside it says *stormunddrang*, but she's fairly sure it's a painting of the tree house in that lovely garden on Brixham Hill, where he and its owner played at setting up an art school before falling out so badly that her mother had to apologize in writing. "Artist's own. Oil on board." There is no date.

Christ it's hot. Where is her mother?

Martyn, very close, emits occasional thoughtful murmurs, like a critic at a primary-school art fair. The real critics had outraged Leah by not RSVP'ing; until half an hour ago, she was cursing the arts pages of all the newspapers. Even the appearance of Bryan Chilton, Ray's old hero, has not soothed her. But now Jess sees her stand beside their father like a bride, laughing, joining in the praise and the mockery of absent friends: the Artist's Vivacious Daughter.

Everyone her father has ever known is here, including the people he says he hates: several of his old girlfriends from the sixties, alcoholic television directors, elderly musicians prone to groping, underwashed pub regulars. The outrageous bareness of the walls, the heat, the booze, the kaleidoscopic roll call of teachers and neighbors who know what he is, yet are still here, make her feel unhinged. There is also, she could swear, a pungent smell of Sunday lunch.

Come on, girl. Do this for . . . for . . . someone. Do not show weakness.

The second painting is familiar too, with that crick-cracking the fixative he likes gets when it ages. It's very pink and orange, faded creamy-white dripping like candle wax down what might be thighs. Three or four brave admirers stand possessively close, commenting on its freshness, the rugged masculinity of the palette-strokes. Beyond them, like an outer planetary ring, lesser disciples prepare their expressions.

Jess stares straight ahead, head up: a scapegoat ready for torching.

Where is her mother?

The third is definitely a nude, just about; blue, thickly applied. It looks very new; the areas of bare canvas sharp and clear. It is smallish but magnificently framed like a cathedral centerpiece: deep mount, double-layered gilt cassetta, as if a child has drawn an elaborate margin to distract a teacher. Even at this distance, over the heads of the populace, Jess sees that it has her sister's eyes.

By the time she has extracted herself and Marie-Claude, Lucia feels pulled thin as copper wire. *Get out my way for this conversation I don't want to have*, she wants to scream at every local dignitary: the weird optician, the horrible woman who once almost won *MasterChef*. She knows her cheeks are ablaze with awkwardness, menopause, lust, all three. Gillian catches her eye, looks puzzled at Marie-Claude. If, Lucia thinks, Sukie Blackstock crosses my path, I might push her over. I could do it.

"I have canceled another party for you," says Marie-Claude, groping in her pocket for a cig. "You know Eduard Previn?"

"Of course I do."

"You see?" she says. "This is serious," and Lucia looks at her feet. She needs an explanation for when someone spots them. She's usually good at this; tonight her mind is blank.

They are in a storage room off the entrance hall, with jingling hangers, precarious stacks of foil serving platters, scuffed plastic salad bowls and, for some reason, several panettone in ornamental tins. Focus, she tells herself, watching Marie-Claude's lips.

Marie-Claude is insisting on excitement. "Don't be a silly girl," she says. "This is not to resist." She could not give a damn that this is Ray's evening, weekend, year. When Lucia tries to remind her, she looks so dismissive that Lucia checks behind her that no Ray-supporter is peering through the door. Fear dies hard, Priya once said.

Love dies hard too, unfortunately. God knows, she has tried to cure herself.

"I can't . . . it's not silly," says Lucia.

Accepting is impossible. She has to make Marie-Claude understand. Ray always says she's an over-explainer, that people wilt, lose the will to live, while she feints at what she wants to say.

It's why I'm an artist, Lucia wants to tell him. But that argument would last for days.

"For goodness' sake," Marie-Claude is saying, "do not be absurd. This is joy. It is enormous success. Biography-defining. You have earned it. And your hus—"

"It isn't," begins Lucia. "It can't be. Look, I truly am so sorry."

"For what? You pay me. 'Andsomely," and Lucia almost laughs.

"Yes, yes, but you've been working on this for ages. My whole career, even. You've been so brilliant," and Lucia hears the echo of how she talks to Ray, the sucking-up, the creeping serf. "The thing is, it really would be amazing. Life-changing. But I can't."

"Tell me. Why not?"

"You know why."

"You could choose it to be possible."

"But . . ." Marie-Claude's life has not been one of marriage, although she has had two husbands ("and," Ray says, "many more"). She lives with a needy Oriental cat and has a series of rich, horrible men as lovers, but Lucia would forgive her anything, cross a motorway behind her like a loyal duckling, because whatever success she has had was brought to her, coaxed and summoned and left at her feet, by Marie-Claude.

And Marie-Claude knows where other successes are buried.

Here's one. Four years ago, Ray was interviewed about his technique by a famous-ish novelist on the radio; they all went out for dinner, Ray and the novelist and the wives. The novelist asked about Lucia's work; Lucia conceded that she too was an artist.

"Tell me about it," he'd said, so Lucia tried, then mentioned Hertz-Chamaut.

Already, this was a monstrous betrayal.

Then the novelist told the radio people, who summoned Lucia's documentation from Marie-Claude. They invited Lucia "in" to discuss recording a big profile; sent her flowers. Lucia felt sicker and sicker. She hid from the postman. Ray kept pointing out that she'd brought this on herself, had clearly chosen her priorities long ago. His friends, he said, thought she was disgusting; Dr. Mac, armed with barely any of the facts, dropped by her studio to explain her crime, hoping for whiskey. Lucia listened for longer than she should have, hurried straight to Hertz-Chamaut, begged Marie-Claude to ring the radio people to retract her interest in their interest. Marie-Claude barely spoke to her for months.

And despite her sabotaging it for him, her endless soothing

and explaining, Ray's fury was infinite. She told no one, at his special request, how upset he was; considered leaving Marie-Claude because now Ray mistrusted her too, questioned her motives, said Lucia was her slave. Lucia cannot say yes to the Biennale and expect to have a marriage at the end of it.

Marie-Claude says: "But this is your life. Your art. Maybe you can choose."

31

Everyone is making the best of a difficult situation, thinks Gillian, and that's what counts. Neither of her children has shown bad manners; Ray hasn't loudly blamed Lucia, perhaps because Lucia seems not to be around. That won't go down well.

And at least there is food. First, Leah was spotted hurtling downstairs; then, after some time, she press-ganged Becca and some of Ray's keener students and they started bearing trays of chopped-up wholemeal loaves and what looked like cream crackers into the Gallery. Relief all round, until Ray started scowling. It seems that he was not consulted; Becca reported that, when Leah realized that the caterer she thought she'd hired had gone to the football, she started to cry. And then, oddly, rather than trying to cheer up her father, she spent a long time trying to get hold of the caterer on the phone. Meanwhile, everyone was starving, so Becca organized the convoy of nutritionally disappointing snacks. It seems incredible that they're allowed to eat near the art at all.

All of which would be a perfectly standard Hanrahan drama, except that Lucia really has disappeared.

Gillian still can't meet David's eye; there is a high risk that he will corpse. So far they've coped very well. In fact, no one is looking much at anyone. They have been pointedly focused on what art there is, which amounts to a couple of splodgy naked ladies, a maybe landscape and a pencil sketch on very rough brown paper of the back half of a horse. If Gillian, not a rural person, can tell it's equine, that's something.

So now everyone has gorged themselves stupid on bleached flour and saturated fats, which arrived too late to keep them sober; except for Gillian, who does not drink. She is a bird of prey, sharp-eyed, keeping a lookout for Lucia's sake. She watches Ray's guests acting as if everything is normal, catches the moment Ray spots his previous wife, always too good for him, with her hand on the flat stomach of a Scandinavian man-god who's laughing with the Japanese curator. This is the point at which Ray storms, with assistance, off.

She will not concern herself with him.

Jake seems tipsy, telling a series of lovely young women about His First. David has managed to return twice to the trestle tables, olive juice and mustard dripping into his cuffs. Leah, that seedy doctor and some of the acolytes have formed a splinter group back downstairs, to comfort Ray. Jess, however, is sitting on a wine box telling her boyfriend that she's absolutely fine, promise, just mingle without me, really, thanks, no, *really*. David is cornered by a rather vivacious woman in a revealing blouse and try-hard heels, at whom Gillian has narrowed her eyes. When he escapes, on his way for more Wotsits, he bends his head to whisper, and Gillian's skin tingles. She smiles up at him.

But what he says is not what she had hoped. "We aren't ever coming back here. It's too much."

Gillian, like a passenger watching her ship pull out of the dock, sees their future financial stability sliding away from her. Sweet coward; he's not going to save them.

Right, she thinks. I'll do it myself.

She bides her time, until she can approach her favorite niece from behind, the better to prise her from Martyn. "Any chance of a chat?" she asks.

Then she sees the look on Jess's face. "Oh. Are you OK?"

"No, I'm—" begins Jess.

Martyn bounces back toward them but Gillian grasps Jess's hand; it's like country dancing. "It has stopped raining," she tells her. "And there's a lovely garden. Let's go for a walk."

Lucia, alone, bites her varnish-tasting fingers, tries to imagine going up the stairs. She can't sneak into the exhibition at this stage without Ray noticing. Jess will be free-range and looking for trouble; Leah, enraged that she was left to do everything; Patrick, probably in a pickle of some kind, or being blamed for the wrong color tape on the cabling. See, she's a mother above all, not thinking about Priya.

Where is Priya?

That she could have been so close by, and has probably already left, makes Lucia feel deranged. This may have been their last encounter; Priya's liking for her is growing lighter. Lucia sits in the cold toilet, knickers down, thinks of not seeing, not breathing, not kissing Priya again. It's stopped raining; there will be a new moon. She puts her hands over her eyes.

When Marie-Claude left, Lucia said, "Please will you run up and say something encouraging to Ray?" Marie-Claude didn't even bother to reply. Lucia took a great gulp of night air as the front door closed, looking out at the brown-lilac sky and thinking of escape.

She told Priya, last time, she'd do whatever was needed for them to be together.

"Would you really?" asked Priya.

Lucia was kissing her neck, hands still on Priya's thighs. She lifted her face and looked at her carefully in the half dark.

"Yes," she said. "I really would. Wouldn't you?"

And immediately she knew the answer. Something evaporated from her heart, her self-respect, when Priya, smiling kindly, replied: "How could I?"

Lucia, now standing beside the baize noticeboards, riotous art appreciation going on above her, thinks: bury me under the cool tiles and leave me here. There's a sound round the corner, where, only an hour ago, so many people she didn't care about were waiting for Ray. She hears it again, and her heart clutches: the tap of a shoe heel against clay.

"There she is, my artist," says Priya.

32

Their feet on the frosty gravel sound like a radio play. Jess is obviously in a state; only after some minutes of sensitive auntly soothing does Gillian approach the subject of the exhibition.

"I don't understand," Jess says, "how he could have thought for a second, how any of them could think, it was a good plan. Not to cancel."

"It was . . . startling."

"My God. It's all his horrible friends will talk about for years."

"Will they really?"

"I guarantee. They are obsessed. With each other's careers. Nothing they enjoy more than failure. Christ. How will we face him? How will Mum?"

Lucia and Priya, deep in the darkness of the Guildworkers' Hall garden, are reaching a critical point.

Lucia has been crying; Priya, despite her dislike of extravagant emotion, of need, almost started too.

"You knew, though, the limitations of whatever this would be," says Priya, "from the beginning. Full disclosure."

"I know," says Lucia.

"When I said, wherever we were, would you choose this, even knowing all the obstacles ahead, or choose not to have it and have peace, and you said 'yes' even before I'd finished the question—remember that I said 'no.'"

"I do know," says Lucia, looking for something to kick.

"And then the next time we met you'd learned to say, 'I love you' in bloody Hindi."

Lucia hangs her head. "I tried not to," she says. "I didn't mean . . ." Stupid hot tears are giving her panda-eyes; her heart could split. There is no pain like being the more-loving one, and it's all she ever is. "Bugger. I hate this."

But even Priya must feel it, sometimes, or why would she risk so much for Lucia? It's not small, what she could lose. And sex, the touching of a hand or mouth to anywhere on another person, is not a small thing. It changes the world forever.

She thinks: what did I do before you? I was asleep. I was keeping myself asleep, for you.

I love you, she almost says, but manages to catch it.

Priya, however, puts her hand on Lucia's shoulder. They are hidden under a ye olde propped-up willow tree; the ground beneath dank and yielding, as if it has been hoarding the winter. Like a teenager she thinks: if the rain holds off, that's a good sign. Every edge glistens, peach-gold or wetly silver. She can smell cherry blossom just starting, black winter soil beginning to stir. The air is rich and she is in it, dangerously alive.

Priya's hand; Lucia's shoulder; Lucia presses her cheek against it, strokes it with her chin.

"My sad brilliant horse," says Priya. "I'm so proud of you," and she kisses her.

She still doesn't know my decision, Lucia thinks. Could I not tell her for a few more months, and keep her proud?

The willow bark gleams; slim sappy twigs she wants to rip off and keep, to remember. It smells of riverbanks and spring and fucking. She wants it all. Every part of Priya turns her on: her touching arm-hair, her veiny hands, the mole on her neck where the sternocleidomastoid muscle rises (how she longs for a chance to mention this). They kiss and kiss, their hands reaching deeper into their winter clothing, toward hot skin. Buttons, waistbands; the kissing is catalyst, accelerant. Lucia opens her eyes, closes them to avoid Priya noticing, pulls away so she can really look. She thinks: I will never get over you.

"Tell you what," says Priya. Are her pupils dilated? The gelid surface of her eyes reflects the lights from the Guildworkers' Hall, where nothing interesting could possibly happen. "I do think Bristol together might be good. I could . . . work on you."

"Oh God."

"I mean about the Bi-enn-ale," and Lucia is too far gone to correct her.

Her fingertip strokes Priya's wristbone inside her cuff. She murmurs: "Do you mean it?"

"Yep."

"Nights? Together? Jesus. I might explode."

"It's a risk. You are an idiot," Priya says, and Lucia takes it. She has to. The thought of sleeping together is like finding gold in gravel. Her skin feels as if it's stretching into the dark.

"God, I love you," Lucia says, inadvertently.

"Stand still," whispers Priya, and Lucia gasps.

Leah has always known that what she has, and her sister does not, is endurance. Her strength seemed limitless; she is a mast, upright and true, because that's what her father deserves.

Something's begun to crack.

The slump was inevitable once people started leaving, and maybe she brought it on by encouraging her father to hang around, in case Pablo showed. Pablo did not show.

"I'm not being pushed in that thing like a vegetable," Ray says, when she can delay no longer. He's mean-voiced, narrow-eyed, ready for Dr. Mac. "So sorry to disappoint you," and Leah turns away to hide her face.

She doesn't try to argue, or ask if she can bring it with them; it would irritate him. I'll go back later to pick it up, she thinks, and knows not to say. So they leave the chair in the entrance; he tsks and sighs while she finds Laz-Nat to hand him the secret check, then walks silently and very slowly beside her.

Only once, hoping for understanding, she comments that "the caterer" should still get some of the fee. Ray is always a champion of the underdog, the working man; she thought he'd agree. He rounds on her.

"That family," he says, "wouldn't know a tapas if it bit them on the arse" and she senses that his patience, even with her, particularly with her, is up. She tries to be led by instinct with him. But, when it comes to what she wants, what she feels, it's a vacuum. That's love, she tells herself. Daughterly love.

But.

She needs another kind.

"Dad," she says. They're beginning the slope up to Brixham Gardens; he's walking well but you never know, and she can't remember how much Dr. Mac left for the rest of the weekend. She has been going on and on about how great the pictures were, using every word she can dredge from her childhood to describe the brushstrokes, Tonking, *alla prima*, but it's nothing like enough to soothe him. He is, her sister once said, a gaping maw.

Does he even realize how scanty his pictures looked? You can't tell; he's behaving exactly as he does whenever upset about anything at all, eyes straight ahead, body stony, responses like a dying cold beast. And what happens when Pablo does come to claim her, scooping her up like the hero she has been waiting for? Leah has always needed her father, but what happens when she moves on?

He has been still for what seems like hours. Wedged here in a corner of the soft orange brickwork he can listen to footsteps and talk, almost believe he's among them. It is essential that nobody finds him; he's holding everything tight, as if not being seen is a question of self-control. The throbbing in his ear and hand and wrists is company; it makes him alive to every scurry in the undergrowth, the little howls of pain. He worries about everyone in every lit-up window. The growl of the Junction Road and the lorries around Archway are so very loud; the half-hearted automatic peal of St-Mary-Cross; the clicks and tightenings of frozen soil. Dew pounds the rough grass. A garden spider crashes its tiny violent jaws.

Ray will not let him have this job. It was stupid even to ask. What he had hoped might be solid ground was mud and dust.

Is he drunk? He doesn't remember drinking. The dark is pressing against his chest, his eyelids, filling his mouth. Blinking makes it blacker. He can't have another breakdown, because that would include remembering the first one. The sky is too big. He is a man without purpose. He thinks: If I can't have that, the one thing I wanted . . .

His blood feels very thick. Time to let it out. Time to do something.

Where is Ray, he thinks. I want a word with him.

"If it wasn't for Mum," Jess is saying, "I'd stay away completely. Well, and Patrick. I . . . do you think they are . . . is he actually mad? Dad, I mean."

"David thinks so," says Gillian. "If you mean medically."

"Really? Does he? Wow. Wow. I hadn't . . . why've we never talked about this? Do you?"

Gillian smiles, shrugs. "I'd have thought indubitably. But I couldn't possibly say."

They pass splayed ferns, a gray wall knotted with vines, dipping down into mossy flagstones and round the side to another, higher, lawn, illuminated by an old-fashioned lamppost.

"Martyn feel the same?"

Jess gives her a look. "Are you joking? He's Dad's true son."

"I was wondering how life in Edinburgh is," Gillian asks carefully. "If you're, I don't know . . . Are you still renting? It must be frustrating, paying a fortune when there's this big house down south."

"No," says Jess. "I love it. It's brilliant being, you know, far—" She hesitates, keeps her own counsel. Come on, thinks Gillian. They all have this irritating shiftiness, Ray's lot, affecting not to care. Ray, David says, was always looking for someone to ruin. Poor Lucia; what was she thinking? It's too late for her but, maybe, with a good man, Jess will be fine. At least, she thinks, Bex and Jake tell me everything.

"You do have Martyn, though," she says. "He's mad about you. Plural and singular."

"Do you think?" Jess tips back her head, looks up at the mess of sodium-light and satellites. "Oh God. I suppose you're right," she says, and winces.

"It's fine," says Gillian. "He's a big boy." Jess gives her an awkward smile. No, thinks Gillian; she's not too far gone.

"I should probably get back. See how it's going. Leah'll be furious I haven—"

"Do you think she'll move out soon?" asks Gillian too quickly, but Jess is turning back, squinting through the trees.

"Isn't that . . . ?"

"Oh, look," Gillian says, "there's somebody out here."

33

In the hot bolt of contact, Lucia has lost herself. She is looking into Priya's eyes, dry-mouthed; they are breathing each other's breath.

"Hello?"

The voice comes from behind topiary; someone must have walked all the way over the grass. Priya's shining eyes dart as she looks for exits. She has not removed her hand, there in Lucia's waistband. Lucia mouths "shit" and grabs her wrist but, with the tiniest movement of her head, Priya stops her.

They stand, pinioned, waiting.

"Who's there?" calls the voice again. "Leah, is that you?"

"Shit," says Lucia silently again.

Priya extracts her hand, like a thief. Lucia's clothes exhale. She needs a tree to lean on; her legs are perilously weak. Priya, however, is steel.

"Hi," she says, her voice almost perfectly calm. "Just chatting out here. Don't tell anyone, it's a secret cig. Who's that?"

"Just Gillian. Fine. And Jess, of course."

"Mum?"

And Lucia says, "No."

Ah, thinks Gillian. OK.

Gillian gives a laugh like a cough.

"I mean yes," says Jess's mother. "Hello. Just catching up on political gossip. You've met Priya, um, Menon, haven't you, Gill?"

She never calls Aunt Gillian "Gill." Is she drunk?

"Hello," says Gillian, much too loudly, but she stays exactly where she was. "Lucia! Here you are! I'd forgotten that you two were such good friends."

"I know, it's been years," says Jess's mother, stepping out from under a tree to see its branches. Jess has spent her childhood dragging her away from interesting lichen, gravel, bark. Tonight the stars are invisible under orange cloud, so what is there to look at?

"Are they friends?" asks Jess. "Since when?"

For a cool-blooded woman, Gillian's all over the place. She keeps starting to speak, gripping Jess's arm unnecessarily hard. "Come on, you," she says, trying to steer Jess back toward the Hall, as if she's an interrupting schoolgirl.

Jess is thirty. "Hang on a minute," she says. "I need to ask—"

"I really think we should go and check on everything."

"But, no, wait," Jess says. "Look, Mum, what are you doing out here? Seriously, you should be back at the exhibition. I don't understand what he's . . . Did you know? How could you let him s—"

A wash of dizziness, faintness, definitely not nausea but something very wrong, hits her so suddenly that she sways. "I—I need to sit," she says, and plumps onto the soaking grass.

Everything is perfectly clear. This is the sharpening of his mind.

Patrick will not go back to the house and the fury. He cannot do it. The exhibition will be blamed on him and that's too many straws, nails, in the coffin. His spirit is barely a skin's-thickness now, a meniscus over a brimming bowl. Even the chance of bumping into Ray, of being glimpsed by him, the side of his face, the top of his head, fills him with a wet trickle of horror. It must not happen, if he is to stay intact. He knows what he cannot bear.

What he should do is confront Ray. Shout at him about the selfishness; burst through this force field until they can have a reasonable discussion about Patrick's job, which he deserves. It makes perfect sense, crystal, except that this is Ray and worms don't turn: particularly worms raised by Ray.

It's stopped raining, which is what gives him the idea.

"Jess? Are you all right?"

"She's fine," calls Gillian.

"Did she fall?"

"Bit . . . spinny," says Jess, and Lucia starts across the grass toward her.

"Lucia," says Priya, and Lucia hesitates, as a dark figure bursts around the side of the building and charges up the path toward them.

"Oh Christ," says Jess, closing her eyes.

"Where are you?" her sister is screaming. "Bloody hell, can you, I can't even see . . . Larry said you were all out here. You have to come home. He needs you right now, as if there isn't enough stupid fr—"

Their mother, in the trees, calls: "What's happened? Leah?"

"Don't be all innocent. He predicted it, he *knew* you'd make a fuss about leaving. It's not even your party."

"Slow down. Breathe. Is Ray OK?"

Leah pushes her hair back with both hands, like a priestess. "What are you doing in there?" she yells, ignoring Gillian. "Can't you show support? That idiot Dr. Mac has totally let him down, he promised th—"

Jess's mother steps onto the lit-up wet grass, rebuttoning her coat. By night she seems slightly transformed. She says, with a snap to her voice, "Oh, love. Can't it wait?"

Gillian catches Jess's eye; she senses it too. Even Leah hesitates.

"OK, OK," their mother says. She looks over at her friend, the MP. "No, of course we won't tell the press you were smoking," she reassures her.

"No one cares," says Leah, rudely.

"Please, Leah, be polite."

"It's an emergency," says Leah, but haven't they been here before, so often?

Ignore it, Jess always begs her, but this time, as every other, their mother chooses to answer the tug. "I'll see you," she says to this new friend of hers and, with only a backward wave, as if they are strangers, almost too casually, the woman walks calmly off. Their mother is theirs again. But never, in the history of the Hanrahans, has something more obviously been up.

"What," Lucia asks, freshly kissed, the taste of Priya's palm on her mouth, skin to tongue-tip, salty and sublime, "is going on?"

"What do you think?" Leah half shouts. She is almost stamping with outrage beside the weird ornamental rose feature; my little savage, thinks Lucia fondly, before lurching back to the present disaster. "He's in desperate pain. As usual. And that bastard Dr. Mac got pissed and forgot to leave the script. He's passed out upstairs like a—"

"I thought you loved Dr. Mac," says Jess.

"Shut up."

"You shut up."

"Girls," says Gillian, "hang on a minute."

Lucia has often thought that, with a co-wife, marriage to Ray would have been a breeze. Imagine having someone to discuss it with.

She needs to make things normal for the girls, but that option died long ago. "Enough," she says, calm as stone. Leah sounds as if she could go for Jess; her hands are clenched. There's a whiff of adrenaline, like in a bad pub, and she remembers fragments of other fights: sofa-kicks; a fun-fair bite; more maternal failure and neglect.

Her daughters almost caught them. She should be cold with fear.

"So how are you going to fix it?" Leah's yelling, as if Lucia has simply lost her key. It would make Ray furious, disharmony in earshot of his cronies, but Ray's not here.

He bullies you, she imagines Priya saying, she of the firm upper arms and clean elegant flat. He betrayed you at the worst time in your life. Why should you care?

And it's this, the thought of Priya witnessing the mess that is her life, that gives Lucia fire.

"That's enough shouting," says Jess's mother. "Come here, both of you."

So Jess does, and Leah. There is a strange stolen moment, as if they've dodged an accident and have a sliver of life to spare; Jess can picture them all without her. She clears her throat; Leah's head turns, swift as a prison guard's.

"So?" Jess says. "Is he?"

"Is he what?"

Gillian's right there. Jess pushes through it. She says: "Bad? Or, you know, 'bad.' The Dr. Mac sort of bad."

Leah explodes. "Don't you fucking start on that whole 'real pain' bollocks. You are heartless, yeah, that's what he always says, and he's right. After so much hard work, exhausting physical, emotional labor, artistry . . . He's just mounted an entire *show*, hasn't he?" She's waving her finger, getting closer; roses of loathing bloom on her cheekbones. "Didn't you notice, or was your head too far up your Puritan arse? You seriously don't . . . How can you stand there saying that? How could pain like his be fake?"

"Of course he *feels* it," says their mother mildly, but Leah blasts on.

"You have *never* understood," she says. "Any of you. Or even tried . . . How much he suffers, and cares, and . . ."

"Mum's done ev—"

But Leah is in her groove. "He is the m—"

"Hang on," says Gillian, and they all shut up. "So, sorry, are we talking about his exhibition now? I know this is sensitive stuff, but really, we need to discuss it. The party line."

Leah, standing straight, chin up, stares at the infidel. "What," she asks neutrally, "do you mean?"

Jess thinks: Careful. Her mother has put her hand on Gillian's arm.

"Well, it's obvious," Gillian says, and Jess feels her eyebrows lift. "How to . . . handle it."

"Why would it need handling?"

"For the . . . because . . . you know."

"No. Say it," says Leah, taking another step toward her aunt.

"Because the exhibition wasn't quite, it was very . . ."

"What?"

Gillian is in peril, and she's on her own. Leah looks powdery orange-white in the fake lamplight. The hem of her dark dress and her tights are muddied; there's something dark on her hand. She narrows her eyes at Gillian.

"Modest," says Gillian. "Shall we not fudge it?"

There is a noisy London silence; sirens, shop-grilles, laughing. A bottle breaks; everyone is always ready for danger, the shout in the night. Or, thinks Jess, maybe that's me. She glances at her mother. She's been known to pace, to do what might almost count as wringing of hands. But not tonight. She is, thinks Jess, only half here.

Leah is saying to Gillian: "Oh, is that what you think?"

"Come on," says Gillian. "With the greatest respect, they were hardly—"

"That show, those pictures that you're mocking, cost h—"

"I'm not—"

"Cost him blood," she says. "Exhaustion. You wouldn't understand."

"I'm s—"

"This," Leah says, her voice shaking, "is his monument."

Jess presses her lips together, looks away. There is a clamminess to the air; she is frightened for her sister, who loves and hates too much.

"You think," Leah says to Gillian, "that you're above us, don't you?"

"No! Of c—"

"You think Dad owes you for the house."

"Well . . ."

"He told me. It makes him sleepless; he has ulcers because of you, you and Uncle David. He's trying to create and there's constant pressure. So don't you dare come here and sneer at his work."

"When . . . I think we only ever said once that—"

"That house, our house, is the only thing keeping him from the grave."

The ground wobbles. Sickness floats over her again; Jess closes her eyes, breathes fresh night air through her nose. Eating is supposed to help, she thinks; discreetly she rootles in her coat pocket for a mint, a nut. Mum'll have something, she thinks, as Lucia steps forward.

"Enough," she says. "Leah, don't be rude. Just tell me what we're dealing with. What he, Dad, needs."

Tears shine prettily on Leah's face. She snaps: "Think! It's not hard. Or it wouldn't be if—"

You can see the effort it's costing their mother to keep calm. "If Dr. Mac is pissed, though, how can we . . ."

"We all know you assume I'm thick," Leah says, and Jess sighs, "but I nicked his book of scripts."

34

Well, thinks Lucia. I'm not going to do it.

"What's going on?" says Gillian.

"Jess? Christ's sake, get a move on," Leah is shouting. "It'll take five minutes to go back for the car keys. Better bring an envelope too. And a pen."

"Wait," says Jess.

"What?"

"I can't do it."

"Why not?" says Leah.

"All sorts of reasons. I'm too drunk."

"I saw you. You were barely drinking."

Jess scowlingly says, "I was! That's bollocks, for a start. You always think . . . I had at least three glasses and—"

"Come on," says Leah. "Easy peasy, if you know the roads and you're careful. Those rules are just advisory."

"Don't," says Lucia wearily.

"They are *laws*," says Jess. "So people don't kill someone. He's not, you're not above . . . oh, forget it."

"What? Say it."

"Nothing."

"Go on. You were accusing our father. Who's suffering."

"I'm just saying, because no one else will, it's not OK. Drink driving, any of it. But when I try to explain, or, or stop him, he just laughs, as if—"

"That's by the by," Gillian points out. "As he doesn't drive now."

"So Jess has to do it," says Leah.

"I would, Mum, but . . . I feel rubbish."

"She does look peaky," says Gillian, reliably war-time.

"Sweetheart," Lucia says, holding out an arm. Jess moves closer; Leah huffs. "Is something up?" and Jess gives her a complicated look.

"Oh," says Gillian. "Hmm. Well, anyway, I can't with my knee. Not that I'm offering. I am not making my poor patella worse for anybody's sake. Even for Ray."

Leah's swearing. Jess says, "Definitely?"

"And it is illegal. Extremely. What if you're caught?"

Leah looks scandalized. "We're never caught. So Mum—"

"Where *is* Patrick?" asks Lucia. "I hope he's OK."

"Can't you just ring him?"

Leah says: "He's meant to keep his crappy old phone on but it'll be off. He doesn't try."

"Oh," says Gillian. Here they are, their wares laid out as at a car-boot sale: their failures and shame. "So, Leah, why can't you?"

Jess says: "She never learned. Conveniently."

"Stop it," says Lucia.

"Martyn would," says Jess, "but he'll be too drunk, please don't ask him."

"So, Mum," says Leah. "Looks like you'll have to be the hero."

"Lucia, I really don't think any—" begins Gillian.

Lucia swallows, sets her feet. "Actually," she says, watching her breath stream, "the thing is, yes, I have, since, you know. My . . .

operation. But, in the dark, stressed, I don't think that I, well, should."

"It's literally falling off a log," says Leah.

"No, it's not. Not for me. It's like all that stored information, Tube routes, everything, has evaporated. I couldn't even tell you how to get to Camden."

"Camden?" Leah says. "That's the stupidest thing I've ever h—"

"Honestly. And even if I could, I can't park."

"Everyone can park," says Leah.

"To be clear, though, you have driven, though, since?" Gillian asks.

"All the time," says Leah. "She'll be fine."

"When Ray insists, only. It's hard to explain but . . . I really can't."

"Well," says Leah. "You're just going to have to try. I can't do everything. It's only the new chemist by Highbury Circus. You've been down Holloway a million times."

"I . . . it's not simply the . . . working the car, or, you know, other drivers." She is trying not to sound like a child, or to give Leah ammunition. "But I honestly can't remember how to get anywhere. Even which way to turn out of the gate. Please try to . . . There must be some other way, isn't there? I could bus tomorrow."

"You have to go now. He needs it. You cannot want to, to deny Dad his medicine. Not tonight, of all nights."

"Is there really no one?" asks Gillian reasonably. "For his, um, treatm—"

"No," says Jess.

"No," agrees Lucia.

"Well."

"We can hardly ask a neighbor, can we," Leah points out, more tired-sounding now. "He hates all of them."

Lucia's visions are not religious, or moral; they are merely art. She's seeing them as ants, threading through dust: she, the biggest, should be carrying something heroic, a leaf, a grain of rice, but she's flagging, tempted to leave it. The Jess-ant is racing in the other direction, toward a promising blob of sweetness; poor Patrick is stumbling along with a bent leg, a bashed antenna. And Leah, determined angry Leah, is jostling to carry the rice grain by herself. If, thinks Lucia, in a dream of mandibles, I dump the grain, Leah has to carry it, and will. She thinks she wants to. But it is my duty to share the burden.

However, the last time she drove a car, giving Ray a lift to the Lord of Anglesey for a lock-in, she didn't go home to await his call to collect him. The Anglesey is barely fifteen minutes' drive, ten at night, but the rearview mirror no longer makes sense; two feet on pedals, two hands in control while managing 360-degree observation and flicking on indicators, fans, gear stick, like a one-man band, seemed unfeasible, reckless. She parked on a side street with Nina Simone and her sketchbook, which lay cold on her lap as she stared out of the window into the past. When he rang to summon her, she counted the minutes, one-Mississippi two-Mississippi, then drove back round and patiently waited until he appeared. Four hours, to avoid two tiny journeys.

"I just can't," she says.

"He could die," says Leah, crying hard now. "You can't suddenly withdr—"

"OK," Lucia sighs. "OK."

35

The Heath; Patrick knows it like a lover. He has picked it, swum in it, climbed it, hidden in it for his entire life, always by himself; that's how you learn a place. When he's collected his sleeping bag and torch and little stove, he'll be fine.

But he's not a wild man. He'd walk among the beeches all night, wants to do it, but a little thread of sense warns him that, unfed, in pain, this might be the end of his mind. So he's stuck. His friends have not . . . persisted. He is alone.

Then he thinks of something. He's heard about the vagus nerve, which somewhere deep in his spine or entrails can be agitated, as now, or calmed. And the way to calm it is cold water.

No wonder he's been feeling so tangled and absorbent. When he washes in the house it's a hurried bath for heat. He never immerses himself, experiences that shock to his core. He's been soft without realizing; weak. A sluice of cold water will make him be a man.

Moonlight slicks the bonnet of their terrible car. It is matt with age and bird-shit; nervously she touches its cold flank. Tiredness makes her brain feel thick as spools of white sausage. Maybe terror, or longing, will keep her awake.

But the drive is worse than Lucia had imagined. She's all right getting started, feeling quite proud of the coordination, but misremembers the Pembertons, which is Terrace, which is Villas, so next thing she's going *up* Junction Road. Ray would be hysterical. Past the flat where her friend Grace Collini lived, before she manages to wheedle her way through to the Holloway Road; a Christmas miracle. And yes, she remembers to turn left toward Highbury Circus but then, because this chemist is miles down the congested Holloway Road and she does seem to be capable of navigating, wants to show off, she boldly nips down Fairbridge, imagining Priya's grin, and loses track entirely.

But it's all going to be OK. She heads the right direction fast along Sussex Way, too much poke on a couple of corners; then, disaster. Any fool knows that the Seven Sisters Road heads up, north, or at least in the wrong direction; sick, breathing quickly through her nose like a trapped mouse, she weaves straight into the worst lane, the one toward the Sobell Center, where, on so many grim Saturday afternoons, she waited in the car for a kid to return from a trampolining party: always tearful, smelling of sweaty elastic, needing an X-ray. There is no escape from the one-way system around it; she takes it three times while a heavy rain begins to pour off the windscreen, blurring the traffic lights, camouflaging all the youths she could accidentally kill. Tears stick to her lashes; she is praying aloud, to the God who clearly does not believe in her. The new Arsenal Stadium; along Drayton Park, past the HOT ROLLS! MATCH DAYS! SUPPORTERS ONLY signs painted on shuttered stalls and front rooms, the silent clubhouse, picked-at red transfers on children's bedroom windows, then another dead-flower memorial to poor stabbed boys. Is that warning-light usually on? Twice she tries to pull over, to rescue the shredded *A–Z* from the boot; twice the hooting stops her.

She has hardly seen Jess, will pine for her, like a fool, the minute she's gone. She's perpetually lost in the micro-decisions of how to fortify Patrick, push him from the nest when he is ready to flutter. Ray's probably right: she's making him worse. And after this evening, Ray will be . . .

Imagine, she thinks, if I could not go back.

She takes a corner a little too quickly, almost clips a traffic island. And then, like a mountaineer staggering up an unexpectedly final peak, the Holloway Road again appears before her in all its betting-shop majesty. Grinning, dazzled, she considers, tentatively indicates left and begins to drive, second gear, don't forget the hand brake, toward Highbury. Priya would be proud, bar all the disasters; she can't tell her a thing. She's focusing so hard her mind hurts, yet she still forgets the permanent roadworks at the roundabout. By the time she follows the diversion signs to Arran Way where the famous late-night chemist waits, her face is a smear of sweat and heat and unhindered weeping.

And she is exhausted. She stops the car at an angle to the curb; that'll do. She heaves herself onto the pavement, squints at the green cross through the rain and there, in the smears of light and freezing wet, she understands.

36

"Dad?" tries Leah again.

"Not interested."

His room is dark. She's sitting on a heap of books, like a troll guarding the gold. Pablo was meant to be at the show tonight, being impressed. That was the whole idea. What was he doing instead? Is this some sort of game-playing she doesn't yet understand? Her father is calmer now he knows his medicine's on its way, although Jess ought to have fetched it for him, shown him she cares. And he's still so angry with everyone who came, who didn't come, who failed him.

What about me? she wants to ask. I'm sitting here, still.

People were lovely about the exhibition. If they thought it was odd that he didn't have more work, they said nothing. She won't let herself think of the bare spaces; what he showed was brilliant, that's what counts. Does he realize? She loves him too much to ask.

"And those people from the library were there. And Jimmy from the pub. Jimmy worships you."

"Mmm."

"Loads of people. So much . . . admiration, though let's face it, most of them won't get it. Oh and did you see—"

"Don't tell me. OK, who?"

"Sure? Well, even the Frog was there!"

"As in Marie-Claude?" He gives a snort of disdain.

"Yes. That's good, isn't it?"

"Mmm."

"Dad. It is. She was showing interest in your work. Maybe . . ."

He makes his ruminating sound. She's starting to hope that he's falling asleep, that she could sneak away, even phone Pablo. It isn't Pablo's fault; he's a busy man, he didn't mean to abandon them. One day quite soon, when they're together all the time, she will help him get his restaurant going again.

"Jesus Christ," says Ray loudly.

He's sitting up, mouth open. Leah's heart pounds. "What? You scared me. What? Dad?"

"Thought of something. Did you see her in the show?"

"Marie-Claude? Sorry, you mean . . ." There are too many unmentionables, his ex-wife, his ex-osteopath, all the ex-friends. She wasted vital minutes herding them away from him, when she should have been keeping his spirits up, insulating him against the dark night, the years ahead.

"Stupid, no. Your mother. Obviously. Did you or did you not specifically see her inside my disastrously hung and staged excuse for an exhibition? Airside?"

"Not . . ." Leah's too tired to spin it. "You're right."

"Precisely. So where was she?"

"At the . . . door?"

"No. Not all the time. Because—remember Sukie Blackstock, you've met her—she wanted to ask her about gluten-free and she wasn't there."

"So . . ."

"And Sukie went to look for her."

"Oh."

"And guess who she spotted her talking to?"

"Tell me."

"The Frog!"

37

Jess's mother should have known instinctively that Jess needed her.

Martyn seemed unbothered when she went off alone. "Though we have," he said, looking over Jess's shoulder, squinting into the night, "so much to discuss. Don't you want to hear what I thought?" She felt too bleak, too monstrously ashamed, to talk; he said she was being rude and sullen, which would hurt Ray terribly. "He'll be waiting for your reaction," he said. "Mine too, of course."

He's a good loving man. It's her fault, for having imagined a world together, for a week or two.

"I'm going back," she said. "To the house. Are you coming?"

"In a bit," he said. "Just finishing up."

And now Martyn, cat burglar, footpad, highwayman, is stalking his prey.

Jess will be fine walking home. It's a very nice area.

He's merely here as an observer; a peacekeeper, if you will. His quarry hurries from the scene, edges through a high metal gate and, unexpectedly, they're in what seem to be suburbs: empty mounded avenues with glistening lawns and signposts, big solid Tudorish homes. It's absolutely quiet, dewy with prosperity, with pools of misty lamplight where even the most happily coupled person can imagine odd encounters: a satyr, a wartime intimacy. Better still, if one of them were one's future home . . .

No, he reminds himself. Be satisfied; remember the flimsy wood-veneer making-do, the hush, of the scrimping world I've left behind. The Hanrahans' house, with new grout and better radiators, will be a very paradise.

He read spy books as a boy; it's a happy accident that his smarter shoes have crêpe soles. He treads on the outer edges, like a professional, and it shows; they walk along in almost-silence, as if the followee accepts his presence. There's definitely something stalwart in that stride.

You're drunk, he tells himself, but it's just the night air, the dazzling mist.

But where are they going? If only they could have discussed it, because it's actually quite cold and Martyn is not at his most relaxed out here in unknown alleyways, where anything could happen. He couldn't find his anorak in the Almoners' Hall so he's borrowed Jess's overcoat; he must be looking weirder than he has time to think about.

Left out of another set of gates, and they seem to be heading toward open country; no, wait, isn't that the pizza place, where you go to the toilet and emerge in the Middle Eastern restaurant next door? London's careless cosmopolitanism will never lose its thrill. So they must be at the corner of Hampstead Heath, the Heath is where they're heading, and a chill fingertip of worry touches his skin.

And, when Lucia was driving, did she feel the reckless ecstatic thrill of a woman in a passionate affair? Yes. Definitely.

Was she happy?

Not exactly, no.

By the time she's heaved open the shop door, held out the prescription in Leah's special shaky doctor-writing, smiled steadfastly into the pharmacist's suspicious eyes even as police sirens whizzed past, she's beyond caring. She could snuggle up here in a bed of tartan hot-water-bottle covers but she gives a firm, non-addicty nod. She must protect Priya, who can't be entangled in her family's mess.

No, she must protect herself. She could have been, as Marie-Claude said, a famous artist.

Walking back to the car, the familiar curl of the paper bag in her paw, she tries to focus on this concept; it barely lasts a second. She'd forgotten that she has to drive back.

Jess, alone outside the Hanrahan house, is counting weeks on her red cold fingers.

If her friends have done this, or had it done, whatever you say, she's never asked. She hasn't ever needed to think about it; she was always too shy, too unsuccessful, for accidents. It's only just occurred to her that dates matter, that there is an age limit, of . . .

Hang on.

It was the twelfth-ish, of November. Now it's the tenth of February. Thirteen weeks. Oh, thank God. That's legal.

But what if the timing's different in Scotland?

Is it agony, even if it's not an evil doctor, Dr. Mac with a crochet-hook? Once, off Oxford Street, she was so enraged by the sight of an idiot with a placard, picketing a clinic, that she ran up the stairs and said to the receptionist: thank you for being heroic, it must be hard, would you like one of these pears?

"Er, it's fine," said the receptionist, and the thought still makes Jess's toes curl: her earnestness, her desire to impress.

There must be places in Edinburgh. What if you have to take someone with you? If it has to be the father?

Patrick is jogging through the darkness, rain slicing his face.

He still feels watched, as if even here Ray can see his failures, his stupid, stupid hopes. His back is in a state of dread; his ear hurts like a burning coal on a rug, which is what once happened because he'd moved the fireguard to roast a potato and then there was a hole. Ray took to his bed for two days; that rug was a present from his mother. The thought makes him retch, but there's nothing left. Significance halos every car, each tree. Could the man following him be his real father? He left a message for Mrs. R's nice publican daughter at the Good Intent; that's over now.

Over the icy grass, slithering past a pale poisoned tree corpse. He manages not to touch it but his knee bangs the side: numb and now poisoned too. It's hard to remember better times but soon, Patrick is sure, calmed by the soothing ripple of the Fleet, he'll start to improve. That's how it works for people like him.

Lucia could go home and tell Ray she can't do this anymore. Or tell Marie-Claude she's changed her mind.

Or she could drive to Priya's and present herself, for their second time.

The first time, Lucia seized the day. Ray was at the cinema. By the time she'd rung the doorbell, she was a beacon, flames shooting toward the London sky. It seemed, by her grin, that Priya was too. They'd only just arranged it; Lucia was already hanging around outside the Tube when she sent her casual message.

"OK, then," said Priya, as if it were a small thing.

Lucia pressed her to the hallway wall. She hoped that Priya would like it, this new bold version. But Priya skillfully turned them both round, took charge of the kissing. It made Lucia's knees weak. How did she earn this luck?

"I can feel you smiling," said Priya. "Time to take you upstairs."

On the bottom step, Lucia stopped.

"Come on, woman."

"Wait," said Lucia.

"What?"

"The thing is . . . hardly anyone has seen, you know. It."

Because, after a couple of months where she couldn't look at it, but it was at least roundish, smooth, it had become even worse. She bought bra boosters, for excited small-titted girls with high hopes. By the time she faced careful Dr. Shah again for polite squeezes with his cold gentle hands, Lucia's body, protecting itself from the alien item, had encapsulated it, the implant, in a net of scars. Maura the nurse has seen it; she exclaimed at Lucia's bra-booster rash, went with her to buy a medical prosthesis in a sad hushed shop near Old Street: German, size XL. "I know you shouldn't need it, but I think the reconstruction didn't take into account your, your . . . voluptuousness."

Ray was kind but afterward mostly avoided it. He still comes into the bathroom for a chat, tells her off about covering it with her arm. "Don't be embarrassed," he says. "It's not as if anyone else will ever see."

"Does it look OK?" Jess had asked her on the phone, maybe

six months later. Jess is young, deserves to love her breasts, not fear them, which Lucia will do for her, so Lucia said: "Yes! It's very realistic," and neither of them referred to it again.

So that's everyone, until Priya. She knows what happened but cannot possibly visualize this lump of repurposed muscle and synthetic flesh, the asymmetry, the excuse for a nipple. Women their age have imperfections, not areas of horror.

Priya said: "You are lovely."

Fear and disgust fell to the floor like leaves. "I might have to keep my bra on," Lucia said.

"Well, you may," said Priya. "At first."

And then, when she took her into her bedroom, pressed her on the cool white bed, Priya wasn't sweet about it. She didn't tenderly kiss and weep and croon. She behaved as if every part of Lucia was worthy of lust.

Which, thinks Lucia, wondering what to do in the cold of the car, unfortunately has blown my mind.

Then, like God, her phone rings.

Leah's father says he has too much pride to let this rest, however much pain it will cause him. He phones up several of his gang, then makes Leah call her mother.

"Why's she engaged? Who's she talking to? Find out, can't you?"

"There's no—"

"Decent people don't behave like that. I haven't raised you to be a traitor. I'm not having this. That deserter has pushed me too far."

"I know," Leah says, watching the future spinning out of her hands. If he's thinking of leaving her mother, he will sink to the bottom and pull Leah with him.

"Simple solution. Find my address book."

"Oh, Pa, don't ring Marie-Claude. It's late. She might f—"

"It's classic Lucia," says Ray. "Talking to her dealer at my PV? You couldn't invent it, that kind of betrayal."

"We don't necess—"

"You know what Barry Nolan used to tell me? 'Ditch the bitch.'"

"Wait, Dad. There's something I wanted to . . ." Cruel to be kind. "Remember what Coralie said about Mum outside Moorgate station, talking to someone from, get this. Telly."

"Hold on," says Ray. "What are you on about?"

"This is what I've been trying to tell you. Yesterday? I didn't think anything much of it, but Mum's been so weird, and even more private, sort of defensive . . . Anyway, that's what Coralie said."

"What would Coraline know about this?"

"Dad. Coralie. You've known her since Reception. Anyway, I reckon it was that mayor, or minister, or whatever that woman is who came along tonight."

"Well, there we go. I attract stars. Though Cora always was thick, let's face it. So," he says, rubbing the sides of his big nose with his knuckles, giving a raggedy sigh. "Where even is Moorgate? I'll tell you this; I don't give a toss about chats outside Tube stations. That Indian politician? Fine, if she wants to suck up to her. But if your mother can sneakily engineer something professional at my own show . . . well, what choice is there? I have to ring Marie-Claude and find out what the hell is up."

"But—"

"You won't leave me, little one? No, of course you won't. We understand each other. I can rely on you."

"I am slightly drunk."

"Me too," says Lucia into the phone.

"Excellent," Priya says, low and promising, and Lucia's body lights up.

38

He's snapping through the pages of his tiny address book for Marie-Claude's home phone, while Leah thinks about how Coralie's always had it in for her family, envied her. Who cares about her gossip; it's Lucia, Leah's own mother, who's messed up tonight.

It is not a long conversation.

Afterward, chin lifted, lips compressed, Ray sits, quiet and still. Leah waits. Very, very occasionally, even in this mood, like a falling person miraculously caught on a flagpole, some chance will save him. The storm will pass.

Not tonight. Stiffly and painfully he moves to the edge of the bed, then downstairs. She follows. He inches to the living room, lifts up papers, puts them back.

"Dad?"

No response. You can see that great brain chuntering. Then, like a small birth in the garden, just a pink wriggling furless thing, she remembers the conversation her mother had earlier, on the phone.

"Dad," she says, and already it's making her breathless, with dread but also an answer, delivered. "Was there something about . . . it sounds mad. But . . . when Marie-Claude rang earlier sh—"

"You didn't tell me."

"Well, no. But . . . I think she might have mentioned . . . Venice?"

Lucia is still on the phone. "What are you up to?"

"I'm in bed, with sixteen million parliamentary reports. I'm eating cereal."

"Tonight was . . ."

"I know."

"I mean, interrupted but . . . You were . . . wow."

"Where are you?"

"Driving! I mean, not at this second. But I had to nip out," she says, hoping to suggest a rich and vivid social life.

"I thought you hated the car," says Priya.

"I do." She sounds pathetic. But Priya's reaction is not as she had expected.

"Well done," she says. "You brave woman."

"Thank you!"

"I'm proud," says Priya. "Look at you, all famous, roaring around London like a boy racer. Sexy. So, what next?"

"Oh," says Lucia, grinning her head off, "I thought . . . stripping?"

"Easy," says Priya but, in her heady state, Lucia is imagining several worlds along; standing together at Lucia's next show, Priya saying, "I'm *very* proud of her." It could even have been the Biennale, if she hadn't said no to Marie-Claude, if that wasn't absolutely final.

"I meant it, earlier," Priya says, confidingly, and Lucia's stomach lurches, that swoop of lust. "You could come to Bristol."

"Oh! I thought you . . . Seriously?"

"Yep. Imagine. A big hotel bed. Two solid nights of . . . well, probably just sleeping," she says airily. "Those of us with actual jobs will be shattered."

Lucia swallows. "Well . . ."

She's been creeping up the stairs to the loft, avoiding the creaks. Now her sister and father have fallen quiet. If he hears her, Jess will have to go in there and praise him, even if she'd rather crawl to Scotland on bleeding stumps. He will be reeking with need.

But what if, for once, he's properly ill?

She couldn't find her coat, couldn't face borrowing Martyn's anorak and the drama when he realized, so she hurried home, freezing. The door, of course, was on the latch. Her back still aches with the cold; she leans softly against the bannister outside her old bedroom, hears her father picking up the phone again.

"Dad, you can't r—"

"Shh," he hisses at Leah. "Yes," he's saying, sounding suddenly politer, as if he's talking to a man. He'll be sitting deep in his squashy chair, ready to hold out a hand to be pulled up, little table beside him crowded with glasses. How can Leah stand it?

And what about her mother? She should be mortified, furious about that mad non-exhibition, that absolute shit-show pyre of Ray Hanrahan's career but, last time Jess saw her, chatting calmly in the garden, she looked . . . unaware.

Jess has spent her life telling people she doesn't want to turn into her father. But, Martyn being what he is, so determined to force their world into his template, if she's with him, could she become her mother? Smoothing things over, tiptoeing as he gets madder, never ever telling the truth?

And there's the slur in her father's voice. Why does Leah

always say it is exhaustion, even when it's only family, when they all know?

The rage is back; sod Leah. Let her give her life to him, if that's what she wants.

"I don't care, Julian," he's saying. "I don't give a toss about your gallery etiquette. I will ask you one thing, as her husband," and Jess stops breathing.

Up on the Heath, despite the lashing rain and brambles, Patrick is smiling. Weather is power. The muddy gravel clasps his shoes; are there anglers at the ponds this late? Lovers? He won't be alone; the Heath is always full of passion.

People do break in. When he was at school some of the scarier lads would dive-bomb in the men's pond on summer nights; the next day they'd laugh about the flashing white bums they'd seen in the wooded bits off Millfield Lane. Patrick wants fuller darkness, the skeletons of bulrushes, a stew of rot. At the edge of the biggest pond, in deep wet black, he hesitates. Clothes seem cowardly. Water dripping from his eyebrows, guiding his stone fingers, he begins to unbutton his shirt.

"Where are you going?" Martyn calls.

Patch turns round calmly, as if he had known he was being followed. He's not dressed appropriately for this foul weather; something's shining at his chest like silver foil. Has he already been rescued? Martyn squints, sways, tries to stand tall and firm although the planet is spinning faster than usual, and he could easily fly off. He peers a little closer; it's bare skin.

"Oh God!"

But Patch turns his back, takes off his jacket. It looks as if he's going swimming; transfuse this scene with daylight, a buzzing haze of honeyed sun, and there they are, lolling on the grass. It's time, Jess would say, to cut down on the drinking, but she's not one to talk. Not usually.

Hang on.

"I'm so confused," Martyn murmurs.

He can't see Patch properly; the night, far from civilization, is so intensely dark, like a soaked sponge. If there is a moon, it's behind a shield of cloud.

This isn't what he envisaged, not at all.

"Tell you what," he says loudly. "Mate. You're not going in there, are you? There must, must be heated places, somewhere. Swimming pools. We could, no, bit late . . ."

But his teeth are chattering and Patch clearly can't hear him. Martyn swipes rainwater from his face and edges closer, although the slope is a death trap. Imagine dying to save Jess's brother.

"Easy now," he says.

Inexorable, unconcerned, Patch keeps his back turned. This has, Martyn wants to point out, gone some way past normal. Jess should have been clearer that her brother was prone to outbursts of instability; when Martyn took her on, he should have been warned. Although, to be fair to Ray, he's always offering to reveal the details of Patrick's teen misery, his daughters' poor romantic selections.

"Wait," he says. "Oh my God."

Patrick is in the water; inelegantly splashing up to his white thighs. When did he take off his trousers? He falls, or lies down. It's a cold night, barely above freezing. He will die, thinks Martyn, as his insides turn, perhaps literally, to ice. His shaking hands begin to struggle with the buttons of Jess's overcoat. Patch will die of hypothermia. Now it's down to me.

"It simply proves, incontrovertibly, what we all knew already."

"Dad, what?"

"That your mother has crushed my career. Of course we can't both operate in the same artistic sphere. It's true, don't lie to me. Don't tell me she's brainwashed you too. And there's more, of course; if only you knew."

Leah shakes her head, but it's like trying to stop water. She's feeling more than the usual amount of despair.

"Everyone else can see it," he insists, "but of course she found the one gallery in the bloody country willing to keep pushing her. Now I'll have to retrain as a postman or something, although my legs barely c—"

"Oh, come on. You don't need to do that. Anyway, didn't Julian say it wasn't even confirmed?"

"That's not the point!" he bellows, pinkening with tears. "And the idea that she's known, she's been cooking this up. She's always been waiting to triumph. I was a stepping stone." His hand is on his chest: the muscular thumb-base, the old painty nails. "My pulse is racing."

"Lie flat. Remember, that's what Dr. Mac said."

Stiffly he lowers himself, still crying. She can't stop, either. She needs to soothe him but, like a traitor, when she hears a footstep in the hall her stupid heart thinks: Pablo?

39

Lucia had barely crossed the doormat when she heard the shouting.

Usually it'll be directed at her, or Patrick. Where is Patrick, she wonders as she hurries upstairs, ready to lie down and sleep. Hopefully already in his caravan, which reminds her sh—

"My God," she says. "Ray? What's going on?"

"What are you doing?" asks Patrick.

"I'm saving you," says Martyn.

Ray is face down on the floor, Leah kneeling beside him, rubbing his back. It could almost be a massage, but he's bellowing into the carpet, beating his fists on the rug: a toddler long past comforting. Leah looks up, looks away.

It hurts without ending, having a child who hates you, almost as much as having a child who hates himself. Even if you know the source of their mad beliefs, the point where the poison was first dripped in, you want your loving silky-cheeked girl back.

But she is Ray's. And here he is, distraught.

"You," Leah's saying, as if Lucia could possibly be a surprise, holding his pills in a paper bag. "I can't believe you'd even dare—"

Ray turns his head. It looks uncomfortable; that was never a good rug. He stares at Lucia as if he's considering a disgusting lunch. Leah pauses; quiet, at last.

"I've found out," splutters Ray. "Everything."

"What the hell?" Jess is coming in from the hall. She takes a breath; Lucia holds out her hand.

"Can you not start a whole—" Jess begins. "You can't, don't take this out on Mum."

Leah and Lucia gasp. Ray hauls himself upright. "I know," he tells Lucia, as if Jess hasn't spoken, with that googly-eyed look that means he's beyond rage, "what you have been doing all this time. All winter. For months, probably."

Lucia, spinning slowly down to the ocean floor, almost says: "Priya?"

So very nearly; it's like a cherry-stone on her tongue, but something stops her. Maybe it's the tone of his rant, the way he spaces every word for maximum impact, and it sounds so mad; he is mad, she thinks.

"I don't know what you're talking about."

"I spoke," says Ray, "to your gallery. Julian Hertz saw it from my point of view, anyone would. What you've done to me. He told me everything."

Lucia, Leah, Jess gape at him. His calves look old and thin, poking out from his rucked-up trouser-legs.

"You," he says. "You . . . snake. You actually are a monster, like everyone said. I—I have no words. Let me finish: when were you going to tell me? This is . . . it's almost violent. I feel it in my . . . the pain in my cortex. If you knew the damage you've caused. I'll never recover. You disgust me, you always have, do you know that? With your ambition, your pushing, your relentless me, me, me? Do you expect me to . . . what, walk in with you, holding your hand, yes, I'm proud of my wife who has stolen the Biennale from me? Italy, which was always my special place? Can you not interrupt? Don't even try to justify yourself. You make me sick with your 'oh I'm just a dusty sculptor' crap but you're . . ." His hand claws at the rug. "My God. That my wife, my student, could do this to me. I trusted you. I trusted her," he says to the girls. "I'm speechless."

"What have you done to him," Leah gasps at her mother.

"And if you think," Ray's spitting, nostrils flaring as if she stinks, "that pretending not to want it changes anything . . . yes, Julian claimed you've said no, as if . . . you can't seriously, even you . . . oh, I can imagine the interviews," and he goes into his special mimsy voice, a touch of brogue, "'to be sure, little me, I was not worthy but 'tis an honor, for a humble peasant woman artist.' I mean, CHRIST. As if you'd set all this up then turn it down. The damage, the disaster this will do to my reputation. After all my striving, my tormenting myself to produce, to keep this family afloat; as if being the breadwinner is an easy task, while keeping this whole show on the road," he extends his arm to take in the room, the house. "As if anyone could ever think there's space for two married artists. You've obliterated . . . You've killed me. You have murdered me for your fucking stupid 'art.'"

No, thinks Jess. This isn't fair. It is not right. "Dad," she says. "Hang on a minute. You can't start blam—"

"What?"

"You, your exhib—the show."

"What?" says Leah. "You leave him alone. You'll do him actual physical harm if you—"

"But . . . don't make me say it."

Leah moves. She rises, walks quickly across the rug, faces her sister. Her lips are pressed together; she tucks her hair behind her ears. "You knew," she says. "Didn't you?"

"What?"

"You knew about this shit, what Mum's done. Doing. You must've. You're as bad as she is."

Jess tries to move away. She is powerfully in need of sleep. She says: "Can you just . . . I was saying something to Dad."

"Can you just accept your role here, as the traitor?" Leah turns away.

"What? You sound insane," Jess says, and her sister does look frighteningly rigid, stuck on something so wrong. "I don't know what, I've no idea what's . . . but, Dad," she says, and anyone would think she was drunk, so filled are her veins with an urgent need to say this, right now, "how can you say she's hurt *your* career? After tonight? You didn't try," she says. "With the show, at all. It was . . . there wasn't much." The only way she can do this is not to look at him. Or at her mother, who has tears running down her cheeks. She closes her eyes, opens them, tries to focus on her sister's profile, but they all know she's talking straight at him. "You, after all the hype, you didn't . . . Mum," she swallows, "is the one who works hard. She earns it, Dad. She does everything, and *she*'s the one who . . . the meals and bills, but your pointless shopping, the hoardi—" and that is when Leah turns and whacks her.

40

Crashing through the bulrushes, he thinks he hears Patch crying, but the feeling is in Martyn's chest. Mud and reeds and water, so cold he can't take in breath. His arms are round Patrick's waist but he can't pull him back up the bank, can't even drag himself up. Neither of them has been fully underwater but he can't feel anything, his mind is solid, his teeth are locked tight. Actually, the water's warm. He tries to grip Patrick's arms, but Patrick swats him off as if he is goose-down.

Someone's screaming at him. His ears are fuzzy; the pain, of freezing or defrosting, is tapping at his skull. "Please," they're saying.

"Leave me alone," Patch shouts.

"You don't mean it. I'm sorry," he says or thinks at Patch. "I only wanted to show you."

Again, Patch pushes deeper in through black spikes rattling like spears, water swishing infernally. There could be anything, pike or rats; fear is so deep in his throat, but he wants something else. What does he want?

Patch.

To rescue him, obviously.

Where are we? He's roaring, or Martyn is; it's so hard to see but, among the water-glints, he possibly sees his own white hand stretching out.

"What are you doing?" he remembers to ask.

And Patch turns his face. Shiny and silver: he no longer looks proud or valiant at all, just sad. He says: "I don't know."

And then they're beautifully holding hands and Martyn is being pulled out of the bog, the swamp, to land. His body is sinking into the sodden grass; his eyes are drooping, and he imagines an old wild-haired woman with two big hounds lolloping up to him, the fallen hero, and starting to shake his shoulders.

Interesting, she thinks before the pain takes hold. So that's how violence feels.

It was half smack, half punch; a closed-handed thump, mostly wrist, on her face and skull. Not even Dad will be able to say that Leah didn't mean to do it.

Then: wow.

It's like being a plum, burst. Only her lip seems cut, but such a weight of bone on cheek, smashing into her undefended flesh, is stunning: a black-red block of pain. Through the crash of it, the extraordinary hot sting and ache, she has two clear pure streams of awareness, as if she has leaped through a paper hoop and found the real world, waiting:

One: Careful. I'm pregnant.

Two: At last, I can kill her.

"You fuck," she yells, feeling her jaw, touching blood. She tastes it, for strength. The parents are shouting, from far away. She checks: am I dizzy? No.

She and Leah, old foes, are pacing the dry dust, snorting through their noses; they are back-to-back in the dewy dawn, no seconds, ready to shoot. She turns to face her sister, looking for where to hit.

Gillian always listens to her instincts: they are clear and true. As soon as she'd successfully coaxed Jessica away from the disaster in the garden and back inside the Hall, where she started fretting about some lost coat, hardly important now, Gillian located David and told him to take the children off and wait for her All Clear.

"Where?"

"Think of something. Pizza?"

"It's after ten. Jake claims to have had thirteen packets of crisps. And Rebecca's teary ag—"

"I don't care. Cinema, then. There must be something they'll both watch. Or a pub. Buy them ciders." She widened her eyes; he understood.

"OK."

"They don't need to see this."

"What?"

"Unhappiness."

"It'll be fine," he said, kissing her: the good Hanrahan. "You can do it."

So, back at the asylum, she's discreetly wiping the hob when the shouting upstairs begins. She does not reveal herself; someone might need to bear witness. When the doorbell goes, she thinks, "Goodness, David, it was a simple instruction . . ." and then remembers his stent.

Even now, Lucia's thinking of Ray; not her daughters, definitely not her son. She is shouting, "Stop it, you girls, stop," trying to squeeze between the table and the big wooden chair, but then, for precious seconds, when pain could have been averted and damage undone, she does not act.

If she grabs Leah, pulls her back from hurting her sister, Ray will be raging. He'll tell her that she's favoring Jess, punishing Leah, will insist until she finally believes him that all their troubles are Lucia's fault. And doesn't she always dither because, even in the thick of trouble, she's thinking how to justify her actions to him later, in the bathroom or bed, and it's exhausting, inescapable, unless—

Leah's smirk is like a scalpel, letting Jess's fury out. She has managed to back her hard against the bookcase; it would be so easy, in another family, to take it further, bang Leah's smug head against the shelf. It would be natural.

But she doesn't even know how to hate her sister. They're nothing but their father's daughters, even as actual blood is spilled.

Christ, it hurts. Don't look at him. Don't do him the honor. Jess says, as fiercely as she can: "Want me to punch you back? I will. Can you stop looking over at him for one minute? I know you think you're getting away with it, no telling off, not even a fucking word, but don't, don't think . . ." She's gasping with tears; it isn't working. Even Leah's barely listening. "I cannot believe that you . . ." but she can't do it, can't thump her. She gives her another shove, shoulder against big exhibition hardbacks, good. But it's no use. It's hard to breathe under this useless fury. "Don't you fucking laugh," she says, but unless Leah looks her in the eye, admits her crimes . . .

She tries to grab her face but Leah screws her eyes shut, twists her chin away. She's not even crying anymore; there's no need.

"Leave her alone," their father yells. "My God, look at them, there's nothing their own mother won't do to manipulate her own . . . Let go! You're hurting her, poor—"

"Who?" says Jess.

"You!"

So she lets go.

Her eyes close; what she'd give for sleep. It's pointless to resist; she's thinking of his reaction even as she goes for righteousness. "It's not good for you, can't you see that?" she starts once more. "Being stuck here under, you know, his, Dad's—"

"What?" spits Leah. "Thanks to all the nothing you do? Poor cotton-wool-wrapped Mummy's little 'let her piss off to Scotland and break our hearts' baby? Leaving me to sort out every single thing, all the problems, the stresses and poor Dad and n—"

"Stop that!" says their mother. "Why are you . . . What's g—"

And then their father's shouting above them all: "Hello?" and everyone stops. "This infantile attention seeking, while I am physically suffering here. This was my day. You always were difficult, ungenerous. Do you really think," he says to Jess, hands outstretched, like an orator, "that your petty little sense of injustice—"

"She hit me!"

He ignores this, turns to their mother. "You have done such, *such* harm. On your head be it. With your borderline criminal ambition, your greed, your toxic mothering." He swipes snot from his nose, grasps the corner of the table to steady himself, although he could probably manage without it. Jess wants to say so, fight him instead; she starts to say, "It's not Mum's—"

Leah won't have it. He's the one she will protect. "Yeah?" she says and pushes Jess's shoulder hard, prodding her away. "Want to compare who has suff—"

There's no point arguing; better to fall to the floor, drumming one's heels at the injustice. But Jess is an adult. "You can't, you can't just turn this around and be the victim. Is no one hearing this? You smashed into my face!"

"Hardly. Bit pink, that's all."

But Jess is breathing fast and hot; she needs to hurt Leah, in her heart, to deal a mortal blow. Her sister's forearm is pushing against her face and she wants to move it, not necessarily do damage but, in the salty blur of tears or sweat, the hammering pain of her own face and her father's screaming, she has no alternative. She takes a bite.

41

Gillian, still dumbfounded, is holding open the front door, barely concentrating while a woman with long white patrician-looking hair and a full-length Barbour witters on at her about boating and reeds.

"So very kindly, Beena, that's the mother Cavalier King Charles, licked his poor feet and hands and . . ."

It's clearly one of those door-to-door scams but, much as she'd welcome an escape from the maelstrom upstairs, responsibility weighs heavy on her shoulders. "I'd really better—" she begins.

Then she notices the black taxi pulling away from the gate, doing one of those sixpence turns cabbies pride themselves on: the decrepit strangers hobbling toward her.

"Wrong clothing for it," the woman says cheerfully. "The short one had nothing warm at all! But I found a woman's coat on the bank so I shoved that over him."

"Thank you," says Gillian again, peering closer. "But I don't . . ." The woman is filling her arms with wet scarves and dog-blankets ("pop them back when you've finished with them"), a phone, a white pen. They're leaving dark splotches on the path, like soldiers fresh from another battlefield.

"Sorry, one second," she says. "Patrick?"

Ray splutters, through tears: "You always wanted to drive them apart. Are you happy now?" Leah is sobbing, possibly a tiny bit more than the wound requires. Jess, white-faced, is crying too.

Ray says: "See? The family is breaking down! You are bad for them, do you hear me? You cannot do this to your children, to me. If you still care at all, about the love, the nurturing you've had for all these decades, you would refuse it. Tell Venice no. You have to."

"Of course," says Lucia. "How could you think I'd accept it, if . . ." and then she hears Gillian say her name. She looks away and a new thought dawns. In Ray's eyes she has betrayed him, simply by being offered the chance. His rage will never stop; the worst is already done. So she could change her mind.

Shit, thinks Jess. I left it in my coat pocket. But where's my coat?

42

SUNDAY MORNING

"I don't understand," says Gillian.

They're drinking coffee like civilized people. Gillian's eating dry toast. Lucia told her, "I can't eat," but is already on her third slice.

"She was going," says Lucia. "Well, she was about to, when I came down."

"Do you think," asks Gillian delicately, "that she'd have, you know. Waited for . . . ?"

"Me?"

"Mm."

"I hope so," says Lucia. She swallows. "We do have a—she knows I love her, utterly. But maybe she feels, I don't know. I can barely think about it. Let down?"

"By who?"

"Me. For not standing up more for her against, you know."

Gillian, not prone to touching, grips her hand. "Don't, do not start that," she says. "You have tried."

Lucia is not going to cry; she doesn't deserve to. "You, you don't know. And Patrick. My Pat, I still don't understand what they were doing out there. Do you think he . . . ?"

"Does he see someone?" asks Gillian, looking at her plate. "A therapist?"

"Ray took against the one I found. He thought she was estranging him." She stops herself. "I have a new recommendation, though. I could pay myself. Ray doesn't even have to know."

"Exactly." Gillian lowers her voice a little. "I've seen how hard it is, he is, to stand up to. Even for me."

"Really?" Lucia whispers back. "I'm pathetic compared to you. You and David d—"

"That," says Gillian, "is entirely not the same thing. What are those eggs out for?"

"Breakfast cake," says Lucia. "You remember. Sunday tradition. Ray . . ." and she trails off. Ray always says, "My family all together, eating cake," even when Jess isn't there, even when he's spent the previous evening listing the ways Lucia's mortally hurt him. "Although I'm not sure I can quite . . ."

Gillian's pecking up dry crumbs with her fingertip. "Can't he have toast like a normal person? God, I could live on it. This is good, doing this. Why do we never do this?" Lucia looks away. "Lovely light in here in the mornings."

"Illuminating the filth," points out Lucia.

Kind Gillian pretends not to notice. "I mean," she says, "I know it's tricky. Finding time. Or even training up to Sheffield. But you can talk to me. All of it. If . . . if you need."

Lucia sighs, covers her face with her hand. Between her fingers, she examines Gillian's expression. She knows. She must do. She lowers her palm, keeps it in front of her mouth as she says, barely audibly: "What's 'all of it'?"

"Whatever you need to admit," says Gillian. "But what I meant was that things are tough, for you. Have been, for years. You avoid talking about it, energetically, but it's obvious."

"How?"

"If one spends, let's see, three minutes near you. You can't decide about anything. Remember that time . . . you didn't even know if you wanted our old water filter jug until you'd consulted him."

"Well, yes, but . . . God. I can't believe it's visible."

"Completely. Last time I saw you, you'd bought him brand-new speakers to make up after some big row. He likes hinting that we don't know the half of it—"

"Does he? To you?"

"Yes! But you're the one on eggshells."

"But that's fine. Normal. And it's my—"

"No, it's not."

Afterward, Lucia's irritable. Please go, she thinks. Just leave us; I shouldn't have confessed all that.

Gillian begins to gather her children's dirty white socks and earphones.

"Sorry, but can you not call up to them," Lucia says automatically. "It'll wake . . ." and Gillian mildly raises her eyebrows.

"I hung the wet things in the hall," she tells Lucia. "Reunited contents with pockets, I hope."

"Doesn't matter," says Lucia.

"Well, it might," Gillian says, and stops.

"They can sort it out themselves."

Gillian says she's heard Martyn snoring from the loft. Lucia's checked twice on her boy, knocked lightly and seen that he was breathing. Once this is all over, she thinks, I'll sort out help.

"Make sure they're really warm all day, and keep an eye on extremities," Gillian's saying. "Herbal tea or squash, not coffee. Do you still not have any idea what they were—?"

"None. At all," says Lucia.

"No. And flat Coke," she says, "for dehydration."

"I'm not sure dehydration was the problem," Lucia says, smiling, but it hurts. Please, she thinks, leave me to my failure.

It is too late to confess her real conversation with Jess. Gillian is a good mother. She won't understand.

Last night, Lucia had no choice. Ray was relentless and, although she held out longer than usual, after midnight he was back to how the girls, his girls, were fighting on his day. So she let him convince her: if she persuaded Jess to apologize to Leah, some of the damage would be undone.

When Lucia came down this morning, Jess was already up, dressed, bag by the door. She did try. "Love, you know how he is. So incredibly sensitive about family stuff. He desperately wants you all to get along."

"Why's it always about Dad?" Jess said.

"Mm? Do you want tea?"

Jess gave her a look. "Come on. It's always 'Your father's upset,' but why can't he tell us directly? Why are you his conduit?"

"Not this now, please."

"When, then?"

"Well . . ."

"Never? Well, I'm sorry," Jess said, as if a cork was out, "if this isn't comfortable, if I'm being impertinent and . . ."

There passed between them the knowledge that, were Ray here too, he'd smirk, say "fancy" or worse. Lucia thought, Oh my love, I've made you small too.

"What I realized I don't know," said Jess, not looking at her, "is whether your mum was like this with your dad."

"Don't start," Lucia said. "Like what?"

"You know."

"Mum? Well. She was very strong, for him."

The moment felt freighted; a chance to fill Jess up with wisdom and security, when so many others have been frittered away. "Which is what love means, sometimes. Marriage."

Jess rolled her eyes. "Not for, say, Gillian, though. She is loved. Haven't you noticed? *She's* strong but so is Uncle David, and he doesn't env—"

"Stop now. Seriously," said Lucia. She looked around, started gathering stray forks. "Haven't y—"

She could hardly look at Jess, but saw her flush. "I just," Jess said, with a hard out-breath. "I don't want to . . . to be . . ."

"Oh," said Lucia, who will not cry in front of her. "My lovely girl. You don't have to be anything y—"

"No," said Jess, moving her hand away. "That's not it. I don't want to . . . to be like . . ."

"What?"

"You."

Lucia looked at her. Looked at the table. "Oh."

"Don't be cross. I just—"

"It's fine," said Lucia. "So. I really should . . ."

"Do you know what I mean?"

"No. Tell me. Actually, don't. You know, oddly, sweetheart, I'm not in the market for a sort of negative relationship-intervention by my actual daughter."

"I'm just scared, Mum," Jess said, her voice wobbling, so of course what could Lucia do but go to hug her. "I don't want . . . Maybe you and Dad, he was so spectacular when you met. But me, me and Martyn . . . I feel he's *telling* me we are happy, and that I'll never find anyone who loves me as much. And maybe he's right. But I can't be with him just because I'm scared no one else will want me. Can I?"

"Why wouldn't they? You're completely lovable."

"I can't be," Jess said, tears beginning to dot off her nose and onto her top, blotting the cotton like breast milk.

"Oh my love, why not?"

"Because I don't . . . I'm not—"

"What?"

Jess took a huge breath, wiped her face. "I'm not going to tell you everything," she explained. "You are my mother."

"I remember. Vividly."

"So, can you just leave it?"

Lucia clenched her jaw, released. "But you were . . . Oh, never mind. Look, you need to stay until after lunch. Dad'll be so . . ." She stops.

"I can't."

"Why not?"

"Work."

When Ray realizes that Jess has left, she will need to suck all the pain from him, take it herself. "But, sweetheart, what about Martyn? Monkey, look at me. Is he going too?"

"I . . ."

"Yes?"

"Don't make me feel bad," said Jess, her voice rising again. "He'll be fine. You know how much he loves Dad. Wants to be like Dad, even, so he can just nestle . . ."

"You have told him, though."

"What?"

"That you're going. Why? What else?"

"I . . . will."

"Jess. It's not fair. You have to. Are you actually going to leave now? Oh, sweetheart. Do you want me to tell him?"

"No! They don't need to be protected, you know. Men."

Lucia gave her youngest child a long, hard look. "Right."

"At least, I won't. I mean it's OK for you, you chose it, but . . ."

"OK," Lucia sighed. "Enough."

Jess went for another hug. A huge wave of tears was rising,

like a fundraising thermometer: green; blue; into the red. If her mother knew what else she wasn't admitting, would she forgive her?

"Mum," she began.

"Christ," said her mother. "I forgot to make the breakfast cake," and Jess thought: She's past saving. It's too late.

43

Patrick, under every spare covering his sisters could find, musty and not all quite dry, has finally stopped shivering. He slept, on and off; the last time he woke up he lay there on his back and understood that he'd never have a night in his caravan again.

But where can he go?

He's read about adventurers, wayfarers bedding down in heather, snaring rabbits, but that was the past. I'm a man out of time, he thinks, and pinches his inner arm until it makes his vision wobble. Idiot.

Painfully, like his future self, he sits, pulls on his trousers slowly. He has to get out of here before Martyn stirs; he cannot bear to face him.

But what about Jess, his fat-legged toddling sister? Could he, for her?

The Gillians have gone. Eric Nakamura, lending Graeme a fiver "for the bus," has gone, without comment on the exhibition. Graeme too, taking the net of Babybels Lucia bought in the hope that Jess still likes them, that she could once again pour calcium into her daughter's lovely bones. There's so much cheese; Ray had planned a spectacular "no fuss" Sunday lunch for Eric Nakamura. They'll never eat it all themselves. Gillian, when she saw the quantity of olives, said, "Only the best for Ray."

"Will you take a salami? I beg," Lucia said as the Gillians were leaving, but Gillian only smiled and made a "phone me" gesture.

No sign of Patrick. She dare not disturb him. Please, she prays as she has done for decades, let my boy have survived the night.

Now Leah's gone, looking tense and tight: "Pablo will be waiting," she kept saying when Lucia offered her tea, toast, anything. "He's always at the pub on Sundays and he'll want to explain about yesterday," and it seemed rude to ask her daughter what she meant.

Carefully she asked: "Oh, the Nathaniel son. Do you think that's a good idea? Isn't he quite a layabout?"

"He's fine."

"It was bad, though, that he left you in the lurch. What a sod. Do you have to now? Sweetheart? Because I wanted to cha—"

"Yes, I have to. And, anyway, I need to clear up the show."

"Not already?"

"It's finished," Leah said, shrugging as if it were a tiny thing.

"We've got another fortnight. Haven't we? Love?" All that money. "Everyone was told . . . The invitations sa—"

"Well, Dad's changed his mind. And it is his show, his work. So can you just forget it? Anyway. He knew this would happen."

"What?" asked Lucia.

"That no one would get it. That he'd be occluded." And what could Lucia say to that?

She followed Leah to the front door. "So what's he said?"

"Nothing."

"Sleeping?" she asked.

"Usual level," Leah said. "Don't go up again. He's too fragile."

She forced herself to wait for ten minutes, then hurried upstairs. The curtains were drawn.

"I know you're awake, Ray," she said, like a polite murderer. "Please . . . stir." But he is obstinate in his rage, would neither speak nor appear to be asleep, merely breathed, angrily, until she backed away.

When Martyn emerged from the loft, hungover, raring to discuss last night's brave rescue, and found that Jess had left, he adjusted his face so quickly that Lucia barely caught it. Every time Lucia looks his way he's fiddling with his phone. I've reared, she thinks, a brutal child.

This is not a dreadful thought.

Everything is broken. She makes coffee, watches it cool, digs her nails into the tabletop. At last, she creeps back up to their room.

Her hand is, or should be, shaking. Right, she thinks. Let's begin.

They're like penguins, faces all tipped toward the departures board, waiting for the Edinburgh platform to be announced. Jess has tied her hair up, wrapped her green scarf round her coat shoulders, as if that'll work. Her breath roars against the wool like an astronaut's; her coat is muddy and stiff, as if the fibers are infected. Buy food, she tells herself; you need nourishment. And she's in pain; her lip seeps discreetly. No one has said a thing.

This morning she went in search of her mother. The kitchen was cold; there was a two-liter container of full-fat milk defrosting in the sink. She has tried before to talk to her about hormones in dairy but Lucia just looked tired and said, "Your father loves it."

The thought of her hurts. Last night's oddness has pinched at Jess all night.

Maybe she should rush back. Her mother was definitely distracted; what if she's ill again? And this is Jess's last chance to see her?

But what kind of rat returns to the ship?

A tear rolls down her cheek and stings her lip; she tightens her fists and touches the white plastic stick, chill in her pocket.

Patrick isn't crying exactly. He needs to talk to his mother, but she's with his stepfather in their room. There is scraping and shifting from the loft, but no conversation. A childhood sense, a buried knowledge of whose ankle clicks on the stairs and who coughs how, is making him uneasy. He knows the sound, the feeling of this house, and something is not right. Where is his younger sister?

A weight seems to have been stripped from his chest in the night. All the dark conflict, how to free himself, whether to be, has been replaced with a new clear problem. What if Martyn believes that he, Patrick, saved him? Or even the other way round? Either way, he'll surely think there's a bond.

Or, worse, what if Jess discovers what Martyn tried to do? Martyn might blurt something out when he sees Patrick again.

If Jess's happiness is at risk, obviously Patrick must sacrifice himself. He needs, he's now realizing, hand on the back door, to hide until Martyn has left.

Then he sees, leaning against the ketchup bottle, an envelope.

"I'm not speaking to you," says Ray to his wife of a thousand years.

Usually he likes to see one's eyes, but he won't look at Lucia. It's as if he's been rehearsing.

"Have you rung her?"

"Who?"

"You know who. Oh, come on, don't look all confused. Or are there two huge fucking career-defining shows on the go, three? Did you bag the Turbine Hall too? A little Hayward retrospective? Although, what am I saying, you'd never manage to keep several in your head at once. You do realize, don't you, that without me you couldn't run a household? You can't even understand the thermostat."

"I—"

"Various people have said, people who care for me, that when we naively started planning my comeback, my resurrection, you should have mentioned that you had other plans. Massive betrayal, distracting all my guests, my journalists, with 'oh modest me has been approached by the Biennale who I've sucked up to my entire life.' That's all. It would have been . . . the minimum, to have said."

"I didn't kn—"

"Oh, come on. You think my friends didn't realize something was up? They know what you are. You were beaming like you'd won the Turner and it wasn't exactly wifely pride, in retrospect. I suppose people will think that I made you turn it down. As if I give a toss what they think. The damage's been done."

She's standing there like St. Sebastian, arguments and justifications spurting from every arrow-wound.

"Remember what Bernard Allan warned me the first time he met you? Christ, if you hadn't cannibalized every chance I had . . . And this is just a pause, let's face it. It'll quicken their appetite, make them want you more another time. Or was that the plan as well?"

She presses her lips together. It's like trying to fill a beach hole with water, drop by useless drop.

"Tell me," he says. "I'm curious. We all know how dangerous you are, but did you, even for a second, think you'd get away with it?" His hair is smudged to one side, his face spongy with sleep and whatever helped him to it. Sour breath and sour sheets. "What this would do to me, my children? And did you imagine," he asks, "when this gets out, that any decent human in existence, my very loyal friends, the entire art world you care so slavishly about, would ever speak to you again? You *have* told her it's a no?"

44

He can't keep hiding in the side return. Where, then? Not back to the caravan, because Martyn will find him, or inside the house, because Ray will ask questions.

I am, thinks Patrick, a solitary atom, and I need to become a molecule, which would make Jess laugh at him, and he smiles for the first time in weeks.

If only she hadn't gone already, wasn't Martyn's girlfriend, didn't live so far away. Her note said: *P.S. obv. don't tell the others I left this for you.* There's shouting upstairs from Ray; this means Patrick won't see his mother for hours. He pats his pockets, checks his satchel. In his strange awakening this morning he packed as if heading off for a full day's work: phone, book, pencil, various pebbles, wallet, jumper, penknife. Everything necessary is here.

He still feels cold and rigid as a park railing, could do with tea. But, quietly, he opens the gate.

Jess hurries along the platform, phone jammed under her ear like Quasimodo, waiting for an answer. She feels sick and so impossibly tired that she could ask the next tallish man to carry her, a beefy child to drape her along the top of her case and wheel her to her seat. There's too much fog in her mind. If her mother picks up her phone, for once in her life, Jess could be dissuaded. It might be the magic sign she needs to be glad for everything she has, whether she wants it or not.

If she answers, I won't get on this train.

Even if she won't really talk, I'll let this train go and then maybe Martyn will catch the next with me, and I'll be grateful to be loved again.

If she answers, she'll definitely tell me to stick with him, keep the . . . the fetus, and it worked for her, didn't it? Hasn't she had a happy enough life?

Awkward though, if her father's already passed the door to Vivienne's flat, and noticed the second George Gregory Pye is missing.

"Hi," says Lucia. "Can you hear me? I'm in the garden, I have to be quick. No, just listen."

Patrick can't get hold of Jess. The bus is too open, a freezing box lurching up to traffic lights. Two shouty sisters and a huge-bellied man wearing a tiny camouflage T-shirt are staring at him; a baby begins to scream. He's thinking he will have to get off on York Way but then a guide-dog-in-training called Billie rests her loose lips on his shoe, the wide calm bridge of her nose like maple, and the fear passes.

Jess, answer your phone.

King's Cross booms with announcements and bellowing laughs and metal scraping. He wastes minutes staring at the Arrivals board, then waiting politely in a long queue for tickets. If he can catch her, he will have to be brave. He will ask her: when you left the first time, how did you dare go to college, how did you summon the nerve to defy him? Was it to save your own life? Am I too late?

Platform seven. The back of the five past East Coast Excelsior Rapide to Edinburgh is receding along the tracks as he arrives.

45

So, thinks Lucia. It's over now.

Marie-Claude was neither surprised nor angry. She simply said "*enfin*" which, as far as Lucia remembers, doesn't mean very much. She began to describe what would happen in the next few days but Lucia stopped her.

"I can't . . . I need to know as little as possible about it. Sorry."

"OK."

"Sorry."

"Please. You need to end this habit."

"I'll try. Also, what you said about visiting, you know, spending a lot of proper working time there . . ."

"Yes?"

"Well. Could—can it start, the staying actually in Venice part, as soon as—well, right away?"

It's dark out, and in. Ray snapped at Martyn when he suggested turning up the heating: "We're not all wee runts." Leah, already in several wispy sweaters, fingerless gloves and something called wrist-warmers, looked scornful, then offered her father a hot chocolate, into which she poured the rest of the brandy. Martyn has never needed alcohol so badly in his life.

"I should leave soon," he says. "For my train. Shouldn't I?"

When Leah's phone buzzes, she knows it's Pablo, ringing to apologize. Life can flip like a coin; now her happiness can begin. She's smiling as she picks it up.

It's her mother.

"What's she saying?" asks her father behind her. "What's she want? Tell her to bloody h—"

"I can't hear," Leah says. She strokes her father's shoulder comfortingly. "Shh, let . . . don't get all riled up. Mum, are you with Patch? What the hell?"

"That idiot," says her father. "Living the life aquatic. Well, you can tell him fr—"

"Does he even know how to catch a train?" She raises her eyebrows at Ray, grins, but in truth her spirit is sinking fast. "Well, it's true. Wait, how do you know if you're not with him?" She doesn't even bother to put her hand over the mouthpiece. "Dad," she says, "you'll never believe . . . actually you will. Jess has gone back to Scotland. And Patch is apparently on the way to stay with her."

"What?"

"I know."

"Unbelievable," Ray says, and her mother has some fiddly explanation, who rang who from which train, but she's not interested.

"Poor, poor Dad."

"They're welcome to each other. Unbelievable."

When she tunes back in, her mother's making no sense. "You're what? Mum, wait, come on, seriously? Well, not today. You can't. There's loads—"

"What?" her father's asking. "She can't dump this all on me."

"No," says Leah. "No! I won't. You do it," and she hangs up.

She doesn't look at her father. Martyn appears in the doorway. "Any news?"

"Oh God," says Ray. "The ghost of sons-in-law future."

"So what's the story?" Martyn asks.

"Listen." She needs to beam calm at her father. "Though the thing is . . ." If Pablo were here, he'd stroke her hand. Her father will love him. "OK. But it's a bit weird."

"Hurry up," says Ray. "I haven't got all day. Everyone wants to discuss the show and b—"

"Mum," Leah says, "also announced that she has got a work thing. Like, really last minute. Something small and boring, she said."

"Where? On a Sunday afternoon? That's outra—"

"Bristol? I think. Seriously. She's such a cow. Poor Dad. Poor Daddy. Don't worry, we'll look after you."

Martyn nods. "How long?"

"Just a couple of nights." The minute she's out of here she's ringing Dr. Mac.

"Seen Patch, at all?"

"Oh, yeah, the other thing is um . . . *he* 's caught a train with, you know. My sister."

"Sorry?"

"I know, it doesn't make sense. They talked from the train. He and she. Or Mum and Jess. God knows."

"She'll ring me soon," Martyn says, nodding. "She probably realized she had leftover marking, that's why she's rushed back. Did she leave me a note?"

"No," says Leah. "Not even for Dad."

Martyn looks up out of the window, wrinkling his nose to keep his glasses on. "It's raining again," he says, and gives a small cough. "I wonder if last night's odd, you know, saving went to my chest."

Ray ignores him. Leah watches Ray.

"I—I, my Year Twelves have a study week, and the rest of them barely . . ." Martyn goes on. "I can say I'm ill, rest a bit. The Head respects me so there's no problem. Or no, I'll tell him that there's a family emergency."

"Well," says Ray. "There is."

46

It is only two nights: not a future together. The future with Priya is grief.

Lucia stands on one leg, then the other, willing the Circle Line train to go faster. She keeps going back through her phone call with Leah; she sounded convincing, to herself, but her daughter is a deep, still pool. At least no one knows about the dusty clothes in the studio, the toothbrush and knickers. She's imagined a sudden summons so often, yet still was unprepared.

Electric light glazes the sooty guts of the westbound Tube tunnel, glinting off corners of pipe and wire. Her hand moves to her suspiciously overstuffed work bag. This time, she takes out her sketchbook. And, although the page stays blank, it is life, not Ray, that distracts her.

She has had her vision.

It's only a short trip. They are separate things: Venice and Priya. Even if Ray never finds out what Bristol was really about, who she went with, nothing will lessen his rage when he hears she accepted the Biennale. She can fantasize all she likes about the thrill of being respected, a name at last, but it will end her and Ray. His fury will burn her to ashes.

But at least she'll be in Venice, far from the blaze.

Every time her mind completes this loop, gazing through the EMERGENCY EXIT sign, she tries to visualize her and Priya together. But Priya is breaking her heart into ever smaller pieces; there's almost nothing left to save. If she's going to do this, face the fire, she might as well throw everything on.

She needs to force herself to end it.

The train's arriving at Paddington. She shouldn't go to Bristol. Or she could go, and Venice will still be waiting.

She can't do it.

But who will save Lucia now, if not herself?

Acknowledgments

Thank you to:

Jess Phillips MP, for so generously answering my ignorant and/or personal questions about life in the House of Commons.

Olivia Camillo, Sandra Turnbull, Nicola Tassie, Raphaelle Bischoff, Rosie McFadzean, Charlotte Mayer;

Charles Asprey and Sunita Kumar, for invaluable help and information.

The British Council and Cortina, Tanya, Youlya, Lidia, Ruth and Nicola Barker, for Moscow, Yasnaya Polyana and inspiration.

Claire Baldwin and Victoria Hobbs for publishing advice.

Kate Muir, Maggie O'Farrell and Sarah Waters for literary guidance and steadfast friendship.

Pat Kavanagh and Gill Coleridge for their faith; Peter Straus;

Maria Rejt, my loyal and brilliant editor from the very beginning; the irreplaceable Camilla Elworthy, Becky Lushey and all at Mantle/Picador.

And, for their endless extraordinary support, kindness and wisdom, which helped me through it: Jane C. and Jane H.; Nicola Roche, Ros Eeles, Brenda Pinnock, Bridie McGillycuddy,

Carly-Anne Lee, Jane Fior, Judy Sanitt, Joyce Lit; Marion Donaldson; Caroline Stofer; Alex, Lottie, Gabrielle, Polly and Shauneen; Elaine, Jean and Martha; Mag Leahy; Rick Mower; my sister; my parents; my children, Theo Mendelson and Clem Mendelson.